SWEENEY

ON

THE

ROCKS

SWEENEY

ON

THE

ROCKS

A NOVEL

ALLEN MORRIS JONES

PUBLISHING

NEW YORK, NY

Ig Publishing
Box 2547
New York, NY 10163

www.igpub.com

ISBN: 978-1-632460-83-7 (paperback)

The best heroes all have a little bit of villain in them.

In the dripping, vermin-rustling basement of a Bay Ridge trattoria, amid cardboard pillars of boxed Chianti and swelling cans of ten-year-old tomato sauce, past a narrow hallway of folded buffet tables and five-gallon jugs of olive oil, a man sits duct taped to an armchair, squinting under the greasy light of a bare bulb, regretting certain, ill-considered life choices.

Skinny in a sallow, cigarette-stained sort of way, up until a couple hours ago he'd been the cat's meow, the bee's knees, the cream in your coffee. An anachronism all the way down to his graying, well-trimmed little Valentino mustache. Which, by the way, and thanks to a swatch of duct tape being repeatedly torn off and reapplied, has been mostly reduced to a row of bloody freckles, a slow-welling pattern of red dots. His tongue comes out for a taste, then retreats.

You wonder, in this business, what you would do—what you *will* do—when somebody sticks a gun in your ear, says, "Get in the car." Will you play the hero? Throw some wild punches, offer a few kicks to the crotch? Or maybe make a break for it, screaming like a cheerleader? Pull your own gun and go mano a mano right there in the street? Turns out, no. None of these. Here's what you do instead: You get in the car.

He sits in his sweat and blood and stale urine, the rich stew of fluids that flee our bodies at the first sign of trouble, then adds a few drops of tears to the mix, sobbing with a little half-hitch hiccup. Each hand has been taped to the arms of the chair so as to the leave the fingers free. Swollen by the tightness of the tape, pink and trembling, there's something obscene about their wormlike, naked vulnerability.

A voice from the dim periphery. "You still with us there, Georgie?"

From the chair, sobs, pants.

"What do you think, he still with us? I can't hardly see nothing." Under layers of dust and cobwebs, the bare bulbs emit only a dim light.

Three men sit splayed in various postures of boredom. Three cashmere coats folded over the cleanest of the wine boxes. Three sets of white shirtsleeves rolled to the elbow. Per union specs, they all wear identical sneers. The smallest man, an aging and obese toad of a guy, a sixty-five-year-old mouth breather named Donnie Moretti, separates himself from the shadows. Limps over to stand under the bulb. The other two, gents not uncommon to the genre, are dull blades indeed, heavy-lidded and slow. Somebody's cousin married somebody's cousin. This older guy, though. This guy has a gleam. Cynicism, intelligence. If he was mocked in high school (which he was), then surely a trail of Molotov cocktails and slashed tires followed in his wake (which they did).

Ominously, horribly, a set of bolt cutters swing heavily at his side: Tick tock, tick tock.

At this point, you wouldn't think the man in the chair would be capable of copping to the details. But yeah, swollen eyes and all, he fixates immediately on the tool. Groans low and doomed, a rusty car door wrenched open.

Twenty feet over their heads, the last few late night diners are polishing off the dregs of their wine, sopping up watery marinara with crusts of sourdough, settling back, inspecting the bills, waving credit cards. Down here, though, a man has come to the reluctant awareness that even if he lives through this night, his days of wiping his own ass are almost certainly behind him.

The duct tape on his mouth is loose enough now it's mostly just a gesture. He sobs through gummy adhesive. "I don't...god, Jesus, I don't *know* where she is, Donnie. Swear to god, swear to god, swear to god. We don't talk no more. She don't like me. Swear to god."

Donnie shifts the bolt cutters, reaches out to toss the tape aside. "How long I known you, Georgie? Grade school, right? Kindygarten? You went to school with my kids. They had you in that gifted program. You rubbed me wrong even then. You was five years old, you thought your shit didn't stink. I gotta tell you, though..." he lifts his pug nose, sniffs conspicuously, "it's stinking now, buddy."

Appreciative chortles from the apes in the wings.

"Here's how this is gonna work." With effort, a popping of joints, he squats in front of Georgie, bolt cutters across his knees. He caresses the handles like the ears of something cute. "Eddie's dead, he don't know the answer. That Russian everybody talks about, Breetvah, whoever the fuck he is, he's off the map. But you, you're right here. Complete with all ten fingers. Plus, plus..." he hefts the bolt cutters, lets them drop heavily on the man's crotch. "Plus a tiiiny little excuse for a dick." Holds up two fingers half an inch apart. "Each time I have to repeat myself? I'm cuttin something off. You answer sooner rather than later, we send you to your maker with yourself mostly intact. Maybe they'll give you an open coffin. If not, they'll be finding you scattered from Utica to Utah, Boise to Joisee. Now..." He rises, groaning slightly, holding a knee, and places the polished jaws of the cutters carefully around a jerking, quivering pinky. "Now. Where..." and he shuts the cutters hard. A crunch of bone, a spurt of bright blood, the small plip of a finger hitting concrete. "...is that sister of yours?"

Four days later and three thousand miles west, Ted Sweeney bounces his weak-springed, 1961 International up one of Montana's kidney-bruiser excuses for a road, head bobbing with the beat.

At a glance, here's a guy who's just flat broke. Tailgate held on with baling wire, windshield a cobweb of gravel cracks. He prioritizes power bills, dodges collection agencies, eats half his meals from a bag. And yet he's thrumming his fingers on the dash, humming along to an old Stones tune. Breaking out now and then into background vocals: "Whoo-hoo, whoo-hoo." A rare occasion in the story of his life, for him to be aware of his own contentment.

He's got a ring in his pocket, is the thing.

Sick of his own equivocation, the endless interior dialogue of pluses and minuses, he finally decided, "Y'know? Screw it." Went to Bozeman, a jewelry store in the mall. Said, "She likes white gold, right?" Turns out there was a little moon-shaped number that Sweeney's pretty sure she'll love. A couple tiny stones set in white gold. Twelve hundred bucks on the third of three credit cards. He can afford the vig to Chase but not the meat. Sixteen percent interest. And if he tries unsuccessfully not to compare it to the museum piece he bought for his first wife fourteen years ago (three carats, twenty-eight grand), maybe he can be forgiven given context and circumstance.

Owner and sole employee of his own handyman business

("Anything for Money" stenciled on both sides of his truck), the last ten years have seen him go decidedly blue collar. Ambition wise, his eyes were bigger than his stomach. He's aging into a fondness for domestic beer and second-tier college football. And while he still jogs his three miles a day, hits the heavy bag occasionally, likes to paint (canvases, not houses), he is otherwise more or less your average American Joe.

Case in point: An engagement ring in his pocket, but his thoughts inadvertently go to the Yankees and A's, the TV ten minutes in his future. They're probably already three innings into it, Yanks six runs up.

Used to be, once a week in the summers, he'd find his habitual seat low in right field. The taste of a sausage dog and onions, the beer so cold, the field so green. Seventh inning stretch, the sweepers sang YMCA, dancing out the letters. Nice days, those. But leaving New York behind, he's been doing his best to betray the Yanks at every opportunity. If he can hate the Yanks, goes his thinking, he can manage anything.

But whatever game is in his immediate future, it ain't the Yanks and the A's.

~

Is there some law, some rule? Newtonian this or that. The older you get, the faster your memory goes. Case in point: He could have sworn he left his dog inside the fence. But now, pulling up to his back door, here comes Zeke out to meet him, panting and grinning, front feet on the truck door. Sweeney steps out, scratches at the collar. "You doing okay, Zeke? You have you a good day? Figured out how latches work there buddy?"

A mongrel mishmash of Australian shepherd and beagle, maybe some blue heeler, Zeke's default stare is equal parts wisdom and disapproval. Wouldn't surprise Sweeney at all if he'd learned about locks.

And indeed, here's the picket gate swinging free. Sweeney's already thinking about another kind of latch. Something with a knob.

At the back door, however, house key in his fingers, he stops. Swallows.

His door frame in splinters, the dead bolt assembly dangling loose, the imprint of a crowbar in the molding.

His tongue thickens and his mouth goes dry. Maybe it's just a robbery. Simple B & E.

He steps back, glances around. Near dusk, and across the yard one hundred yards away, the ranch house's windows are already lit yellow. The old folks, Carl and Pauline, will be at their ease in front of the TV. Half deaf, eyes milky with cataracts. No help there.

For years you live your life tiptoeing around certain imagined scenarios. Gun barrels that turn out to be folded baby carriages, stubborn starter motors that might be car bombs, a rifle-scope glittering on the rooftop of Western Drug. Afterwards, of course, you berate yourself for being jumpy, twitchy.

Get a hold of yourself, Sweeney. Burglar, just a burglar. Just some kid lifting your laptop.

He touches the door, eases it open. Peers into the gloom. "Get back," he whispers to Zeke, pushing at him with his heel, ignoring the dog's accusing whine. He slips inside, linoleum sighing under his feet. He should have taken off his shoes.

Back in the old days, he'd have remembered to take off his shoes. He does it now.

Originally a bunkhouse, his home is a bare-essentials kind of place. Tiny kitchen, half-assed stove and sink, ancient turquoise refrigerator. It's all clean enough, but done up in the used furniture and threadbare curtains of bachelor-melancholy. No dried flowers or jars of potpourri. The fridge innocent of old Christmas cards and family photos.

He almost flips on the overhead light, then takes his hand back. On his way past the stove, he lifts a frying pan off the rack.

Here's the living room. His over-inflated couch and kitschy lamp (bucking bronc etched into a leather shade), half-ton, yard-sale TV, an easel set up by the window with a half-finished study of the mountains (too much blue), his brushes in their coffee mug of acetone. And then the back of his soggy recliner. If they're still here, they're either out in the parking shed (wooden tennis rackets, a folded-up ping pong table) or in his bedroom. He thinks of his old laptop, the fireproof safe in his closet. His hundred bucks in emergency cash, his passport.

And so his hand's already on the door to his bedroom. But then…No. Those open drapes? He'd left them closed. And his recliner. It's facing the picture window, away from the TV. It never faces away from the TV.

He cocks the frying pan like a baseball bat, advancing on the back of the chair. "Hey!" The word jumps out, startlingly loud. "Hey. Outta my lazyboy."

Nothing. No movement from the chair. Not even a tremble. Glancing at the half-dark glass of his window, Sweeney sees, in reflection, a figure slouched low, a ghost of a ghost, a small man with in a crooked fedora tilted over his eyes.

Sweeney touches one corner of the chair with his socked toe and twirls it around.

The motion of the chair rolls the fedora onto the floor.

And a shotgun, arranged under the crossed hands, drops barrel-first between the man's ankles.

Sweeney lowers his pan.

In Sweeney's chair (his *favorite* chair, his old pal of a piece of furniture) someone's arranged a tidy little corpse, ankles crossed, lapels neat.

Sweeney feels a faint tinge of nausea. Then nothing but violation. *His* chair, *his* house.

The guy's head lolls, rocking slightly. Cheeks pale and waxen, dead eyes staring out toward a questionable eternity. Under the man's chin, hinge to hinge, see the wink of white bone, a cartilaginous mouth in the esophagus, gaping. The clean slice from corner to corner, ragged only where the cut is the shallowest. A dried bib of blood.

Sweeney, who has some experience in this regard, can't help but admire the efficiency of the work.

~

Ted Sweeney, thirty-seven years old, getting soft and complacent in his near old age, mumbles to himself. Pacing, running his hands through his hair: "Okay, don't panic, now. No panicking here."

What he needs is a few minutes, a window to think this through. He pulls the drapes (glancing out to the horse barn, the two-story house, the south pasture) and sits on the couch. He swivels the dead man around until they sit facing each other. Dark, hooded eyes and a hundred dollar haircut.

Sweeney's been trying to quit the Camels, these slow, three-inch increments of an early end, but he feels now—with a warm and satisfying regret—that he's about to fall off the smokes wagon in a big way. He takes a pack from the coffee table drawer and finds his matches. Even when you're quitting, you keep a pack somewhere. In the flare of a kitchen match, Sweeney's scowling brow. The smell of cordite and tobacco; the smell of wars.

The face before him is unfamiliar. Narrow cheekbones, close set eyes, dark black hair brushed back with a gel thick enough to reflect light. Sweeney knows the stereotype. Purple silk shirt. A fedora the color of dull chrome. Loafers built up half an inch on the soles. Whoever this guy was, he had some scratch. Wearing the cash equivalent of a good used car.

The more he stares into his face, however, studying the half-closed eyes, the slight sprouting of black hair in the nostrils, there's something ...

The shotgun has a rough, brutal utility about it. A little pump-action .410, the stock scarred with a dozen different dings and scrapes, the mouth of the barrel still frayed silver where the hacksaw had worked. These big city wops. They talk a good game, but none of them know firearms from formaggio. A .410. Jesus.

Dizzy, now, and it's not just the cigarette.

There's not much blood. Just a dinner-napkin-sized swatch on the front of his shirt, a ring of dry rust around the collar. A guy gets his throat cut, there should be blood sprayed on the walls, sopping into the carpet. Ipso facto, the body got moved. Sweeney almost congratulates himself for this simplest little bit of deduction.

A rain patter on the roof, and from the back yard, his dog barks once, a single, bossy exclamation. Sweeney opens the screen door. "Okay, all right." He fills the food bowl with a scoop from the pantry. "Little glutton, then, here we are then. Go to it."

Then Sweeney's back on the couch, smoking his second Camel.

Who are you, buddy? He leans forward, runs his hands around under the man's hips, feeling for a wallet. But no, that'd be too much to ask. Then he reaches for the right hand. The skin cold, the joints reluctant. Under the sleeve, a Bulgari watch. Sweeney flips the face over, hoping for an etching on the back. To dear so-and-so from your loving wife. Again, nada. Waterproof to 500 Meters. Finally he turns back the collars of the man's suit jacket and shirt. No tags, no labels of any sort. Custom tailored. Even more expensive than they'd looked. He pats the front pockets, feels an interruption in the smooth fabric, pulls out a few quarters, a pack of spearmint gum, and a car key remote with a plastic Avis tag.

So. Okay. Any minute now, if this is a setup, the drapes are going to light up with rolling red and blue cop lights. "Open the door! Police! Freeze! Hands up!" Yadayadayada.

If not, he's got time.

There's something about the face. Something...Take ten years off the guy, he might have been one of those kids, a bag runner, maybe, one of those greasy, evil little shits loitering around the tire shop, teaching himself to smoke cigarettes. He might have once hurried to open Sweeney's car door.

Zeke pads in, burping Iams, hops up on the couch and drops his fox-snout nose on Sweeney's hip, Sweeney lets his fingers play under the collar, around the ears.

An hour ago, his biggest worry was paying for an engagement ring.

He sits and smokes. Okay, if he's anybody else, if he's Joe Blow, you call the cops. You're innocent, Sweeney, you got alibis…

You got alibis, right? Time of death? Rigor, but no odor. Call it six hours. And Sweeney—thank you, Jesus; I ain't religious, but thank you, Jesus—was in Bozeman all day. Used a credit card at the jeweler's.

If it's a setup, it's a sloppy damn job.

But he's not nobody else, and never has been. It's a small town. Word about him gets out, he either has to run or hang tight. And Sweeney? If you hang tight, inside of a week you're a dead man. Not to mention your family back in New York. Sister.

Running's no good either. He *likes* it here. He's put down *roots*.

Fuhhhuck.

If not a setup then what is it? A warning? Maybe. But why? If they could get to him with a dead body, why not just get to him?

And where's the other one? These guys always travel in pairs.

Sweeney walks through the crime scene he used to call a living room, resisting the urge to hurry. Outside, the soft, muddy grass of his driveway—soft enough to show tire tracks. It's chopped and scarred with his own comings and goings. But there might be a slightly smaller tire track beside his shriveled caragana. And in the mud beside his gate, just off the cracked cement walk, that might be the impression of a smooth-soled shoe. Whoever walked that body into his house had to be strong enough to carry him (no drag marks in the mud) and either had to know that the old folks would be away or have confidence enough to risk it.

Inside Sweeney's house, he turns on every light. Okay, if you're the guy, you've jimmied the door, and you're a little nervous, keeping an eye on the ranch house behind you, kicking your feet at Zeke; yapping little dog. You have the body in the backseat, maybe wrapped in a blanket. You go back to the car. Moving faster, in a rush, you fireman's carry the body into the house, dump him into the chair. You're going to track in a little mud. And, yup, there's smudges on the linoleum. A slight little path of reflection, heading from the door to the living room. Not a lot, though. The guy was careful.

Okay, but once you get the body in the chair, you're going to be relieved. Maybe in the mood for a joke. I mean, this is funny, right? You're chuckling. Do you leave a little souvenir, maybe? A little fuck-you to Sweeney?

Sweeney goes through the room more carefully. He has a pair of cheap Charlie Russell prints on the walls, faded to blues and greens. The glass on both, he's only briefly ashamed to note, is covered with dust. Be an easy thing for a guy to finger smear a little note. Ditto his lamp with its leather shade, the heavy stitching and crude painting of a bucking bronc. The old folks do love their western kitsch. But no. No message.

The problem, he finally decides, is this: Rock, hard place. Sweeney in the middle.

Fight or flight or stasis? Nobody to fight, nowhere to fly. And anyway, he *likes* it here. Stasis? His ex-wife—the proud possessor of a Ph.D. in the history of Sweeney's failings, a post-doc in the intricate, expanding list of his fuck-ups, past, present, and future—always said he'd rather drive off a cliff than sit spinning his tires in the mud.

Sheeeyiiitt.

~

Seven years ago, looking for beer money, a side of cowboy mystique to go with his entrée of ennui, he'd answered an ad for a night calver. Said over the phone, "I'm honest, I'm reliable. Two things you just don't see much of anymore." Exactly the right tone to strike with any rancher over the age of fifty.

But honesty and reliability can only get you so far. Late nights, early mornings, here's Sweeney out there with his first-calf heifers, pointing a flashlight, looking for bulging vulvas, twisted tails. Big bad Sweeney, babysitting cows. And his first time reaching into a birth canal for those soft, tiny hooves? Urine in his face, a blurp of green cow shit around his hands. Sweeney's stomach, stainless steel for thirty years, emptied itself onto half-frozen mud.

He'd stayed with it, though. Whatever had gone missing within Sweeney, self-confidence or self-esteem, these ranchers had it in their blood. Sweeney rented the bunkhouse, trading room and occasional board for helping out. Maybe it'll rub off, whatever they got. Seven years later, he's still here, still kind of waiting.

Nine-thirty at night, Sweeney knocks at the back door. "Anybody home?"

"Teddy?" Pauline struggles up from her knitting. "Everything okay?"

Carl's got his remote, kicked back with the misshapen

knots of his feet up on a hassock. "You don't got plumbing problems over there again? Toilet still working?"

"Just thought I'd come over, say hello. Haven't seen you in a while."

"Well, aren't you the one." Pauline wobbles into the kitchen. "I baked yesterday. Feel like a piece of pie?"

"Apple?"

"Cherry rhubarb."

"Even better." Stepping through this door, you expected to be fed. "A little early for rhubarb?"

"Costco. We went into town today."

"Jesus god, that Bozeman." Carl hasn't taken his eyes off the TV. "Bozangeles, they're calling it and I think that's about right."

Sweeney notes the dishes still in the sink. While Pauline cuts him off a piece of pie, he runs water, squirts in dish soap.

"Oh now. You don't have a do that, Teddy."

He scrubs at a hardened crust of ketchup. "You didn't happen to see anybody come into the yard today, I don't guess? Drive up, turn around?"

"We was in that goddamn Bozangeles all day."

"Carl," Pauline says absently, "*language*. We didn't see a soul. How come?"

"Note on my door? Said they came to say hi, but didn't sign it." The lie comes easy enough to bother him.

"Well, that wasn't very polite."

"Yup." Sweeney dries a final plate. "Anyway, you don't mind, you see anybody around, let me know, okay?"

He considers their living room. Lace curtains gone yellow with cigarette smoke. A burled-cedar coffee table polished on the two spots, left and right, where they put their heels.

A wicker basket on the fireplace with ten years' worth of Christmas cards.

All of it as dear to Sweeney as his own childhood.

~

He parks in the middle of the Highway 89 bridge, the Yellowstone rolling black and silver below. Two o'clock in the morning, there's half a moon and an empty road. Deep water down there. Roiling, splashing, grumbling, anxious for the Missouri. *Full* of big fish. Brown trout, sulking. Once a year, some old fart gets his picture in the paper holding a twelve pounder. You got retired time on your hands, you can dredge streamers all day long.

Stepping out of his truck, it's quiet enough he can hear the squeak of his truck springs. An odd feeling, standing in the middle of an empty highway. All this road just for him.

Five hundred yards behind him, long haul truckers growl down I-90. Ahead, an empty scroll toward Clyde Park, Wilsall, Ringling. A series of diminishing small towns nested like Russian dolls. The Crazy Mountains in dark horizon. To the east, nothing but wind and sage and a downhill run toward Appalachia.

Not quite hurrying, he lifts the body out of the bed. A few strands of loose hay trickle out onto the road.

The body sags into a U, and he catches it with his knee, quick-steps it toward the edge of the bridge. Lets it rest briefly on the railing—"Father, son, holy ghost."—and rolls it over into the river.

A long moment, then a splash.

Later, there will be regret. Thoughts of the body tumbling along maybe even now, rolling on the gravel bottom, the hard current playing with eyelashes, exposing blank pupils. What was his name, his nickname, his mother, father, brother? What were his dreams, his sins, his penances? Nobody deserves to rest unmarked and unremarked upon. Sure, I mean, he probably had it coming. But nobody *deserves* it.

Until now, Sweeney hasn't had time to feel anything but panic. First thought? Save my ass. Now, however, staring down at the dark water, the glint of silver on ripples...If old times are an indication, he'll soon turn into a maudlin mess. How much we take for granted, all these small miracles. Buttons, chewing gum, zippers, unlocking his truck, turning the ignition. His cell phone, his microwave. Jet contrails. In aggregate, our extraordinary days. And yet we die.

Maybe the body's already caught against some tangled root, the current making a floating gauze of his hair, minnows swimming into the open mouth, picking through his teeth.

But for now? No cars. No cops. No issues.

Cool.

~

An old habit, Sweeney likes his late-night walks. Back home in Brooklyn, collar up to his ears, he'd hit the pavement three or four nights a week, stroll along anonymously, enjoy the slow segue of neighborhoods. Chinese to Russian to Hasid. In Rockjaw, though, there's no such thing as anonymous. A guy walking alone at night arouses suspicion. He trails barking dogs and porch lights, 911 calls. Silhouettes in screen doors.

With Zeke, though? I'm just a guy walking my dog.

Through the windows, house to house, there's a teacher bent over his desk, grading papers, blowing lightly on the coals of his disillusionment.. A few doors down, a young woman stands at her stove, hair in her eyes and a spatula working. Her heart has been broken. But whose has not? Further down, an old man limps away from the fridge, white box of Chinese takeout in his hands.

Sweeney is well aware—although he doesn't dwell on it—that they are always they. He is not among them. He is a stranger here, and always will be.

Signing up for witness protection comes after a dozen discussions. The first one, you're in handcuffs chained to an interrogation table. You and two detectives play an intricate game of approach and avoidance. "Sure yeah. Maybe you could help us out. *Maybe*. Whatchyou got?" Bad coffee, cigarettes awkwardly lit. Finally, a week or a month later, you're staring at a half circle of Feds in cheap suits. The Assistant DA, in a slightly better suit, is handing you a pen. At no point do they tell you the entire truth. I mean, they make an effort. If they gave you the whole, Price is Right, Com'on Down spiel, and a year into it you discovered the lies, you're going to pull a Lazarus and roll back the rock, which would be embarrassing for everybody. So they tell you about starting over, cutting connections. But they don't tell you about how you'll never fit in. Not anywhere.

There are fourteen motels in Rockjaw, Montana. At the Super 8 by the Interstate, Zeke leads him from tire to tire. To anyone watching from a window (say, a Bensonhurst wop with blood on his mind, schadenfreude in his heart), Sweeney's just some guy with a dog. Meanwhile, his left hand's working overtime in his pocket, clicking at the remote. Unlock, unlock, unlock. But no...nada. No beep-boop-bop. No flashing headlights. Nothing. Would have been too much to ask, the first motel he tried.

Three places later, however, and by the faint light of the dormant movie theater marquee across the street, a Ford Taurus beeps a cheerful little welcome, unlocks its doors.

Sweeney glances around. Cars, hotel windows. A late model Chevy truck idling outside the Hawk's Nest Saloon, driver's forehead on the steering wheel. Sweeney allows himself a moment's pause, enjoying the sense of his own competence.

The car? Bronzish. Nondescript. Clean. A few million others in America just like it. He covers his hand with the cuff of his sleeve and pops the trunk. Empty. A flap of carpet over a spare tire. He goes to the front doors. In the back seat, an empty Avis folder. But in the front seat floorboard, half hidden under the floor mat, a thin brown briefcase. Smooth calfskin. Expensive. Don't congratulate yourself yet, Sweeney. Don't get cocky. You don't have the upper hand here. You are miles away from having the upper hand. He tucks the briefcase under his arm and tugs at Zeke's leash. "Let's go, boy. Getting late."

~

Sitting Indian-wise in his living room, he goes after the briefcase with a screwdriver and mallet.

By his knee, Zeke works over a leather bone, gnawing it around with more anger than hunger, keeping half an eye on Sweeney. In Zeke's world, there are leather bones then there's everything else.

Two combination locks on the briefcase, one on either side of the handle. But rather than try to pop the hardware, Sweeney goes after the hinges. Couple hard whacks and the case falls open. He dumps it across the carpet.

Looks like…a stainless steel .357. Cobra. Nice pistol.

Utilitarian. Got some punch. Sweeney spins the cylinder, checks the loads. Unexpected from the same guy who carried a rat shooter for a shotgun.

And in loose cash, there's seven hundred and...fifty-*five* dollars. Sweeney folds it, tucks it into his jeans. Call it payment for funeral services rendered.

Then there's a manila envelope full of photos. Black and whites, printed out on a laser printer. Surveillance shots. The flat depth of field that says telephoto. And they're all of the same woman. Lighting her cigarette, laughing wide-mouthed at a bar, reading a magazine, face half-hidden under those big sunglasses they wear these days.

He knows her. Knew her, anyway. Oh boy and oy vey, did he know her. Brooklyn born and bred. Knew her inside and out. Tina Harrison, his piece on the side.

What is her photo doing in a briefcase in Montana?

Sweeney owns an ancient laptop, an early Dell. Thick as a family Bible, heavy as an endloader, most days he more or less successfully resists its charms. The dim screen, the fan loud as a blender. But he fires it up now.

Within a few minutes, after the router headaches and the half minute spent wrestling with his own cynicism (privacy? what privacy), he'll Google her name. Find nothing on the woman herself but instead a missing person's report for her brother. Cocky, obsequious, burdened with the unfortunate name of Georgie Harrison. Thought he was a gangster, that kid. Always angling for a way into the life, posturing, talking words he learned from a book. No surprise it caught up to him.

But Tina? There was always something feral about her, something with teeth. A Venus fly trap for a heart, snapping at Sweeney as he buzzed past.

~

How many dead men has he seen up close and personal? A rude question, even according to the generous terms of his own ongoing interior monologue. Self-flagellation masquerading as introspection. The worst ones of course were the ones he tagged himself. Number three, cleaning up, he'd found a bloody molar rattling around on the floor boards, lost in taco wrappers and napkins. "Sorry, Sonny." The guy's name had been Sonny.

But to his credit, Sweeney never did nobody that didn't deserve it. What he told himself, anyway. But from whose perspective? Not theirs, surely. And *that* kind of thinking is slippery as a bar of soap.

Sweeney has this recurring dream. Can't get rid of it. The people he's killed, their heads are mounted on the wall of a log cabin. Some kind of ski lodge. Montana meets Brooklyn, right? And the heads are never quite right: ears too far forward, eyes slightly askew, lips too red, the cheeks sunken. And here's where it gets creepy: They're all still alive. Talking. Sneering. Keeping up a running dialogue about Sweeney's failures, his shortcomings. "Can you believe this is the schmuck that offed us?" kind of thing.

Sweeney has a problem sleeping late. Three hours and here's Sweeney blinking at the ceiling, tobacco-colored water stain in one corner. Depending on Sweeney's mood, the water stain looks either like a happy Labrador retriever with floppy ears or a mutilated hand with the middle three fingers missing. This morning it's the hand. That speck off to the side could be a thumbnail somebody pulled off with pliers.

His cell phone vibrates on the bureau. He picks it up without bothering about the caller ID. "Sweeney. I'll do anything for money. Who the fuck calls at 6:15 in the morning?"

"Judge, jury, hangman, my friend. Got a question for you." Cal Merchant. A fugitive from the Army and the Laguna Beach surf scene. Maybe the only man in town with a more complicated history than Sweeney's.

"Ask me anything but the state capitols." And where the bodies are buried.

"What is it about white people that makes 'em get up on a Saturday, spread all their shit out on their front lawns?"

"You tell me, man."

"Reason I'm asking, I'm wondering if you're free to come over, help a brother conduct a little experiment. I want to see what happens when a black man has a lawn sale. I'll pay the hourly."

"Called a *yard* sale. Let me look at my schedule." Sweeney half sits up, glances through to his kitchen, the Ranch Supply cowgirl calendar on his fridge. A single red X over last week's forgotten dental appointment. "Yeah, I'm free." He reaches for his smokes.

A few minutes later, pulling on yesterday's jeans, here's the square velvet box of Aggie's ring heavy in the front pocket. Relic from another lifetime. And then brushing his teeth before the mirror, a freckle of blood on his cheek, a beauty mark just under his left eye.

He smears the dot away hard with a washcloth, scrubbing a faint blush into his skin.

Good as new.

~

The friendship of men, Sweeney believes, is built on an

armature of respect hidden under a veneer of derision.

Twenty miles south of Rockjaw, Cal Merchant owns a narrow stretch of ground squeezed between cliff and creek. Cal built the cabin himself, piecing it together with hand-hewn logs and quarter rounds. Added a gas stove and a bank of computers. Shelves full of books and a dozen small oil paintings (biased toward early California, toward Monterey). It's a life almost painful in its picturesqueness. Fly rods, fitted shotguns. A reloading bench. Cal's said, "Being a black man in Montana? It's a full-time job, defying expectations."

Sweeney goes running with Cal now and then. A two mile grunt to the top of Windmill Falls. Sweeney would suggest sparring with padded gear—his gym keeps gloves and helmets—but suspects that Cal probably knows jujitsu or tae kwon do or some such. Guy has that feel of exotic bad-assery about him.

They've been friends for, what...seven years now? Met shortly after Sweeney's divorce. Shooting pool at the bar, they knew each other the way dogs know each other. A look, a snarl, a sniff. In this town of seven thousand, how many share a background in real violence?

Sweeney parks down the road from Cal's, leaving room for other vehicles in the narrow driveway. Strolls up to the door, Zeke at his heels. Eight in the morning, there's already a hot summer smell of sun through the pines, the seared scent of needles and sap and bees.

Cal meets him on the porch, desk lamp in his hands. "Just in time. Grab some boxes there, maybe start spreading some stuff around on tables?"

"You can buy my time but you can't buy me."

"*Every*body's for sale."

"There's a profound truth."

A pair of picnic tables on the sloping lawn, a makeshift clothesline stretched between two aspens. For the next hour, Sweeney arranges vintage suits with butterfly collars, Lycra ski pants, raveling sweaters, t-shirts advertising shoes. "This mean your mother's moving up here?"

Cal's bent over his old mountain bike, inflating a tire with a hand pump. "How you get that?"

"This is all from your spare room."

"Nah, man. Just a white man experiment, like I said."

"Hard to imagine your mother in Montana."

"You don't know the half of it."

Cal considers the sacrificial spread of his possessions. The existential transition, mine to yours. "I can see the attraction, man. Yeah, dig it, right? It's like a purging, it's like a capitalist enema. Just cleaning out all this old crap." Somewhere Cal's picked up a Copenhagen habit, and he pinches up a chew. He keeps his head shaved, and now rubs his hand thoughtfully around the baldness.

They come to sit on folding chairs on Cal's porch. It is on this porch, pine boards still bleeding drops of sap, that they have pronounced judgment on national politics, Kanye and Kim, on female CNN anchors. What they have *not* done, of course, what they have both assiduously avoided, is talk of their own childhoods, mothers, fathers, first jobs, graduations. For years Sweeney's resisted the urge to confide. I mean, where do you even start?

Startling, how a friendship could thrive in such thin soil.

Cal sits with a gray cash box, making change and flirting with women in summer dresses, expounding to Sweeney on the apocalypse. "I been thinking about putting in a bomb shelter. I'm no prepper, but I mean, you need to be *ready*. Know what I'm sayin'? Get your brass you can recycle, lead bars, gallon cans of smokeless powder. Caps. Jars and lids for canning. A good seed vault. Passive dehumidifiers. A good root cellar. You need..."

His mind elsewhere, Sweeney interrupts. "I got a hypothetical."

"Lay it on me." *Hypothetical*. An entrée into any number of decent chats over the years. Sweeney and Cal both with an interest in the criminal mind. A hypothetical assassination, terrorist plot, bank heist. How's a guy get away with it? How's he get caught?

"So an ex-criminal, maybe somebody from LA or something, right? Hiding out in Montana. *Pulp Fiction* meets *Lonesome Dove*."

"Farfetched, but yeah, okay."

Sweeney sneaks a sideways glance. "Guy comes home one day, finds a body delivered to his house. Waiting for him on his front porch."

"Past catching up to him kind of deal?"

"Maybe, maybe not. He wouldn't know. He's isolated."

"So where's the hypothetical?"

"Yeah, okay. You take a guy, no resources, cut off from all his old connections. Does he run, does he stay, does he fight it out?"

"Depends on what he's got to lose, I guess."

"Maybe more than he thinks."

"No man is an island, right?"

"Maybe."

"Well, everybody's got more to lose than they..." Cal shifts in his seat. "Is that Marilyn?"

A sheriff's cruiser pulling into the driveway, idling past the parked cars.

"Looks like it." Sweeney hunkers down low. "For my sins."

Marilyn steps out, leans her forearms on the open door. Busty in khaki brown and a gold star. Mirrored sunglasses and red hair pulled back tight enough to thrum. "Hey Cal. How's the yard sale?"

"Not bad. Another day like today, I'm going shopping for a Cadillac."

"I've always seen you in a Lexus." To Sweeney, she says, "Feel like going for a ride, slick?" She ignores the half-dozen or so browsers around here, all of them conspicuously minding their own business.

"In that? Uh uh." Sweeney hates cop cars like he hates taxes and higher math. You can't argue with it.

"Com'on hotshot."

He pulls out his truck keys. "I'll follow."

"Get in. Or." Her fingers jingle-jangle the cuffs hooked to her belt.

Sweeney's eyes bounce back and forth. He finally nods. Steps down toward her cruiser.

"Just climb on in the back there."

Backseat of a cop car. No handles, windows permanently up and locked, a screen which, from Sweeney's personal experience, it's impossible to kick your way through (a problem of leverage). Not to mention the stink. Lysol over a foundation of urine and vomit. He says, without much hope, "I'd rather not."

"Oh Sweeney," she grins too many teeth at him, "you can't charm your way out of *this* ride."

"Arrest me, then."

"Don't tempt me. I lie awake nights." She's never made an empty threat in her life. "See that there…." She steps closer to lower her voice. "On the front seat?"

Sweeney puts his nose to the window, cups a hand against the glare. Sees a stamped and canceled manila envelope, unflapped. Her name above the copshop address.

She says to his ear. "That's your ticket to Deer Lodge, you don't cooperate."

Resigned, he grabs the rear door handle. "That day I married you? Worst day of my life."

~

Twelve years ago this August, him and Marilyn sat in a steel gray limousine, chilled as produce in a drawer, watching as every soul they knew in the world lined up for their paired funerals.

Through the open door of the church, he glimpsed a cascade of roses, an avalanches of lilies. He'd have maybe expected a dozen cousins, ten or twelve high school drinking buddies. Not this receiving line, not this neighborhood parade halfway around the block. I mean, *damn*.

Maybe it made sense. They'd died young, right? And tragically. Young and tragic makes good box office.

It put a lump in his own throat, especially when he saw his mother. If he's to be damned for any sin in his life (putting them in alphabetical order would take time and a half), it's for giving his mother this grief. Hunched in her dark finery, clutching a trembling bouquet of baby's breath. They brought her a chair, and she sat shaking hands, lifting a cheek for kisses.

Beside him, Marilyn sniffled.

"Jesus, woman."

"I know, but."

Their limo was an indulgence, a whim he'd paid for out of his own pocket. How often you get a chance to see your own funeral? The Fed, disguised as a chauffeur (if you call a borrowed hat and a pair of sunglasses a disguise), was short tempered, spending his Saturday driving an ex-con around. He looked at Sweeney in the rearview. "She's not falling apart back there, is she?"

"You should see the opportunity here. Look at that line. You got your felons, you got your parole violators, a couple arsonists." His cousin Eddie was all three. Twenty years before, Eddie had shown Sweeney how to slimjim pinball machines. Now he stood thin and pale, sideswiped by grief.

Sweeney said to Marilyn, "He looks good, don't he?"

"Who?"

"Eddie."

The Fed turned interested. "Eddie Adamo? Is he, what, that guy with mustache?"

"None of your business."

Sweeney's tone pissed him off. "All those folks crying and carrying on? I roll your window down, there's two or three probably wouldn't mind seeing you go tits up for real."

Good point. Jimmy Basconti, Mike Harmon...

Sweeney poured two bourbons from the fold-down bar. Handed one to Marilyn. "Step on it, son. Airport."

~

Back in Brooklyn, Marilyn had been a petite, fragile kind of thing. A gum chewer preoccupied with her nails. Poisonous in her barbs, able to flay him to the bone with a single sharp word. In retrospect? We're all just trying to get to there from here. She had her own struggles. Hanging out with the wives of Sweeney's compadres, talking jewelry, sex, shopping. Her own disappointments.

But now, where had she gone, that mean-eyed little firecracker? Some part of him wants to start excavating, find his wife buried under the layers of sheriff's deputy. You could imagine this woman running a chainsaw, cutting firewood. A sunburn in lieu of makeup. A couple of simple sapphire earrings. Skin peeling off her nose and a galaxy of freckles across her cheeks. Similar constellations presumably still across her breasts. You expect redheads to be lighthearted, fun-loving. But with Marilyn? Those two words never seem to enter the conversation.

They sit at the back of Brownie's cafe, insulated by the invisible, ten-foot buffer that comes courtesy of her uniform. They have their mugs of coffee and the manila envelope.

Not quite lunchtime, Brownie's is still crowded. Run by Haight Street expats, their namesake desserts, prominently displayed under glass, are crusty, melt-in-your-mouth little pieces of heaven. The illicit versions, Sweeney knows from personal experience, are kept in foil in the basement freezer.

Incongruously, the restaurant's clientele consists mostly of railroad retirees and ranchers, old men who hold their newspapers with the stubs of missing fingers.

Marilyn notes Sweeney's plaid shirt, tattered jeans rolled at the cuff, the belt tightened an extra notch. "Still the same old snappy dresser."

Then the waitress is at his elbow. "Warm up your coffee?"

"Thanks, Pearl." After the waitress leaves, he says to his scowling ex-wife, "You're prettier every time I see you, I swear."

"So here I am on my way to work. Just another average day. Looking forward to a few speeding tickets. Maybe breaking up some domestic abuse…"

"Every ex-wife's spesh-ee-al-ity." Among their rituals of disdain, here's Sweeney rejecting the dim coals of his own slow-smoking fondness. You ignore it like you ignore the smell of mice under the floorboards, hoping it'll go away.

She opts for a cop's blank stare. "And so I get into the office, and what do I find in my morning's mail but this…" She pushes the envelope across the table. Sits back. "I blame you for ruining my day. My life, my career, god knows what else."

When he goes to open the envelope, Marilyn puts her hand over his. The waitress is back, adding another quarter inch to his coffee. Flirting. "Heard you went to Bozeman yesterday."

"Oh?"

"Kinsey saw you in the mall."

"Just going to that Barnes and Noble."

"What are you reading? I picked up that new James Lee Burke? It was almost…"

Marilyn says, "Thanks for the coffee, Pearl."

Pearl touches Sweeney's shoulder. "You have you a good day, *Ted*." Glances at his ex, who has forgotten the politics of women.

"You still got a way with the locals."

"Open the envelope."

"Birthday present?" He slides out a sheet of white paper. "You keep forgetting, but I always knew…" He turns the page over. Sees a photo printed on a laser printer. Could have been the same printer that produced the images in the briefcase. A gray-toned digital snapshot of the body. *His* body. The dead wop. Posed in Sweeney's living room. Charlie Russell on the wall, TV in the corner. Whoever had the camera, they were sitting on Sweeney's sofa. Where Sweeney had sat not a dozen hours ago, smoking a cigarette. Under the photo, written in blue ballpoint and careful, block letters, Sweeney's old name.

Sweeney slips the photo back into the envelope. "Anybody else seen this?"

"Yeah, you bet. I made copies and tacked them up on phone poles around town. Jesus."

He pushes the envelope back to her. "It's okay."

She leans forward. "Don't tell me it's okay," she hisses. "Don't you *dare* tell me it's okay. How is this in any way, shape or form okay?"

She's as angry as he's ever seen her (which is saying a *lot*). A bright red flush rises up from her collar. Her ponytail starts to work loose. A frizzy halo.

Sweeney glances around. Sees coffee cups paused mid-sip, forks poised above free-range eggs. A small slice of the infinite multitude of people who all live secure in their illusions of justice, of right and wrong. Happy to believe that there is a cosmic scale, that "things will work out," that as heroes of their own ongoing triple features, they will all triumph in the final act.

Him and Marilyn, they know different.

He stands, tosses bills on the table. "Let's take a walk."

~

Blind love. She'd been so beautiful. The feel of her small smooth hand when he'd slipped the ring on her finger. A siren to his passing ship, the rocks upon which he'd slung his hull.

It all went bad, sure, but he still had that feel of her hand.

Couple years after their wedding, she'd said, "You got a heart like a sieve, Cosmo. Everything runs right on through."

"Yeah, but I got a dick like a can opener."

At the start, his fierce, post-adolescent fumblings had brooked no argument. Contorted with ankles and elbows against headrests and window knobs, it'd been all, no no no, then yes, yes, *yes*. The waters of the Hudson a dark ocean out the back window. A good Catholic girl with a taste for guilt, retribution, she wanted the opposite of safe, predictable. After date one, she'd been the one to suggest date two.

But in Montana, Sweeney had gone tame, had become something less like a downed electrical wire sputtering sparks and more like a dog coming to you with a stick. She'd been the one to suggest divorce. "It's not like it was, honey."

Sweeney now has a couple of stale bagels from the counter, and they stand on the weathered dock in Sacajawea Park, tossing crumbs to geese. "I didn't kill him."

"Never said you did."

"Came home last night, he was in my chair just like that picture. Somebody broke into my house, crowbar work. Left him for me like that." He tosses another piece of bagel. The geese squabble before the largest of them scoops up the soggy crumbs. "Old folks were in Bozeman. Didn't see a thing."

"Where's the body now."

"Probably somewhere around about Big Timber."

"Jesus, Sweeney. You dumped it?"

"What else?"

"You could have called the marshalls."

"I'm not moving again."

"How about the state police? Or me? Just a thought."

"Yeah, right."

"You dumb wop. The things you still don't know about this town."

"Just think about it for a second, okay? I mean, Jesus, Rachel."

"Who's Rachel?"

Her old name. A slip he hasn't made in years. "Yeah, sorry. Damn. This thing's got me rattled."

After a moment, "Any idea who he was?"

"Nope." Another chunk of bagel. "Looks a little familiar, though. Something about him." Sweeney briefly considers bringing up the briefcase. The photos. Decides for a hundred thousand reasons to keep them to himself.

"Yeah, I thought the same thing." She sighs through her nose. "So we're blown, then. It's over."

"We don't know that. Somebody's sending a message, we just can't read it yet. That's what I figure. But if this guy's from the families, whoever killed him is likely from the families, too. Which means that New York knows we're alive, which means the Russians know, which means we should be dead already. And we aren't. Which means we got a puzzle on our hands."

"Sheeyit."

Hearing his own affected expression in her mouth, the pipes of Sweeney's heart sigh out a few brief notes of nostalgia. "Maybe it's a partner dispute. Like they were here to tag me, and one partner changed his mind. They fought. Then, etcetera."

"I was going to run for sheriff next year."

"Charlie's retiring?"

"Running for state senate. I'm trying to take his place.

Give me some of that bagel." She tosses a pinch of bread. "*Was.* Was going to take his place."

"Good for you." He means it. Does a quick tally of the advantages behind having his ex-wife as Park County Sheriff.

She asks, "So what are you going to do?"

"Did it already. Get rid of the body. Now wait and see what happens."

"Where's my kneecap breaker, the guy who kept a pipe wrench in his trunk?"

"Buried under pink marble in Newark."

She chews her lip, not quite conceding the point. "Okay," she finally says. "They're messing with you, which means they're messing with me. So let's just think a minute here." She tosses the entire bagel into the water, soliciting a brief, fluttering rumpus among the geese. "First, it takes balls to put a body in a chair like that. You've got to *have* a pair, right?" She raises her fist. "But you've also got to know when your two old geriatrics are going to be gone. Which means watching the place, keeping an eye out. You seen anybody hanging around? Any cars, trucks, hunters with binoculars?"

"No. I wondered about that, too. And no. Nada."

"Okay, so somebody at least not bad at surveillance. Staying inconspicuous. Also, somebody, safe to say, that didn't like that guy in your chair none too much."

"Safe to say."

"Okay. So what we're going to do. First thing, I'm going to find out who the Italian was. Find out who he ran with. Second, you're going to browse the bars, look for, you know, fedoras. Anybody you might recognize. Third, you're going to read some newspapers online, some *New York Times*, some *Post*. Browse some chat rooms. See what's been going down back home. See what the families are up to."

He could almost kiss her. "All right."

"You got anything that might have the dead guy's prints on it?"

He thinks about it. "Shotgun. He had a sawed off .410 in his lap. It's under my couch."

"A .410? Good lord."

"Yeah, right? It'll have prints, though."

"Okay, get it to me. I'll say I found it in a parking lot. Sawed off enough to be illegal?"

"Yeah."

"Meantime," she grabs him by the arm, shakes him. "Meantime, hey Sweeney? Lose the puppy dog eyes. I mean, Christ. Be a man."

~

When Sweeney was a kid, wise guys were well on the wane. They didn't know it, Sweeney and cousin Eddie, but they were coming late to the party. The tide was ebbing, pulling away from the pilings to reveal a beach wrack of retro-chic cement shoes, quaint pinky rings heavy as brass knobs, gnawed missiles of damp, dark Cohibas, money clips etched with the Virgin Mary. Paul Castellano got his ticket punched on the upper east side and opened the dam on a flood of RICO wiretaps. The good days were gone and maybe they weren't coming back. The Italianos, La Cosa Nostra, the muscle, the well-tentacled men's club of thousand dollar shoes and cashmere scarves, the embodiment of swaggering entitlement, of insulated privilege and petty hijackings, money laundering schemes and protection schemes and numbers schemes, of gears over gears, of a hierarchy of favors and obligations as

intricate and messy as spider webs tangled around a broom...
it was all going the way of the dodo, analogue in a digital universe. The Feds and RICO. The exiled Russian yids down on
Brighton Beach. The Dominicans up in Queens. Irish Westies
on the docks and greasy cocksuckers from Albania that spoke
no English past the hallowed seven epithets, unwashed deal-
ers from Columbia, as boneless and lethal as coiled snakes.
They were all converging on the twitching corpus of the five
families, buzzing like houseflies.

Sweeney was thirteen, Eddie four years older. They were
a rare thing these days (though they didn't know it)—the
next generation. Italianos with a mean streak, a love for
money and their own stereotyped narratives; no concern for
repercussions, for parents or cops or the feds with their cold
gray monolith of the Manhattan Penitentiary on south 18th.
Fuck em, was their attitude. They didn't fear nothing.

You want to make a hood? Give him a few early successes.
For six months, and initially under Eddie's direction, Sweeney slimjimmed game rooms up and down Brooklyn. Twen-
ty-seconds at a machine and a cloth coin bag held under a
cascade of coins. Like hitting cherries in Atlantic City. Then
out the door. If you were fast on your feet and kept your eyes
peeled, it was free money. The world rewards quick feet and
sharp eyes, was Eddie's philosophy.

In August of Sweeney's thirteenth year, Eddie had been
working at a tire shop on New Ultrecht and 84th, under the
ell. A job of some suspicion among the aunts and uncles. There
were rumors, ominous overtones of unruly dealings. Aunt
Florence had used those very words. Legs crossed, varicose
veins bulging, she blew a thread of smoke, said, "Eddie? I just
pray, god save him from all those unruly dealings over there."

But for the younger cousins, their admiration was undiluted. Eddie *knew* things. How to fake a fall on the subway, pull a wallet. The best bolt cutters to snip free a bike. Knew who said what to who and why. Who profited, who paid. Debts owed, debts received. Eddie knew it all, and doled out the knowledge like dimes. Just last week, he'd shown Sweeney a small silver key from his hip pocket. "Know what this is? Universal handcuff key. I ever get arrested? It's always right there where I can get at it. Don't leave home without it, right? You see what I'm saying?"

Coming home three-thirty in the afternoon, Sweeney was sweating through his shirt, laboring under a twenty-pound school backpack. Here's Eddie, cool at the bus stop. One foot cocked up on the glass, smoking a Camel. Back then, Camels were an old man's cigarette. Even his choice of smokes felt daring, unpredictable. The acne that would give him his scars, the pockmarks along his cheekbones, it was all in full bloom. An angry, painful pox of whiteheads and blackheads and half-squeezed sores. Sweeney envied even the zits. Wished he had a few of his own.

"Yo Cosmo. Little brother under a backpack. You're like a turtle with that fucking thing."

Sweeney's name, to pull the tooth early, was Cosimo Aniello. And while the Aniellos were, by and large, respectable people (longshoreman, cab drivers, pavers, an orthodontist, circuit court judges, a priest or two) Cosimo was a throwback name, an anachronism, a nod to his father's sense of history. "You could do worse, kid, than be named after the first Medici."

"Bum a smoke?" Thirteen years old.

"Sure." Eddie was nonchalant handing over the pack and

lighter. The movement pulled up his shirt sleeve.

"New tattoo?"

"Yin yang in barbed wire. What do you think."

"The fuck?" A turquoise circle the size of a fist, bifurcated with a faint S. The skin around it still red and irritated.

"Look it up." Eddie stepped on his cigarette. "Come on. Got somebody I want you to meet."

"I know what it means. I just never pegged you for no kind of finoochiu."

"It's *finocchiu*, and go fuck yourself. Let's go before I change my mind."

Friday afternoon, the city was out on stoops with coolers, electric fans blowing across blocks of ice, quart bottles of beer in paper bags, elbows on concrete and leisurely, the world-is-fine laughter. Maybe it was the cigarette, the pleasant dizziness, or maybe the proximity to his cousin, but Sweeney felt *fine*. Strolling through the vast acreage of Brooklyn's humanity, the rich stew of swirling city odors: Unwashed bodies, frying meats, garbage, melting asphalt. It was all so good.

"Little brother," Eddie said, putting his hand on Sweeney's shoulder, "you have a gold-plated invite to meet one Mister Jimmy Greco. Courtesy of your good cousin."

"The Nose?"

"Yeah, but you don't get to call him that. Nobody gets to call him that."

Sweeney was only briefly subdued. And sure, it might be true that in the larger ocean of the five families, the Nose was a small fish—a midlist soldier with a smallish crew of associates; a good, if unextravagant, earner—inside Sweeney's world, he was the equivalent of banker, mayor, newspaper editor. A man with power and occasional largesse. Fathers and uncles came to him for favors. Meeting him would be admittance to a certain kind of manhood.

"He likes respect," Eddie said as they walked. "Yessir, nosir. That kind of thing. Think you can handle it? Little smartass like you?"

"Yessir."

"And don't stare at his nose."

"Okay."

"He said he needs a new kid for the tire shop. A young kid, he said. Twelve years old. You're twelve, right?"

"Thirteen."

"Tell him you're twelve."

Why did Eddie choose Sweeney? Among the various litters thrown by their shared aunts and uncles, the twenty or thirty other children to whom they were related by blood but alien by preoccupation, he reached into the box and pulled Sweeney out by the scruff. Because the kid was quiet, maybe. Knew how to keep a secret. Maybe it was because, a year earlier, Sweeney had tossed bricks through each of the four apartment windows of a despised math teacher, a guy who had first flunked Eddie then, a few years later, given Sweeney a B. (Sweeney did *not* get Bs.) Or maybe it was because out of all of the parents, only their two mothers had married other Italians.

The tire shop sign, in flickering blue neon, read, "Tire Shop." Sweeney knew about this place the way you knew which delis had blind spots under the curved mirrors, which stoops to avoid past nine o'clock at night, knew the ephemeral but real jurisdictions of Brooklyn Latinos and blacks and Italians. That is to say, he didn't know how he knew but he knew.

Housed in an inauspicious, three-story red-brick building, there were apartment windows on the second floor, and, facing the street, a pair of bulkheads and two scrolling metal doors. The first was always open, admitting legitimate traffic from the street. Tilted, teetering columns of retreads and a cave of pneumatic wrenches and water basins and oil spills. The second metal door was opened only three or four times a month, its bay separated from the legitimate business by half of a brick wall, open just above eye level.

Most of the building, despite appearances from the street, was hollow. And the south end, the second floor, was the domain of Nose. From here, from his swivel chair with duct-taped arms, beside his smoldering coffeepot, between a pair of gray metal filing cabinets leaking forged receipts, he watched his blue-overalled kids pop beads and seal leaks and glue retread, touch up Goodyear lettering with white paint. And over the brick divider, he sometimes watched the offloading of untaxed cigarettes, cases of booze, stereo equipment meant for New Jersey.

The Nose wasn't a *bad* man. His ambitions were tempered by his pragmatism. His specialty was hijacking. Not especially bright, he knew enough to know his limitations. Liked to keep things simple. No numbers games or dope dealing for old Nose, no protection rackets or herds of whores. No, he liked the basic equation of shit coming in, shit going out. And because he paid up the ladder without complaint, and because he was careful with his kids (no rats, ever), he was respected. He got the good tables, sat with the capos, kissed the right cheeks, swung his admirable schnoz out across the constant trickle of cash, the tidal ebb and flow, without apparent envy or calculation.

He also knew how to manage his employees. If he caught one of his kids with his dick in his hands, leaning on an elbow, taking more than a few minutes to smoke a cigarette, he'd rap hard on the glass with the ruby ring on his second finger. The sound penetrated even the echoing clatter of the tire shop. One rap, a warning. Two raps, think about looking for another job. Third rap, finger across his throat, pack your shit, get out.

Eddie led Sweeney into the first concrete bay, into the odors of rubber and oil, the hollow cacophony of ratchets, and up a rickety wooden staircase against the southern wall. He knocked on the wooden door.

"Yeah, what is it?" A voice like nails in a rock tumbler.

Eddie opened it a few inches. "Boss? I got my cousin." Gone was the cocksure Eddie who strutted into church picnics with a six pack. In his place, an obsequious peon, a court jester already apologizing for bad jokes.

"All right, all right. Jesus, don't stand out there all day."

Jimmy the Nose sat with his feet up on his desk. Clipboard in his hands. Gnawed pencil in his hands. Smaller than you'd expect, slimmer. An old man gone ageless. He was Milton Berle, Dick Clark, George Burns with a rotten apple for a nose. And *Jesus*, what a nose. A robust, rosacean, bloom. It was J. P. Morgan, W. C. Fields, Bill Clinton on a bad day. Make matters worse, the Nose had the bad habit of compulsively sniffing at things, smelling the most random crap. He'd touch his desk then smell his hands. Sniff his tie, his shirt cuffs, sign a check then sniff the paper. Just *try* not to look at that thing.

"What's your name kid?" The pencil found a home behind his ear.

Eddie said, "Cosmo Aniello."

"Was I talking to you?"

Sweeney waited a beat, then said, "Cosmo. Sir."

"Aniello. You related to Pauly Aniello? Up in the Village?'

"Down the line somewhere, I think. Yessir."

"How old are you?"

"Twelve, sir."

"Don't overdo the sirs, kid. You're making me blush." But he looked approving.

"Okay."

"You got a bike kid?"

"Had one, yessir. Got ripped off a couple weeks ago."

"Yeah?" He showed interest. "You catch the punk what did it?"

"I got some ideas."

"Never let em get away with it. My advice to you? Never let nobody get away with it. You show weakness, they keep coming for you. People are jackals."

"Yessir."

"What's in the bag." A backpack by Cosmo's ankles.

"Books. Schoolbooks."

Eddie chimed in. "This kid's smart, boss. Reading all the time. Always got a book. Regular Shakespeare, this kid."

"Shakespeare, huh." The Nose said it with equal parts contempt and calculation. He rubbed his forefinger under his nose, sniffing. He touched an eyebrow, mentally rearranging a chessboard. "All right, kid. We need somebody to clean up the place, push a broom. Think your big brain'll let you be a janitor for a while?"

"Yessir. You bet."

"You bet. Okay. Shakespeare, broom pusher. Time to time, you'll be running pick ups and drop offs. You'll need a bike."

He leaned up on one hip for his money clip. Found a couple wrinkled bills and pushed them across the desk. "Here's an advance. I'll take it out of your first paycheck."

A twenty and a ten. What kind of a bike cost thirty bucks? "Thank you."

"You're welcome." He sat back in his chair, turning his attention to his window overlooking the bays. The boys working down below. "Now getcher asses out of here."

~

Despite himself, Sweeney's become attached to his old International. Every backfire and steering wheel wobble has the comfort of the familiar. Attachments are unavoidable, he supposes, if only because the alternative eats you alive.

His long term plan? Keep the air moving in and out of his lungs.

Short term? Take Aggie out to a nice dinner. Wring out his credit card for its last few hundred bucks. Maybe pay cash from the dead guy's wad, though that feels like flirting with fate. Feed her a decent bottle of red wine and drop to a knee. Show her the ring.

He's already running late, though. And so opts for the scenic route.

Five minutes out of downtown, he turns east, drives under the interstate on gravel toward the Absarokas. After a couple miles of washboard, he finds his favorite wide spot in the road. The town of Rockjaw distant behind him; ahead of him thataway, his cabin.

From under the seat, Sweeney pulls out his binoculars. As the crow flies, the cabin's less than ten miles away. Half-hidden in ponderosa, a brown metal roofline amidst the clutter of pine branches.

The name of his handyman business, "Anything for Money," tends to sometimes be taken literally. Harmless old Ted Sweeney, sure; neutered by circumstances, yes. But there must still be some last vestige of the old Cosmo, some lingering scent of past violence, because people keep coming to him with problems. "Anything for money? I might have some work for you." The last few years, he's once or twice done some strongarm stuff, jobs on the edge of ethically iffy. The guy who owns that cabin? A rancher, a millionaire, but seven-thousand scenic acres on the edge of National Forest couldn't keep him from losing his only son to skinheads up by Troy, Montana. Some kids get hooked on dope, meth, but this kid, sixteen years old and jerking off to Sarah Palin, found a compound full of neo-Nazis.

Sweeney followed the kid's stolen credit cards up to a third world cul de sac of Airstreams on blocks, German Shepherds on heavy chains. Sapped the boy off a bar stool and drove him back to Rockjaw, sedated and handcuffed to the door handle. One day to drive up, half an hour to find the kid, one day to drive back. Three thousand dollars. But better than the money, the old man made Sweeney a promise. "That cabin up there? Soon as you can get me a decent down payment, it's yours."

Next year Sweeney'll be thirty-eight. Two orbits away from forty, which is a whole new ball of wax. And here's what he's got to show for it. A good dog and an old International. A ring in his pocket and the hope for a cabin in the woods. A place where he might finally shake the sad etch-o-sketch called Ted Sweeney and start twisting all knobs anew. And while he's honest enough to know that the idealized vision could never survive the light of reality, he's romantic enough to hang onto the vision by his ragged fingernails.

Used to be, he'd walk down 86th street and cars would slow. Blonds would watch him in their makeup mirrors. The toughest men would pick at a spot on their lapels. His car (a *sweet* old Caddy, forget about it) was known from Dyker Heights to Coney Island.

In Montana, though, the Feds found him a pressman's job with the local paper. Rolls of newsprint, forklifts, electric dollies. He'd come home smelling like a house cat doused in diesel, his throat thick with the insults swallowed off his prissy little shift manager. Sweeney in blackface printer's ink, yasser yasser, thinking, *I'll break your knees, cocksucker.* He was going through a screwdriver phase, and when the orange juice ran out, he'd swig vodka straight from the bottle. He used to *be* somebody.

Feds had encouraged Billings. But he'd taken one look at the oil refineries, the badlands rimrocks, the strip malls, and said no, uh uh, no way. Ugly little city. For once, his wife had backed him up. "Don't you have anything, you know, *pretty?*" So they'd settled on Rockjaw. Where the mountains came down straight to the river and the river ran through the middle of town and geese swam in the park.

Five years and a divorce later, him and Aggie became an item. His bad luck to fall for a woman who's got all these unreasonable expectations about truth. Two divorces behind her, a pair of pre-Sweeneys each of whom kept saying, love you, love you, *love you*, right up to the point where they hit the road, she has said often that what she digs most about Sweeney is his honesty. Their first date, as the salad plates were being taken away, she said, "Nothing I hate worse in the world than a liar. What about you?"

And Sweeney, no stranger to the Reid technique of criminal interrogation, kept non-aggressive eye contact, maintained even breathing and refrained from swallowing (a bobbing Adam's apple is a dead giveaway). Said, "I couldn't agree more."

Tony Castori's always been vain. Even as a teenager, a dime bag schwag dealer in the South Brooklyns, Castori (AKA, Tony Castle, AKA, Tony the Trigger) dumped half his nut into clothes. His first collar? He was thirteen years old and walking out of Bloomingdale's in a jacket with tags tucked up under the cuffs. A security guard came out of nowhere, twisted up his collar. Sweet little silk number, that jacket. He still regrets the loss.

Nowadays, working second to Donnie Moretti, five years away (tops) from capo, he's got the scratch to indulge himself. Imagines that good clothes give him an extra, more fearsome edge. In any case, there's nothing like standing in front of a three-way mirror, fitting a new pinstripe number while some spic kneels with chalk, marking the hem. Who's short now, motherfucker. Who's a dago now, asshole. He's told his kid brother, his protégé, "First impressions, Fontana. I ever see you out the front door without a tie, I'm kicking your ass back upstairs."

But three days in pissant Montana? Damn if his world hasn't gone completely upside down. The place is all felt shirts and baseball caps. Hiking boots. Yesterday, he sat on the edge of his motel bed, one foot up, putting a final shine on his loafer. Said to his brother, "Okay, I'm going over a that little town with the airport. Flash them photos around, see what I come up with. You keep doing what we been doing. Eddie's wife shows up, keep an eye on her, gimme a call."

In Bozeman, he found a decent barber shop, which put him in a better mood, getting a nice wet trim. The barber said, "Brooklyn, huh?" Turns out the guy's got cousins in Dyker Heights. "You ever eat at The Seven Hills?"

"You kidding? They got my picture on the wall. They got a drink named after me. The Tonytini. Two olives, two onions, kicks you in the ass."

Back in his car, he called his wife. "Yeah, hey, how you doing. Yeah, still in Miami...no, it's all right, we got a pool, hey listen...okay, you listening? What? Okay, well you tell that punk kid he ever gets his ears pierced...hey, chiudere il becco. Your fuckin mouth, okay? You listen. Tell our son he ever gets his ears pierced I'm cutting them off and nailing them to the fuckin wall, okay?" His next call went to his piece of ass on the side, an effeminate queen named Eric or sometimes Erica. Don't ask, don't tell. Tony's voice went gentle, tender. "Heya bella, it's me. Just you know wondering what I could do all the way from Montana to make you happy." Those were personal calls. The next call, however, was business. Using a burner he'd just bought from Walmart. "Yeah, hey, it's Tony. No, nothing yet. How long you want...Okay, okay, Donnie. Just asking here. Just asking. Okay. I'm just, Fontana and me, we're just getting tired of, I mean, Montana. Like the Sahara only without the sand, you see what I'm saying?"

Then he called his brother, but the kid didn't pick up. Tony got tossed straight to voice mail. Said, "I tell you to keep your phone on, you keep your fucking phone on. You going to remember that next time, or you need to start writing it down, or what?"

Later that evening, feet up in the motel, the kid still ain't picking up. Tony said for the tenth time, "You get this, you fucking call me, you fucking call me now."

"Dancing with the Stars" was on the tube, but he couldn't really enjoy it. This was his kid brother here. The youngest of four, and the only one with Tony's ambition to get things done.

But Montana, right? What kind of trouble could he get in?

Tony dozed off, red wine in one hand, cell phone in the other.

Aggie's the kind of woman, you catch a glimpse of her on the street, and just before recognition, you find yourself thinking wholesome thoughts. Julia Child and Christmas, 1950s TV, early Chevy ads.

And Aggie's house? For Sweeney's money, it's America boiled down to grit. The last bastion of the unironic, the eye in a cultural hurricane of insincerity and cynicism masquerading as sophistication. The kind of place that makes you want to comb your hair, straighten your tie. It's got shade trees, sprinklers, kids on bikes delivering newspapers. It's got…

But then no. No, it doesn't. No truck in the driveway. Everything but the woman herself.

He loves her, sure, but. The woman's *always* late. Seven thirty, he'd said. And now he's disappointed. Another reason he knows this is love, how he looks forward to seeing her at the end of each day.

He has a key. Coming up the walk, he doesn't quite dodge a sprinkler. Sticks his head in the door. "Anybody home?"

From the front hall, it's a straight shot through to the sliding glass back door. Aggie's daughter, Elizabeth, responds faintly, "Back here."

Sweeney goes to the junk drawer for a wine opener. Uncorks merlot.

On the kitchen table, a fan of carelessly tossed mail. A

bill from Northwest Energy, a couple magazines (*Vogue, Guns & Ammo*), and then…god*damn*it. Another manila envelope. Aggie's address spelled out in the same block handwriting.

In the back yard, Elizabeth is sunbathing, kicked back, singing along to the radio. Faintly: "Roll over Beethoven, tell Tchaikovsky the news." Through the kitchen window, the empty driveway.

Sweeney gingerly pops the seal of the envelope, opens the metal catch. Inside, a single sheet with the same photo that Marilyn had received. Same body, same Charlie Russell print on the wall. This time, a caption: "He's worse than you think."

Okay, okay. What's a guy do in this situation?

Only thing he can do: He folds the sheet into fourths, slips it into his back pocket. Replaces the flap on the envelope and flattens the metal ears. Inexplicable, of course, an empty envelope in the mail. But inexplicable is better than unforgiveable.

Sweeney takes his wine into the backyard. "Are you Lizzie today, or Beth?"

Aggie's daughter sits in a black bikini patterned with white sailboats, painting her toenails, knees to her chin. A Horowitz of the sarcastic comeback, a Lolita of the lingering look, she's one of those teenagers who should only be dealt with by moon-faced monks constrained by vows of silence and chastity.

She's also still unemployed two months out of high school, and cute enough to expect the world to come to her. Maybe it will. In her bedroom, she sleeps among the pinks and mauves of a sixth grader, stuffed animals arranged on pillows, boxes of Barbies that never seem to make it to Goodwill. But in the backyard, she's all teenager.

She glances up, then devotes herself again to her toes. "Always Beth to you, Mr. Sweeney. Mom tell you about quitting her job?"

"Told me she was thinking about it."

"That's just her way of opening the subject."

Conceived when Aggie was fifteen, these two women circle each other within the awkward boxing ring of not-quite-parent, not-quite-siblings. They clench and uppercut in equal measure, weeping, bleeding, sacrificing, occasionally biting off an ear. Elizabeth resents and loves her mother, barely tolerates her, while Aggie has to deal with seeing her daughter attract more attention than she does. It's a difficult thing, Sweeney supposes, for a young mother to watch her daughter become competition.

"She already quit?" Sweeney ponders the implications of an insolvent Aggie.

"Uh huh." Elizabeth puts a final dab on a pinky toe and caps her polish. Sets it aside and stretches languorously back. A kitten on a windowsill. "She's going to ask if she can go into business with you. Be your secretary or something."

"Elizabeth..."

"Whaaat...?" Drawing it out, teasing him, stretching.

Sweeney leans forward on his knees. "You want to fuck me, is that it?" Tired, he can feel his veneer cracking. Some putz trying to set him up, meanwhile here's his future stepdaughter, playing cheap hooker.

"What?" She half giggles, then sits up. "*What* did you just say to me?"

"Want me to give it to you *good*, huh?" He makes a motion. "Hard?"

"You can't talk to me like that..."

"Well stop fucking acting like it." He tosses off his wine. Her problem, no authority figure. "I won't stand for it. You're like a cat in heat, sticking your tail up under my nose."

She turns on her lawn chair, giving him her bare shoulder. "Leave, then."

Sweeney's phone vibrates in his pocket. He checks out the number. "That'll be the day."

~

Cousin Eddie used to have a theory about balance. About the universe keeping itself on an even keel. Let's see if Sweeney can remember this right. A riff on philosophical materialism, a la Fodor. Everything is energy, right? E equals MC whatever. So let's say there's a fixed amount of energy in the system. Energy dissipates, it don't disappear. But if *everything* is energy, shouldn't that apply to how folks behave toward each other, too? Good and evil, there's only so much to go around. Every bad thing, it only follows that there must be a good thing out there to balance it out.

The notion stuck with Sweeney. The trick is, though, what's good, what's evil? And what about repercussions? Unintended consequences? What's good for me is evil for you.

Sweeney says into his phone, walking back into Aggie's house, "Yeah hello, what."

In his ear, the laughter and musical confusion of a downtown bar. A woman's voice: "…sweetheart, I don't smoke Kools. What do I look like, I mean, hellooo? Here. Here's five bucks. Get me some Vantage's…hello?"

"Yeah, hello."

"Who is this."

"You called me."

"*Sweeney?*"

"Yeah, who's this?"

"Teddy baby, Teddy boy, lover boy. It's Cheryl, sweetheart. You don't recognize my voice. I'm *dev*-uh-stated. I'm *heart*broken. I'm, uh, hey, you got a, don't forget the matches there…"

"What's up, Cheryl." Rubbing his eyes. God save him from drunks with cell phones. "And aren't you supposed to be in rehab or something?"

"What's up. Um, yeah. Okay, oh yeah, right. There's this chick down here, you got to come down and say hello, I mean, *got to*. Okay?"

"Why's that?"

"She's talking about this guy, and he sounds just *like* you. Like he must be your twin brother or something."

"What'd she say?"

She pulled away from the phone again. "I gave Patrick all my change, go find him. *Dying* for a smoke…"

"Cheryl?"

"…no, I said Vantage. What?"

"What'd she say?"

"Oh! She said one of her old buddies was living out here somewhere. New York accent, New *Yawwk*, right? Tall, good looking. Quotes fancy pantsy writers nobody else has ever heard of. Has these scars around his eyes. I mean, right? How many of you guys could there be in the world."

"Where are you?"

"God, I owe you my *life*, thank you, sweetheart. You're a savior. What's that now?" The sound of a lighter, then a vast inhale. Montana has smoking laws, but enforcement is spotty.

"Where. Are. You."

"Oh. The Spur, sweetheart. Where else?"

~

Sweeney pulls out of the driveway just as Aggie pulls in, bag of groceries on the seat beside her. They roll down their windows. "Thought we were going out," she says.

There's something of the water bird about Aggie. One of those women who grows more interesting with age. Not quite haggard, not quite mannish, light blue eyes and tobacco-brown cheeks. Good calluses in her handshake. Since leaving high school to have Elizabeth, she's juggled jobs and checkbooks, a weekly roulette spin of heating bill versus phone bill, prom dress versus gas money. She works forty hours a week at the Park County Library. In slow periods, she's read her stalwart way up and down the shelves. The only person he knows who has trudged through the entirety of both Balzac and Trollope.

It amazes him that no one else in this small town recognizes this woman for what she is.

"Just got a handyman call. Gimme an hour? You okay with a late dinner?"

With Aggie, the tiny lies are more dangerous than the big ones. She has a nose for duplicity. "Okay..."

"I opened a bottle of wine on the counter. Have a drink. I'll be back before you can finish it." Sweeney puts his truck into gear, the transmission bitching a little. "Oh, and your daughter's going to be talking shit about me. Lies, all lies."

Familiar territory, complaining about Elizabeth. Sweeney's relieved to see Aggie roll her eyes, briefly distracted. "That girl, I swear."

"Okay. See you in an hour. Love you." This last said quickly.

Not the first time, but still one of only a handful. Special occasions all. He leaves her staring after him, squinting.

Not necessarily a bad thing, to keep a woman guessing.

~

There are twenty-one churches in Rockjaw but twenty-three bars. Self-absorption and regret have, for now, beaten out self-congratulation and piety to the tune of at least two taverns. People keep count.

The bar lately calling itself the Rusty Spur is, as it happens, one of Sweeney's favorite joints. Sipping his Scotch, swirling the ice. Amid the haze and mirrors, the wink of bottles and the smell of ancient cigars, here, at least, he is not confronted with the cheerful and scrubbed faces of the more successful, the younger and less regretful.

A long bar and, at the back, a pair of cigarette-scarred pool tables. Two TVs and yesterday's newspaper spread out in pieces. A small, late-eighties boombox churns out an endless melancholy mix of Patsy Cline and Willie Nelson. Ten years ago, he'd been a Mahler fan, liked his Berlioz. Now it's outlaw country.

He stands in the door, letting his eyes adjust to the gloom. He hears his name in a boozy, feminine flute of a voice. "Sweeeeney!" And down the bar, just ahead of the beaded curtain that leads to the bathroom, a tiny platinum-haired shadow peels away from a circle of drinkers.

"Cheryl. Light of my life. How's tricks?"

Ninety pounds of cheerful, over-exuberant meth addiction, Cheryl's one of Sweeney's less successful social projects. Five years ago, she'd been a high school volleyball player of genuine talent. But a stripper mother and an absentee father, turns out volleyball's for losers. Sweeney had encouraged college. Helped her navigate some student loans. But here's where good intentions get you. Two weeks out of rehab, she's twitching like one of those windup toy penguins that dance across your desk. The complexion and lips of a porcelain figurine but the teeth of a Kentucky tobacco chewer. She grabs him by the arm. "Come on, come on, come *on*. Getcher ass over here. *Got* to meet this gal, got to meet her. I mean, hey. Is that a new shirt? Lookin' smaaart! How's Aggie doing, by the way. Hey, you ever want to take a break from that same ol' same ol', you be sure and let me know..." She hauls him forcefully up to the bar. "Ted Sweeney, here's, uh, what's your name again sweetie?"

"Tina." The woman straightens, turns. Gives him La Giaconda with attitude.

Sweeney's heart stutters and backfires. His next breath is something less than a theory.

She. Her. Them. Ten years ago, one day before Cosmo died, he'd laid in bed, studying this woman's naked body. He'd thought then, knowing it was the last time, *Remember this*. And now he does.

"Lazarus is arisen," she says, "walking west on the pieces of broken hearts. You're a hard man to find, Cosmo."

Think fast. A dozen faces around them, all staring expectantly. Despite the various levels of intoxication, there's collectively enough consciousness here to scuttle Sweeney good, to pull the chain on this whole lengthy charade. The word will spread: Cosmo is Sweeney, and vice versa. If he doesn't do the opposite of the wrong thing here, he's done in Montana.

He sticks out his hand. "Yeah, I know. Everybody says

you, *you* got one of those faces. But we haven't met, I'd have remembered." Going all flirty, clearly (as far as the audience is concerned), making a play. "Ted Sweeney." Sends a thought her way: Please, please, *please*.

He watches her tumblers turn and click, click, click toward a conclusion.

She reaches up to touch his chin with a knuckle. Turns his face this way and that. "Yeah, my mistake. Sorry about that, Mister, uh, Sweeney? You're the spittin' image of this guy I used to know back in Brooklyn."

"Brooklyn, eh? What part?" Sweeney lifts a finger for a beer.

"Bensonhurst."

"Gangsters, huh? Williamsburg, me." Sweeney can't stop sneaking glances. Tina, here, in Montana. The incongruity of it. It's like gravity reversing itself, the sun rising at midnight. She's aged, sure, but...damn.

"Hipsters. Even worse."

"So they tell me."

The beer arrives, and Sweeney gives it a distracted sip. Says under his breath. "Parking lot. Ten minutes." Then to Cheryl, "Gotta go, sweet little thing. You stay clean now, okay?"

"Eh? Oh, yeah, hey." Her half-shuttered eyes flutter fast to a private tune.

Us and our poisonous appetites. The luckiest among us are devoured across our lifetimes. The rest go fast as paper matches.

~

Sweeney's weakness is women. Chin, cleavage, calves. Over the years, he's loved them indiscriminately, unwisely, urgently. They're his idols and his altars, his chalices of wine. A pair of tight, sunburned calves under a sundress will pull him clean out of a conversation. Is she a tennis player? A careful tuck of hair behind an ear and a laugh big enough to reveal her molars. Is she really such a happy person or is she compensating, covering up? He wants answers.

And because he's tall and thin, and because he has self-confidence, the interest is usually reciprocated. Best drug in the world, that initial meeting of the eyes, the mutual appraisals. Even after he got married, he couldn't stop. It became more dangerous, of course, but...no choice. His love of Marilyn didn't legislate against his interest in the tennis player's calf.

Sweeney sits on the hood of his International, thinking about Tina. It's like gnawing at a thumbnail, equal parts pleasure and pain, peeling away satisfying strips of himself.

She walks toward him under islands of yellow light, heels echoing on asphalt. Used to be, her beauty was effortless. A Hunter College sweatshirt and hair pulled back with a hank of yarn. One touch of her fingertip was enough to send him off like a tuning fork. But she's wearing makeup now, and keeping the fingertips to herself.

He says, "I forgot how tall you are."

"Part of it's these boots." Calfskin numbers in lavender and rhinestones.

They'd met in a bar in the East Village. An afternoon of stained concrete floors, tattooed bartenders, Tom Waits on the stereo. Off Sweeney's turf, but he was just looking for a place to read the racing sheets and get quietly fucked up. Make notes on tomorrow's bets. Over in the corner, here's this twenty-year-old Mediterranean-looking chick. Beautiful in a Staten Island sort of way. She maybe had a little Arab blood back in there somewhere. That smooth, smooth skin and dark eyes. Her crooked teeth kept her from flawlessness, but with her mouth closed, she was Salome, Helen, Beatrice. The kind of woman, every time you looked at her it was like a tiny little vacation.

Her date was a dump truck of a man. A weight lifter, rebel flag stitched on his jacket. He had her by the arm. "I can't trust you to do a single simple goddamn thing? I tell you to make just one..."

Tina, squirming: "*Offa* me!"

And so much for a quiet afternoon with booze. "Hey buddy."

"Mind your own goddamned busin...."

Sweeney twisted the guy's wrist up against his back, hit the shoulder with the heel of his palm. Just that quick, he'd popped the joint. Watched the guy go pale as Elmer's glue. Doesn't matter how big you are, nothing hurts like a dislocated shoulder. You're helpless, emasculated. The guy slipped to the floor like a sodden towel, patch of piss darkening his lap.

Sweeney looked at Tina. "Buy you a drink?"

Twelve years later, here she is in a parking lot in Montana, saying, "I don't know whether to hug you or shoot you, you sonofabitch."

"I'm ready either way." He raises his arms like a rood.

She sighs, produces a pack of smokes. Sweeney's helpful with his lighter, and they have a moment. Sweeney says, "You need to get off the street."

She blows smoke. "No chit chat, huh. Just straight to bed."

"Not for me, no. I'm kind of engaged. You know, more or less." Still, some part of him—the basic, reptilian, reproductive core back behind the cerebral cortex—wakes up and smells opportunity. Their sex had been so, so good.

"So, you and Rachel...?"

"Her name's Marilyn now. Yeah, somebody left the coop door open, we both flew."

"I'm married now, too." Glances away in what could be guilt or grief or guile.

"Congrats to the lucky fellow and all that." Some part of himself, he's appalled to note, deflates. "But seriously," Sweeney hops off his hood and walks around to open his truck door for her, "let's get you off the street. We could drive out to my place, be about fifteen minutes..." he remembers his sink stacked with dirty dishes, the beer cans overflowing out of garbage bags. "Or where are you staying? You got a motel room?"

She's staring at his door. "Anything for money, huh? Kind of ironic, seeing as how that's why I'm here and all."

"You got a motel room?" Sweeney looks up and down the street.

Sure she does. The Blue Sky, half a dozen blocks to the east. The same fleabag, in fact, that had harbored the dead guy's rental car.

Inside his truck, she slips off her boots, puts a bare foot on his dashboard to massage the arch. It's a gesture so unguarded, so familiar, it sucker punches him right in the heart. "You *live* here, Cosmo?" she says. "This little town? Jesus, how do you stand it."

Sweeney pulls into the parking lot. "So how'd you know which...uh, town?"

He notes the parking spot that had last night held the dead guy's Taurus. The car's gone.

Tina says, "What's wrong."

"Nothing. What room, again?"

~

Sweeney should call Aggie. Instead (what's another ten minutes?) he gets comfortable on the second of two beds, ignoring the No Smoking sign to tip ashes into a plastic cup half full of water. "So."

"How do I look, Cosmo. Do I look good?" Touching her hair. Used to be, she'd be coy about her second glass of wine, making it last. But now she has a silver flask from her purse and pours gin over ice from the hotel's machine. She doesn't offer him one. Curled up on the other bed, putting her stockinged legs together, dig the sound of silk against silk.

"You look good. So." He holds up his ring finger. "Who's the lucky fellow?"

"You're talking different now. You got that Midwestern twang thing going on now. All Brent Musburger and shit. I like it, it's nice."

"Thanks." He waits.

She drinks her drink and pours another. Rubs her face. In the dim light of the bar, what had looked like an artfully-arranged, cascading mess of hair is, in fact, simply a mess. Take a step closer to the comb, Tina. Her nails have seen better days and the collar of her blouse is raveling at the corners. "How long you been dead now, Cosmo?"

"Call me Sweeney."

"Ohhhkay. How long?"

"Ten years. More, I guess."

"Lot can happen in ten years."

"You ain't shittin'." Some portion of every day spent wondering about the tiny dramas playing out, even now, back home in Brooklyn. "You keep in touch with anybody from the old days?"

"Yeah, I mean. *Yeah.*" She takes one of his cigarettes. Lights up. "After you died, me and Eddie started a thing. Kind of. Kind of where you and me left off." This last said in a tentative, wistful way.

"Eddie? *My cousin*, Eddie?"

"Yeah, we been married, what is it, six, seven years now."

How do you even start to digest this? "So. Uh. Wow. Okay. How's he doing?" Back then Eddie hadn't even *liked* Tina. What was his word for her? Hoity-toity.

"Not too good right now. Neither one of us."

"Okay...?"

"Eddie's the one sent me out here. He's, *we*, we're in a pinch. He's kind of laying low for a while. Waiting until you and me can take...some of the heat...off." Her voice dwindles to a whisper. "Fuck it. I'm scared, Cosmo."

During the subsequent long silence, Sweeney thinks: *Shit*. Tina sees him wrestling with it. "I gotta take a leak."

"Always the lady." One of the things he'd liked about her. Coarse and crass, but the poise of British royalty. Nobody could flick a cigarette like Tina.

He can't help comparing her now, though, to Aggie. Who wouldn't say piss if she got dunked in it.

With Tina out of the room, Sweeney finds his ring box. Flips open the lid and gives himself a second or two. Trades the box for his cell phone. "Yeah, hey, it's me...Yeah, I know. I'm sorry baby. Yeah. Okay, well, let me fill you in on all this later. Okay. Trust me? Okay, yeah. Thanks, babe. Talk to you soon...Hour or two, at the most. Okay. Bye."

Tina's standing in the bathroom door, blouse untucked. "Short leash, huh?"

~

Tina settles in with her third glass of gin. "So what I want to know, I mean, why the car crash and funeral, right? Why not, just, you know, *phew*...." she kisses her fingertips, "... disappear."

"My mother, my sister, Eddie. Ma familia. You too. Those Russians, they got no....decency. Is maybe the word. That guy got sent up to Sing Sing? Bytchkov. He ever thought I was still alive? He'd have gone after everybody. Sisters, cousins, whatever. When I turned states, I didn't want a chance, not a single chance, there'd be a vendetta on the table. My one condition."

"You did it for me."

"Yeah. In part."

"You never thought about...." She stares into her drink. Opens her mouth, shuts it again.

"What?"

"Nothing. Forget it."

"So you and Eddie? How'd that happen?"

"Dangerous men, Cosmo. You got me hooked."

"And college?"

"Couple years into it, well. It lost its spice."

"Now here you are."

"A man who states the obvious."

"How'd you find me?" The question of the hour.

"Eddie. He figured it out. I got the idea it weren't too hard." She stares at him, acting cool.

Sweeney can play that game. "And how'd he take it when he found out I was still alive?"

"How you think?"

"Pissed?"

"Yeah, I mean...*yeah*? Cousin Cosmo? You know how much he grieved over you? That first year after the funeral, he lost like twenty pounds. And he was already skinny. You meant more to him than I ever will. I'm just being honest. Then once he found out, couple months ago I think, he figured, yeah, you must have had your reasons, Russians and all."

"I'm surprised he's not out here himself."

"He's been, yeah uh, preoccupied." She twists hair in her finger.

"Well, whatever shit you got yourselves into, you're still in it."

"Meaning?"

"There was a guy in town showing around a photo. Asking about you."

A little drunk, she's taking it pretty well. "What'd he look like?"

"Does it matter?"

"Might, yeah." —

"Short little guy. Clothes horse. Shoes built up on the soles. Ring a bell?"

"Not even a bit," she says, but might be lying. Tosses off her drink and taps on the plastic rim with a fingernail, beating out a rhythm. "Wanna know why I'm here?"

~

He does, of course he does, but what Sweeney finds now, more than anything, is that he wants to hear about home. He wants gossip. Ten years. Ten years of squeezing pennies like they were pimples, ten years of lying in bed and wondering about his sister, his cousins, about Eddie, he needs information, needs details he can roll around in his head during the next fifty years of sleepless nights. "So where are you guys living?"

"Bensonhurst, on Seventy-second? Got a little red brick townhouse. It's *nice*, Cosmo. Two stories, three bedrooms. These gorgeous big pictures windows on the second floor. Eddie put em in special so I'd have good light for my houseplants. Neighborhood's gone wall to wall Chinamen these days, but we got good parking."

"You keep in touch with any of the old gang? Mike Maio? Jimmy Ruggino?"

"Oh yeah, I mean. Some."

"So?"

"Well. Mike's down at that penitentiary in Atlanta, twenty to life. He got drunk and ran over some old lady."

"Wouldn't that be involuntary, though? I mean twenty to life for a hit and run?"

"Yeah, but. He drug her under the car for a while? Claims he didn't know she was under there, but you know Mikey. He's got that weird sense of humor? Anyway, there was this school, PS 128? Out for recess, and yeah, all these fourth graders stood at the fence, watching him drag this sweet old lady for like half a block. Some of those kids were in therapy for, you know, *months*."

"He never was the sharpest knife. What about my family? Uncle Joe's kid Cathy was dating some Mexican. How'd that ever work out?"

"Yeah, Cuco. He's Puerto Rican. Owns his own plumbing business in Newark. Has like *twenty* guys working for him. Cathy and Cuco, they got a couple kids. *Cuties*. But I mean, we don't see them much. Eddie and Mexicans, right?"

They talk for half an hour. Finally, Tina stubs out her

cigarette, says, "This is great and all, memory lane, don't get me wrong. But I drove all this way in my little Toyota, which doesn't get great gas mileage by the way, and..."

"You drove?"

"Through South Dakota, Cosmo. I mean, Jesus. You ever *been* to South Dakota? Just to find my old flame. And now he apparently doesn't give a shit why."

"Yeah, all right. So. Why?"

She exhales. "Finally."

~

"You never used to carry a purse."

Smoking, using both hands to dig around in her handbag, she squints up. "Yeah? You never used to wear blue jeans or apologize. Pot kettle black, right?" She comes up with a clenched fist. "Okay. You remember how you and Eddie were always talking about efficiency of effort? The big kahuna score, the one you could use to leave the life?"

"He told you about that did he?" This, more than anything, brings home how his lady on the side and his best friend have been living lives intertwined. Efficiency of effort had been Eddie's favorite phrase. Rather than nickel and diming all these little hijackings and blackmailings, he was always looking for that one. Big. Score.

"He got it, Cosmo. He *got* it. Problem is…" She opens her fist and tosses him a piece of crushed gravel. "Problem is, we got no way to move it."

Sweeney snags the stone out of the air. Opens his palm.

Poorly lit between his heart line and life line, here's some kind of *rock*, man. A blob of a stone. If it weren't for the sides flattened out into octahedrons, he might have just spit out a wad of bubblegum. He holds it up to the light. The surface winks palely opaque. He bounces it in his hand. "Is this what I think it is?"

"What do you think it is?"

"The biggest fucking uncut diamond I've ever seen in my life."

"Ding ding ding. The man goes to the bonus round." Tina stubs out her cigarette in her gin. "Take that times four or five dozen. Enough rocks to fill up a ten gallon hat. That's what we got. And given the people Eddie pissed off getting hold of them? Yeah, pretty much the whole wide world. We got no way to move them."

"What do you want me to do about it?"

"You'll get your cut, don't get me wrong. Ten percent? Management fee?"

"You want me to find a buyer? Out here in Montana."

"*Shake*speare in Montana. Take the wiseguy out of the city, is our thinking, right?"

Ten percent. Despite himself, he's already thinking: Why not half? "Where's Eddie during all this?"

"Laying low. The heat he's got on him right now? It's like the limbo. How low can you go."

"And who's bringing the heat?"

She lights another cigarette, smoking and staring, judging. "I'm not sure that's a need-to-know sort of thing. Need-to-know basis. That was always what you were always saying, remember?'

"I'm in Montana. I'm dead. What harm could it I possibly do."

She shrugs.

"So how's Eddie expect me to move a hatful of diamonds?"

Standing up, she twists her silky legs his direction, him on the edge of the bed. She folds his fingers over the stone and straddles him slow, arms crossed around his neck. "Cosmo, mi amore." She kisses him lightly on the forehead, then the nose. The mouth. Her lips open slow, and her tongue gives him a tentative tap. "We got faith."

You ask Tony Castori how many people he's killed, he'll say thirteen. Thirteen's a good number. He'll talk about car bombs, digital actuators, Mohawk caps, Semtex wired into ignition systems. He'll talk pipe wrenches and .22 slugs in the back of the head. Truth is, though, he's personally responsible for only one mortality, a hit and run in Midwood. Some short little waspy fireplug of a guy come running across Thirteenth Avenue on a Saturday evening, trying to make the light. Maybe he was heading to see his girl. Dressed up in cashmere and khakis, he was forced to meet Tony's Cadillac all of a sudden like. Twenty-eight hundred bucks in body work later, Tony had a notch on his bandolier.

Unlike most killers, and maybe because his hit was an actual *hit*, Tony's still got a tiny little bit of heart in him. Shriveled and underused, sure; wrinkled like fingertips coming out of a bath, yeah, but it's a heart.

Friday morning, alone in the motel room, this feeling he's got in his gut, it's no damned good for nobody. It's like when he saw the legs under his Caddy, red blood pebbling through the broken asphalt. He tries his brother again. Gets popped straight to voice mail.

You start imagining accidents. Cops. Coronaries. Twenty-eight's not necessarily too young. Plus, I mean...*Montana*. Rattlesnakes, bears. He stares off at the horizon. Maybe he'll try the hospital. Cop shop. Fontana's not much of a boozer, but he likes his dope. Maybe he tried to score and got collared.

Tony knots a blue-and-black striped tie in the mirror, a limited edition silk number from Seigo. Slaps the blood into his cheeks, breathes deep through the nose. Okay, he'll get this figured out. The fucking kid. Poppa's dead, but Momma... God won't let it happen.

In the rental car, he wets a fingertip, touches his eyebrows. Does a double take.

Briefcase. He'd left it on the floor there right there, right fucking *there*. Fifteen hundred dollar Brooks Brothers calfskin. Now it's gone.

Okay, so yeah. This changes things.

Motherfuckers. I mean, mother*fuckers*.

He hits the steering wheel with his palm. Winces, inspects his hand for a bruise. Sits for a while, absorbing the implications.

Ten minutes later, he goes to a pay phone across from his motel. Dials Donnie. "Yeah, hey, it's me. Call me back at..." He pulls back, gives him the number. It rings five minutes later. "Yeah, hey. Fontana's gone missing. Fuck if I know, we split up yesterday. I ain't heard from him since. But, yeah... but the thing is, is my briefcase, see, it's gone too. No, yeah, Donnie, I know. What? Yeah, pistol, pictures, some cash. No, he wouldn't a just took it. But Donnie, hey, just listen...okay. What I'm saying, they got Fontana. What I'm saying..." Tony takes a breath, looks up and down the street. Dirty pickups parked at angles. A fishing shop. Some kind of art gallery. A half dozen cowboy bars already open for business. "I think we got competition out here."

For the next ten hours, Tony finds himself going through the motions. Feel the tension, man. He's a hammer thumbed back slow, he's an overinflated tire, tight as teak. If this little shitheel excuse for a town is in the least way responsible for one single hair gone missing on little Fontana's head, it'll be a Bruckheimer movie. God's wrath will come down, and it shall be called Tony Trigger. Fire, brimstone, a voice thundering from the clouds.

Poor kid. Tony fights back tears.

In the hospital, he clears his throat at a couple nurses. "Yeah, heya. I'm looking for my brother? Late twenties, about my height, yeah. You had anybody breaking a leg or something?" Nothing, of course. Then he considers asking at the sheriff's office, the city police, but whichever way he can imagine that conversation going, it don't go his way. If Tony Trigger got on the radar in Montana, he'd get blamed for every half ass bank job and convenience store holdup inside of a hundred miles.

Lack of a better plan, he starts a slow rotation through the bars, sipping Johnnie Walker, feeding bills into poker machines. Hell, this town ain't so bad. He wins fifty-two dollars at Mustang Sally's, loses it again (plus a twenty) at The Lazy Bar B. A series of affable, booze-hardened bartenders give him a little bit of shit about his hat, his tie, his suit. "Some kind of convention in town?"

He doesn't mind. "The tie? You like the tie? Hundred and twenty dollar tie, you ain't seen none of these in here before. Not unless you seen my brother. He likes the bars. Looks kind of like me, right? Little shorter? Dresses sharp?"

Finally he gets a hit. "Yeah, he was in here yesterday about this time. Looking for some woman. Had a picture?"

"That'd be him. What time was that?"

"I don't know. What time..." He shouts into the back. "Carol, what time was that kid in here with the pictures?"

Come dusk, all Tony's got to show for his time is a Scotch drunk. He stands wobbly under a streetlight, squinting at metal numbers on the phone. "Yeah, hey, it's me. Call me back." A minute later, picks it up on the first ring. "No he's still gone. I figure tomorrow I'm shaking down some Russians. You know how they stick together. Gotta be somebody in Montana they'd want to connect with...No, yeah, no sign of Eddie's woman either. Fuck no, I'm not giving up...I'm just... Donnie, hey man. Please, you know how much I...No...what it is, I just need me some more guys out here. I'm flying solo out here. How about you get Nick Scarpa and that buddy of his, what's his name, Jake, Jack, something. I need me some ballbusters out here. Get me some ballbusters..."

Talking to Donnie, Tony keeps an eye on the street, the motel, the parking lot. Notes a drunk staggering down the sidewalk. Across the street, a broken-down pickup pulls into the parking lot, bleeding exhaust from the side panels, limping on bald tires.

Tony squints in the dim light. Something about that driver....

The truck pulls into the motel lot. A woman steps out of the passenger's side. Not too hard on the eyes, good set of wheels. And sure the light ain't too good, but maybe that's, yeah. That could be her. No, no. Uh uh. That *is* her, that's fucking *her*. And the guy she's with...something about him. Right on the tip of his tongue. Looks like that guy, that car wreck guy, got his number punched by the Russians. Everybody said it was the Russians. The rat, what was his fucking name...

"Donnie. I gotta check something out. I'll call you back, gimme half an hour. You ain't going to believe this..." Against protestations, he hangs up the phone.

Turning back, here's the drunk up against him, slouched

and slovenly, eyes hidden under a homburg. He's got his hand out. Slurs, "Heya buddy, chew gotya couple bucks you might could..."

"Fuck away from me." Tony shoves the drunk to the side, watching as Eddie's wife and that *guy* (what's his *name?*) disappear into the hotel.

It's like a poet or something. Like Pound or Frost or... Shakespeare! Shakespeare. Risen from the dead and hiding out in Montana. One part of the puzzle falls into place. *That's* why she came all this way out here.

The drunk is back in front of him again. "Just a few bucks, man. Com'on. Heave a heart." He bumps against Tony, raises his head. "Please? Tony?"

And then the drunk swings his hand around quick, a blur with an eight-inch lead sap attached. It collides with Tony's temple, cracking like an axe into wood.

Tony's head fills with a shower of silver confetti. Nausea, and a quick, coalescing curtain of darkness. His last clear thought, even as he feels himself slung limp around the shoulders of the drunk (who is not, of course, a drunk), his last dim, coherent thought, even through the confusion and disappointment, is an apology: Oh I'm sorry, I'm so sorry, Mama, Fontana, me I'm so, oh, I'm....

Sweeney's no cop, although in a parallel universe, an alternate reality wherein black is white, up is down, etc. etc., he might have made for a badass detective. Indeed, having watched his ex-wife shed her carapace of earrings, scarves, and minks in favor of starched khakis and a star, anything is possible.

Exhibit one: He's never been able to let go of a question.

Every question, Eddie used to say, has to have an answer, otherwise it ain't no question at all. The kind of roundabout reasoning Sweeney used to love.

The problem now? Too many questions. It's like an old Buster Keaton movie, like opening a closet to let loose an avalanche of hats and coats and wooden tennis rackets.

Leaving Tina's motel room—"Just stay close, keep your head down. Anybody knocks on this door? Don't let them in, okay?"—he thinks, what do I do with all this? The image that comes to mind, right after Buster Keaton, is a juggler with chainsaws, maybe a flaming torch. You can't slow down, you can't stop.

On the concrete stoop outside the motel's office, he lights a Camel. Hands in pockets, tilts his head back to the stars. A cool night. An hour alone in a motel room with Tina and his virtue is still intact. Cause enough for a few seconds of self-congratulation. Ten years ago, they'd been famished for each other. Biting shoulders, licking ears. So, yeah, he's held himself together not-so-bad. Performed well viz Aggie.

Still, he finds himself shaken.

Bourbon, he thinks. American whiskey.

In his flannel shirt pocket, the rock from Tina. "You mind if I keep this for a while?"

She'd been suspicious, until he added, "Down payment on future services rendered."

His marriage with Marilyn had been childless. No matter how they'd tried. They'd kept at it, though, despite the train wreck they could see coming down the tracks. Marilyn blamed Sweeney, of course. Sweeney and his gimpy sperm. What he never told her, all it took for Tina to catch was one broken condom. The Saturday he'd chauffeured Tina to the clinic, he'd told Marilyn he was playing eighteen at Dyker Beach.

Birth is thus incongruously on his mind when he comes up to his International, parked five or six spots away from the nearest light. Key in hand, Sweeney, Jr. in his thoughts (the kid would be eleven years old by now, he'd be dribbling a basketball with both hands, he'd be wearing a baseball glove twice too big and pushing up a batting helmet from over his eyes), Sweeney nearly misses the second body dumped in the bed of his truck.

~

Tina opens on the fourth knock.

"Thought I told you to keep this shut."

"Knew it was you." Tina still dressed, but with a toothbrush in hand. "What's a matter? Forget your libido, there, Cosmo?"

"Come with me out to the truck. I want to show you something. Oh, and uh, yeah. Let's get one of these sheets off the bed."

He'd kept Tina largely shielded. The word is

compartmentalize. Marilyn too, of course. But Marilyn had stability to think about, mortgages, checking accounts. Sure, she'd been known to make a gesture, hurl the occasional toaster, but her heart wasn't in it. If you're the wife, there's virtue in blindness. Sweeney remembers holding a compress to his swelling eye. "It's not drug money, sweetheart, and I didn't get it for killing nobody. That's about all you need to know." Never the entire truth, but enough to calm her down.

But Tina, she was living inside a whole other kind of narrative. Wouldn't take no for an answer. What Sweeney eventually learned through hard experience: the girlfriend has no reason to meet you in the middle.

Sweeney had this place he liked just off the R train on Seventy-seventh. Owned by a second cousin of Castellano's, it was halfway up to legitimate, and had a blue collar bar where off duty cops from the 68th precinct drank free Budweisers. There was good seafood in the back. Waiters said Sweeney's name and brushed off his chair before he sat down.

Makes a man feel good, being treated well in front of his girl.

In the couple years him and Tina were a thing, it was their Thursday night date. They'd walk down from their apartment and have pasta and fresh oysters. Folks knew to find him there. A hand on Sweeney's shoulder, a kiss to the cheek for Tina, then Tommy Contadino or Marky Gee would turn a chair around backwards, wave for another bottle of red. "That poker game we been talking about, that thing up in Red Hook, a bunch of us are getting together tomorrow night. We need a sober driver. What you think, you ready to win some money?"

And later, Tina, digging it, would whisper, "*That* was Tommy Contadino? From the papers? Wasn't he part of that cigarette thing, oh, man, what was that thing. You read about it?"

"Nah, wasn't him."

"And he's not talking about *poker* poker, is he."

"What." Half smiling, enjoying the dance himself. "I like my poker games. That a crime?"

Turns out, the lifestyle turned her on.

And so, yeah, he's interested now to see her reaction.

He has her by the elbow. Pulls her around to the side of his truck. "You wanna tell me who this is? And what he's doing in my truck?"

Another thin corpse, another custom suit. The silk picks up a blue-sheened reflection from the street lights. Even inert, there's something of the serpent here. The way the guy's twisted; too many vertebrae in his spine.

He lies in the grease and grime of Sweeney's truck bed, one arm caught over his head, elbow resting on the handle of a handyman jack, a heel twisted on Sweeney's spare tire. Shirt untucked and knees akimbo, pants hiked up to show a slice of pale, hairy leg. His hair, previously worn slicked back from his crow's peak Gordon Gecko style, has exploded.

Tina makes a noise in her throat. Equal parts cough and question. She puts a foot on the rear tire and lifts herself up for a better look. The corpse has a heavy blue contusion on his forehead. But that's not what killed him. She reaches over to touch the guy's chin, to turn his head, exposing a deep slice just under his throat.

As opposed to the body in Sweeney's chair, a guy whose ticket got punched before he was moved, this guy's throat was clearly cut in Sweeney's truck. A fresh wash of blood, puddled in the grooves of the truck bed. The nice suit is soaked with it.

Sweeney says, "Look at the blood, huh. Pretty awful, right?"

Tina turns the head further, leaning into the truck until she's close enough for a kiss. She gathers the spit in her mouth and hawks a healthy one onto the forehead.

"Uh."

She hops down, dust off her hands. Takes the sheet from Sweeney and unfurls it over the body. "Let's get this piece of shit dumped somewhere."

"I know a place." Thinking, even as the world's saddest film score plays in his head: Oh, Tina.

Twenty minutes later, they stand side by side at the guardrail, unwinding the bloodstained sheet, twirling the body down, down, down to the now-familiar splash. Then Tina releases the sheet. They watch it blow and furl over itself, pale as an abdomen, ballooning briefly in the water before being swept away. Tina says, "I need another drink. How about you?"

~

Him and Aggie, they've never spoken the word marriage. Not once in five years. Aggie with two divorces, Sweeney with one. A good night's sleep, that's what they both want. High fiber and the good opinion of peers. But then the bruises start to fade, and maybe you forget about the pain.

The hardest part about lying? One lie leads always to at least two more, in a j-curve of predictably-increasing falsehoods. Good liars perforce need good memories. These last ten years, Sweeney's devoted a lot of effort to keeping his stories straight. He keeps a notebook.

Having dinner with Aggie, for instance, as he's opening the second bottle of wine, she'll ask him, "Your parents ever drink as much as we do?"

Sweeney has said he's ambivalent about his fictional

parents, enough to explain his own long pauses, but she still needs an answer. "Dad had a problem when he was younger, had to quit. But Mom still liked a couple glasses with dinner. More than a couple? She'd get mean, sarcastic." Later that night, he'd write in his notebook, "Dad, former alcoholic. Mom, mean drunk. Wine with dinner."

Over time, he's come to be fond of his dog-eared old notebook. Smeared with the dirt and blood of his handyman work, here's the human condition in microcosm. A nutshell of love and sex and ambition, of flawed self-image and perceived insult, deceit and melodrama and addiction. And all of it entirely a product of his own imagination.

One o'clock in the morning, he uses his key to slip into Aggie's house. The kitchen table lit by a candle guttering down into melted wax. Beside it, a slice of cold meatloaf and a single, uncut potato. A cold dinner. Maybe it's a rebuke, or maybe it's Aggie being thoughtful. Hard to tell. Aggie's a Monet of the mixed message.

He does not feel like an intruder here. Slipping quietly through the carpeted hall to the bedroom, he does not feel out of place.

In Aggie's bedroom, partially lit by a nightlight from the hall, her slight, sleeping form.

He sits beside her and stares for a time at the rise and fall of her breasts. A slight snore every third or fourth breath. Marriage, he thinks, is what happens when you'd rather die than disappoint her. It's the pinball tilt, it's the default position.

The kind of money Tina's talking about, it's going to bring trouble like a needle pulls thread. That rock? Fifteen carats, maybe twenty. Hard to tell with rough, but assuming it's gem quality...Jesus. And then she's talking about a few dozen of those stones?

Aggie's a light sleeper. All he has to do is touch her shoulder (warm as a peach on a windowsill) and she jerks awake. "What is it?"

"It's me."

"Ted?" She sits up, sheets puddling around her lap. She's wearing his old Bobcats t-shirt. "What time is it?"

"Late."

"Where've you been?" In the dimness, her face is unreadable. She's a stewer, and would have been sitting at the table, drinking wine, staring at his empty chair, numbering her grudges. But she is equally a generous soul, and will often give him the benefit of the doubt. At this point, it's a coin toss which way she'll go.

"I ran into an old friend of mine from back home."

"Brooklyn? Here? What's his name?"

"Her. And she's uh, she's kind of in trouble."

"Oh Ted. What kind?" She takes his hand, preparing herself to be sympathetic. Maybe thinking cancer, unwanted pregnancy, debt collectors.

"The kind that could follow her out here."

"What's that even mean?"

"Do you love me?"

She's supposed to repeat it back to him. Sure, hell yeah, damn tooting. Instead, he gets the world's most suspicious look. "What's her *name*, Ted."

"Do you trust me?"

"Not too goldern much, no, not right at this particular moment."

Sweeney considers the upended chessboard that, thanks

to the last thirty-six hours, has become his life. "Sweetheart, this isn't the way I wanted to do it, but here's what I've been carrying around in my pocket all day."

He leans up on one cheek and finds the box. In his closed hand, the crushed blue velvet. He avoids her eyes while he tilts his hand, shows it to her. Gives it a long two or three seconds, then tucks it away again. "That's how much you mean to me. And, I, well, there's things from Brooklyn that are catching up to me. And I want to talk to you about them. I do. But not right now. Okay?"

He finally looks at her. Waits. "You can blink or something."

She closes her eyes. Keeps them closed.

"So yeah, okay. You have time to think about it. Do I want this screwed up New Yorker in my life for good? Is what you should be asking yourself. But what I want to ask you, in the meantime…you quit your job, right? I heard about that. Okay, you got some time off. Would you mind if I paid for a little trip? Something to get you and Elizabeth out of town for a while?"

Her hands work at the bottom hem of her shirt, picking at a loose thread. Finally, she says. "I don't think I've ever been as mad at you as I am right now."

Not the response he'd hoped for. "Sweetheart…"

"What are you thinking, Ted? Show me a ring box, then put it back in your pocket. Tell me to get out of town on the same night you basically just proposed to me. Please, what are you possibly thinking?"

"Well, I…"

"I mean, what'd you do. *Kill* somebody? And then! Then you're already treating Elizabeth like some kind of abused stepdaughter. She told me what you said, and that is not okay, Ted. That is not okay. Show me the ring." She holds out her hand.

"What?"

"I want to see the ring."

Reluctantly, he hauls out the box again. Cracks it and holds it to his chest. He elects not to put it in her hand. If they're having a fight, call this a symbolic stand.

"Well," she sniffs, "you got good taste in jewelry, at least. That's something."

"You like it?"

"I guess it's beautiful, yeah."

"Listen." He stands up, tosses the ring box on the bed. "Put that on if you want." He digs for his wallet. "And here. Take a credit card. This one's got a few hundred bucks on it. Go up to Fairmont, or whatever. Give me a call when you get back. You still want me to propose, I will. We'll go out to a good dinner, maybe try that new place in Bozeman. Something romantic so I can do this right. Meantime, don't take candy from strangers."

She ignores the ring but accepts the card. Pinches it up between two fingers. "Call this hardship for putting up with another man who won't tell me the…" her voice catches, "the *god*damned truth."

~

Twenty minutes south of Rockjaw, Marilyn has hung her hat next to the Yellowstone River, feathered her nest in the kind of bland, soulless modular that sucks the eyes right out of a bright summer day. Paradise Valley, they call it. And it used to be. Before it got filled up with subdivisions, with toy windmills on porches and lawns patched by dog-urine. House after house, vaporous yard lights and garden gnomes, ceramic deer and sickly cedar shrubs. Two centuries ago this valley was a winter encampment for the Crow. Teepee rings and arrowheads. Now each house has its five acres of rocky pasture. Thank a generational series of myopic county commissioners. Here's where we eat, is the thinking; let's go shit in it.

In his ungenerous moods, with too little sleep or too much drink, Sweeney looks at these houses and sees lost souls, dupes, automatons, small horizons and limited means. We are all of us just each trying to capture some last vestige of romance, of true West, a slow ride off into the sunset. Cynicism, under a certain light, is the only rational response to the age. Depression isn't an illness so much as evidence of intellect.

But if he's rested and sober, and as part of an ongoing project of self-betterment (a very private determination to make of himself a more generous soul), he sees a tribe, a community of struggling, aching, failing, sweating Sisyphuses, all of us striving from morning alarm to late night infomercial, and for what? His theory? To feel good about ourselves, to feel admirable in our own eyes. Sweeney is capable of envying the chutzpah, the courage it takes simply to get out of bed.

It's an effort, then, to be around Marilyn. This dour reminder of his own failures.

Three o'clock in the morning, he pulls into her subdivision. His dog's been in the cab of his truck for six, eight hours. Sweeney parks briefly next to the stacked clutter of mailboxes, lets Zeke jump down onto the hard gravel road. Sweeney idles slow down the circuitous drive while Zeke runs along behind.

He'd hoped to find Marilyn awake (she's an inconsistent insomniac, an early morning tea drinker and crossword cheater), but he finds the house dark and quiet. Instead he sits in his truck between her prowler and Subaru. The wagon has bumper stickers: I heart My Shih-tzu, I heart My Persian.

Zeke falls asleep on the seat beside him, nose by his knee, twitching paws, blowing at his cheeks.

Through his window, and even above his cigarette, Sweeney can smell burning trash. The last remnants of somebody's backyard fire.

From behind the seat, he pulls out the dead wop's pistol. Stainless steel Colt .357. Six shooter. Odd choice for a gangster. By and large, they preferred the stage props, semi-auto dis and dat. Sweeney, however, having been known to spend time on a firing range—that basement range in Alphabet City, what was it called? Bull's Eye, Inc.?—always favored cylinders. The good heft and weight in your hand. The balance.

It's been so long since he was in the same room with real money. Dig that energy, man. What would it take to move it? Handicapped as he is by his past, by his geography, it would be a trick. Not only move it, but wash it. There's the real problem. Say you've got two briefcases full of bills. You can go buy groceries. Get some chewing gum. Everything else draws attention. If you buy a house, buy a car, open a checking account, the feds are knocking on your door twelve hours later.

Used to be, they had dodges set up. The launder came readymade. The Nose had his car washes, for instance. Three different coin-operated bay washes, always shut down, always with orange cones in front of the bays. But they allowed

Nose to siphon cash through his accountant, call it carwash income. These days? Sweeney's got Zeke, he's got the old folks at home, he's got Aggie. Basically, he's got buptkus.

Still, Cosmo would have jumped at the chance, the challenge. Would have bluffed his way into it. Sure, I'm your man. Trust me. Made it up as he went along. Would have found a solution. It had been one of his strengths: improvising. You project confidence, people believe in you.

His other strength? Eddie. Who had his back.

Eddie. Who's known that Sweeney's alive, and hasn't been in touch. The thought hurts.

Unless Eddie's been protecting him. Unless he's been so hot that...but no. The shit they'd been through? That time in Philadelphia?

Okay, number one, take it for granted that Eddie, wherever he is, he's got your back. If you can't trust Eddie, you can't trust nobody.

Okay, two, Eddie's wife is here asking for help. Forget about your history (the small sprinkle of moles under her breasts; her black lace nighties, her candles; that one time with the cuffs.). It's Eddie's *wife*, man.

Three, somebody's knocking off gangsters in Montana. At the juncture of Sweeney and, what, ten million dollars? A body shows up in his lazy boy.

Whoever it is, they know Sweeney well enough to want to fuck with him. And *that* list of names, brother, it would take time and a half to put them in alphabetical order.

Marilyn has a rooster-shaped weather vane on a banister. It turns slightly in a breeze; and a wind chime under the eaves starts up with the tinkling.

Sweeney flicks his cigarette onto gravel, slides down into

the seat, tilts his cap over his eyes. Tina's the key to it. Tina.

Twenty-five-year-old Cosmo would have had ideas, been able to see solutions. Thirty-seven-year-old Sweeney feels stranded, confused. Tired. Alone. Most of all, he's alone.

~

"First thing," Eddie said, "we get your bike back."

Thirteen-year-old Sweeney, flush from his audience with the Nose, could care less about a bike. "It used to be all right. This old Greg Hill signature? But I've beat the crap out of it. All the stickers are off."

"Hey Cosmo? Looka here."

They were killing time on playground swings. Smoking Camels to keep it ironic.

"Drag your feet, man. Look at me."

Sweeney slowed until he hung loose. "What."

Eddie smacked him a quick one upside the head. Sweeney's cigarette span away, blooming sparks.

"What the fuck?"

"The Nose tells you not to let people fuck with you, which means, next thing, you get your bike back, demonstrating, ergo, that you don't let people fuck with you."

"I'm not even sure…"

"Don't gimme that. You know who took it. Who was it?"

Sweeney *did* know, in fact. It was a small world him and Eddie inhabited. A cohort of Bobby Badasses and Tommy Tough Guys. The lucky ones, like Sweeney, had a home. Their bones were hung with the firm flesh of three solids a day. The unlucky ones were fuzzy about the notion of dinner, and didn't see the rationale behind showers, toothbrushes. The unluckiest kept their sleeping bags in abandoned warehouses, wore always the same jeans, used the public school system like a pawn shop.

"You know those brothers? D'shawn and what's his name. Darious? Something. The older one. He's into bikes."

"Where they hang out?"

"This construction site around Seth Low? Off Thirteenth."

Eddie glanced at his watch. "Com'on. We got some daylight."

There are certain memories, it's better you don't poke them too often. They're fragile in their scabbing. And this one, the first truly epic ass kicking of Sweeney's young life, is more tender than most.

Eddie, at least, left him to his own failure. Eddie had a pistol in his pocket. But beyond flashing it at the start to insure that Sweeney didn't get mobbed, showing it to the small gang of kids they'd found lighting firecrackers among the rebar and broken concrete of the construction site—he did nothing to help.

Sweeney, even then, was smart enough to see that it's in such moments that we find the trajectory of our lives. Quail and quiver at the wrong moment? Maybe you never stop with the quailing and quivering. Nothing in life is worse than shame. Nothing.

So Sweeney was reduced to blind and stumbling round-houses, crying out his frustration. Darious shoved Sweeney down one last time. Muttered. "Shit, white boy. *Take* the bike."

Afterwards, left eye swelling to a cracked plum, both lips split, Sweeney walked his bike away slow, breathing in small sips out of consideration for his bruised ribs. But he felt *good*. Yes, this was better. This was why you didn't let people fuck with you.

Eddie had snatched a handful of firecrackers, and he lit them as they walked. "The Nose is going to dig the scars, Cosmo." *Pop.* "I tell that story about how you never quit?" *Pop.* "Nose'll eat that shit up. Trust me." Eddie stuck his cigarette to the fuse of the entire string. "He's a sucker for a good story."

A machine gun rattle of firecrackers at his feet, under his heels, but Sweeney resolutely refused to flinch. Flinching was for suckers.

~

Coming awake in Montana, in the cold gray light of near-dawn, the sound of firecrackers fades to Marilyn tapping her nails against his window. "Ted. Hey, Ted." She's clutching her bathrobe tight at the neck.

Zeke and Sweeney both startle awake. The dog growls low. Sweeney rolls down his window. "Heya."

"You stalking me now?"

"Fell asleep." He rubs at the crick in his neck. Smacks his mouth at the taste of ashtrays.

"Question is, why are you even here?"

"We need to talk."

She glances at the neighbors' houses. All the dark windows. "I'll put coffee on."

He doesn't keep track (he's definitely *not* keeping track), but Marilyn has had a *few* lovers here and there, a few that he knows about. A physician's assistant, a high school biology teacher, an ambulance driver. She's still a good-looking woman, although increasingly padded. She's a farmer's wife, a potato grower. She's a portrait by Daumier.

Sweeney slumps low on her couch, brushing at pet hair. The longhaired Persian stares murderously at him from a throw rug. The shih-tzu comes up wagging. The cat's name, if Sweeney remembers, is Max. The dog's name is Catherine. Two names, not incidentally, that they had discussed in the dusty long ago as potential names for their children.

The living room is open to the kitchen. He watches her putter, moving from sink to coffee maker. The robe falls partially open. "Is that one of my old Yanks t-shirts?"

She clutches the robe tight, then visibly concedes. Fuck it. "Yeah. It's comfortable." She brings him his coffee mug and sits across from him. Putting up her fuzzy-slippered feet. Her legs need a shave. "Don't be thinking I'm sentimental."

"You and Aggie both. It's a wonder I got any t-shirts left at all."

"How's she doing? I like her. She's good for you."

"We kind of had a fight."

"Let me take a stab. You told her to get out of town, right? For her own good. But wouldn't tell her why."

"Jesus, woman."

"You're no big mystery."

"You get any prints off that shotgun?"

"Yeah, a good thumbprint and half a forefinger. I sent them in to the Feds, that IAFIS system. End of the day yesterday, they should be waiting for me this morning. I'm just praying those prints ain't yours."

"They're not. Were you sticking your neck out at all?"

She studies him over the top of her coffee mug, sipping at it with both hands. "Two ways to answer that. I said I found the gun in an alley. Sawed off and illegal, right, so I could justify it. So, no, not really."

"Second way?"

"I'm trying to be a good cop here, Ted. This is my life, what

I want to do with the rest of it. And lying about evidence? Nobody would ever call that, you know, *merit badge* behavior. When that body shows up down in Big Timber, when somebody's bright enough to make the connection, they're going to be treating that alley like a crime scene. Which means a lot of wasted effort on somebody's part, probably mine."

"Sorry." And he means it.

"Apology accepted."

"It's not really my fault."

"Yeah, stop while you're ahead."

Past Marilyn, an east-facing window catches the rising sun, illuminating her deputy's uniform hanging off the pantry door, cleaned and pressed. On the counter, her coiled utility belt and pistol. He'd always wondered how cops lived when they were home, and this is it. "How much do you want to know about what else is going on? What I mean is, would you rather go about your day? Merit badges versus jail time?"

She carefully places her coffee mug on the table and rubs her face hard. Goes to the window and picks up her cat. Brings it back to her chair, sits rubbing it. Brings its tail to her nose. "I'm going to leave that, uh, moral conundrum, all up to you. You tell me what I need to know, help us get through this, but not enough to make me an accessory. How's that?"

Marilyn in a nutshell. Marilyn in her frustrating, power-play, calculating, disingenuous glory. Sweeney and strong women. Sometimes he wonders if it's worth it.

Two things occur to him. First, and despite himself, he's a little turned on right now, fuzzy slippers and all. Maybe it's his lingering fantasies about Tina, but he can't keep his eyes of her knee outside its robe. That scar under the kneecap, he's the only man in Montana who knows its story. Moving into their first apartment, carrying a box of books, she'd slipped on concrete stairs. He'd wiped the blood away with a damp cloth, then kissed the wound. The iron-rich taste of her blood on his lips. Second, she's right. It's like chewing on foil, but yeah, she's got a point. He should be able to do this without asking her to compromise herself.

"Okay," he says, leaning forward. "Can you do some digging about my cousin Eddie?"

"Eddie?" He's succeeded in surprising her. "What's Eddie got to do with this?"

"Um."

"No wait, right," she holds up a hand. "I don't want to know. Okay, I can make an arrest record search, that sort of thing. Same ol', same ol'. Just old Ted Sweeney curious about his homicidal family. Anything else?"

"Nope." He puts his hands on his knees and makes to rise.

"You know who you should talk to about Eddie though. Al Broch."

"I thought about that." In fact, it hadn't occurred to him. The Federal Marshall assigned to his case. His supervisor, in a way.

"You should drop in anyway. Say hello. It's the right thing to do."

"What're you talking about?"

"You haven't heard?" Marilyn's housecat, annoyed by the increasing, nervous pace of her petting, squirms off her lap, walks imperiously over to its food bowl, glancing back. Marilyn watches it go. "He's sick, Ted. Really, really sick."

~

Sweeney spent three years in the Nose's tire shop. Three years in the cacophony of wrenches and ratchets, air compressors and the hollow clang of rims on cement. What he seemed to understand from the first, but what so few of his fellows natched, is that the real engine of the world, the currency of it, isn't money but connection. Who you know, how well you're received. People need to smile when you walk in the room.

Having recovered his dirt bike, Sweeney soon gave it up again, passed it down to a younger cousin. Used Nose's thirty bucks to buy a good pair of bolt cutters. Found his next bike in midtown. A ten speed racer that weighed less than a pack of cigarettes, tires thin as smoke rings, shifters smooth as butter.

Five nights a week found him popping beads and patching leaks. Once, twice a week, Nose had him come by in the morning. Handed him a backpack heavy with three bundles of bills. "You got time before school, kid?" Sure he did.

This was Sweeney's own little tour de New York: Brooklyn, Greenwich Village, the Bronx. A kid on a bike. A ruse, a feint, a dodge. The Nose's nod to his own pragmatic paranoia. Who in his right mind would entrust thousands of dollars a week to some greasy-haired punk? It was the age of big hair bands and rap, lift kits and glasspacks. But Sweeney pedaled to a private soundtrack of trumpets and trombones, snare drums and jazz piano. He was on his way up, hitting the big time.

First stop, Tricky Ricky's Tavern in Dumbo. A basement level dive with a scarred plywood bar and exposed pipes dripping condensate. A green velvet card table under lights. "Heya, it's the kid!" He was welcomed with the bonhomie of the guy with tickets to the game, the schnook who buys every round. Ricky's sheaf of bills was thinnest of the three, and it disappeared always like a magic trick. "Have a beer, kid."

Second stop, Sciarra's place in the Village. A walk up off Cordelia Street. A front door of mahogany and brass and a doorman bored with the *Times*. The back door, though, past a wrought-iron garden gate and up the fire escape, was sheet metal, and opened to a combination. He'd find Sciarra in his kitchen, reading his paper, smoking. He glanced at the delivery—thickest of the three—then let it sit on the table, ignored. "Coffee, kid?"

"Sure, Mr. Sciarra. Thanks."

Third stop, a mail slot in the Bronx. A weedy front yard, a wire fence missing half its panels. A bird feeder hanging upside down on a loose nail. Heavy curtains and the occasional fat orange tabby blinking sleepily on the sill. Opening the mail slot, a whiff of cat urine, coffee, an undercurrent of departed fathers and sad childhoods. The Nose's mother, Sweeney assumed.

This went on until his promotion.

~

Sweeney has his ideas about cops. For a period of his life, they were his study. State-sponsored thugs and ball breakers, power junkies and over-compensators, you ask his opinion. What kind of personality wants to spend his life like a school marm packing heat? And the Feds? The Feds are the worst of the bunch. Arrogance meets entitlement. Small town cops pulling down thirty grand a year are, by definition, not the sharpest tools in the shed. They don't have the cojones for more than a little traffic-stop intimidation. But the Feds, in the absence of evidence, will manufacture their way to any conviction they want, rationalizing it away as being in the service of a larger good. Put a practiced Fed on a witness stand, show him a Bible and an oath, watch him dance like Martha Graham.

Sweeney had it all figured out. Then he met Albert Broch. A Baltimore Jew displaced, for unnamed but surely profound sins, to a field office in Bozeman, Montana, Broch was the Federal marshal assigned to Sweeney's rehabilitation.

His first few years, Sweeney was obliged to check in a couple times a month, give updates. Ten minute sessions with what he'd thought would be a distracted Fed, maybe a therapist. Instead, what he got was this six-foot-two linebacker with a skullcap and a third-degree black belt in karate, a couple marine tattoos smeared on his shoulders, and a cynicism as profound as his empathy. An office with tilted photos of fish caught on trips to Belize, Alaska, Maine. First day in Broch's office, Broch said, "You need me to take you fishing."

"Not really my bag."

"Bag, no bag, I'm not asking." They were both smoking, an ashtray between them. "Say it's like golf. You've just been sentenced to spend the rest of your life slumming it in Hawaii, working a retreat for dentists and dermatologists. You either pick up golf or go nuts. It's Montana? You go fishing."

So they'd floated the Madison River in Broch's scratched and battered old Clacka, Sweeney up front in the knee locks, slinging a fly back and forth, wrapping every third cast around his neck. During that long, frustrating day, Broch gave him a running tutorial on fitting in. "Don't lose yourself, Ted. You want my advice, that's the main thing. I mean, button up your shirt, get rid of the gold chain, maybe go shopping at Corral West, but don't forget who you are. I mean, who the fuck do they think *they* are."

A cop who gave a shit what was going on inside Sweeney's head. It made no kind of sense at all. But it gave Sweeney the deepest sense of gratitude.

Sweeney parks in the ten acres of asphalt surrounding the Bozeman hospital. Ties Zeke up in the bed of his truck and pours him a dish of water from a jug. "Don't bite nobody." Zeke curls up on his rug, resigned.

Inside, after a visit to the nurse's station for directions, Sweeney finds Broch half-upright on a mechanical bed, lost in a forest of flowers, enough Mylar balloons to float a lawn chair.

Broch himself looks something like a collapsed umbrella held together with dried leather, swollen at the stomach. A needle hangs from the back of his hand. Nostrils plugged into an oxygen tube and the TV remote trembling in clawed fingers. "Ted Sweeney," he says, his dark eyes brightening, "as I nearly live and breathe."

"Jesus, Broch. You look like shit."

Broch wheezes out a feeble, squeezebox laugh. "First honest thing I've heard in weeks."

"How's that now?"

"Doctors, nurses, cousins, uncles, my own mother, they're all giving me that whole, another six months, another year spiel..." Broch turns off Dr. Phil and waves the remote. "My own mother. Ninety-two years old. You're getting better, she says. Trying to convince herself, poor thing."

"How bad is it?" Sweeney finds a chair in the midst of the flora.

"The cancer? It's doing *fine*. Ate up the lungs, had a taste of liver. Now they tell me it's in my head. They say, Can we cut you open again? But I say, tell me, what good will come of it? Apart from giving you the practice. And practice you don't need."

"Anything I can do for you?"

"Shoot me?" But then he considers Sweeney's face. Unlike most cops, Broch never lost sight of the serendipity of circumstance, the roll of the dice. Given a bit of bad luck, *he* might have been the one running for cover, ducking down into WITSEC.

Sweeney swallows against a bolus of pity. Here's the price, right here in front of him. The cover charge for the good days. For the top shelf booze and first lovely cigarette every morning. It's like one of Eddie's theories. We're finally allowed only equal measures of happiness and pain. Broch has enjoyed his life. Four kids. Because, he said, there's nothing like watching someone else come awake to the world. He fished because there's nothing like the hard metallic zing of your reel as a Florida permit finally, finally takes your fly. And he smoked because it makes everything better. But this is where it goes, this is what it comes down to. A stomach swollen with fluids and a patronizing purgatory of Dr. Phil.

"Jesus," Sweeney says, "Al..."

"Nah, sure, you know. I'm just kidding. I mean, hey, right? Look at this setup." He waves an arm. "I got twenty-four hour morphine. I just punch this little button, right? I never seen what the big deal was, but man, this junk is dyn-o-mite. They're telling me, another few weeks? I start getting the Dilaudid. That's how I know I'm terminal. They don't feed you the quality junk unless you're ready to go. So how you been?"

"Oh, you know." Sweeney turns his baseball cap in his hands.

"Got something on your mind, though, yeah?" Reduced to a skeleton, Broch's eyes remain sharp, interested. He's always had the ability to flatter by interest.

"Nah, nothing." Sweeney's problems fade under the cold, faint smell of formaldehyde, of feces.

"Keeping your nose clean?"

"Yeah. Clean nose."

"Listen, hey, Ted. Come over here a little closer. Give me your hand."

Sweeney cradles Broch's fingers between his own. The arrangement of unnaturally heated bones.

"You're my poster child. You know that, right?"

"For what, Al?"

"WITSEC. I mean, *look* at you, man. When you got here, you were a wreck. I'd have laid even odds on your backsliding or, forgive me, worst case, a suicide. Now you got your own business. Got that level-headed girlfriend of yours. And Marilyn? Who'd have ever guessed, right? You're getting on with your life. I'm proud of you, my man."

Sweeney holds that skeletal hand. "I appreciate it. Means a lot. It does."

Broch eases back into his pillow, wincing. "You wouldn't believe the derelicts we're getting through the program now. Who'd have thought that wiseguys would be the good old days? Gangbangers? Don't know how to keep their mouths shut. San Diego put this Hispanic chica up in a hotel room... next thing you know she's got all her old MS-13 amigos up there in the Jacuzzi...week later, she's washed up off...Imperial

Beach pier." Broch's fading, closing his eyes.

Sweeney sits for a long minute, watching him breathe. Then he stands, touches the clothes-hanger shoulder.

On the cold concrete stoop of the hospital, Sweeney sits smoking, turning the cigarette in his fingers.

Life's what kills you, not cigarettes. Smokes may trim off a few years, sure, but what are those years worth? Those last five years, from seventy-five to eighty? Take 'em. Take 'em.

If he's on top of his game, Sweeney can rationalize his way through a pack's worth of cynical philosophy a day.

A pair of cheerful nurses walk toward Sweeney, chattering. Coming up the stairs, they part for him, giving him a good eighteen inches on either side. Despair might not be contagious but why risk it.

Donnie Moretti's getting too old for this shit.

Capo in the dissolute Luchesse borgatta (a good family in long, *long* decline), these days he's more or less sanitized. Twelve, fifteen years ago, if any of his old *amicis* had ever read a paper, they'd have seen how their days was numbered. RICO comes along, it's only a matter of time. Moretti's many things, but he ain't no fool. He'd read the tidal charts of bad news, started putting his money in chain stores. All these retail skid marks up and down Brooklyn? Payless Shoes, White Castle, Subway? Half of them are his. He's a civic leader. And that may sound good but it's no free lunch, believe me. Air conditioner's breaking down here, exhaust fan's taking a dump over there. It's like having a job.

But now and then, just a few times a year, along comes a score that's too good to pass up. An excuse to dip a toe back in the life. He's careful about it—there's more to lose these days—but he looks forward to it, too. He likes getting that feeling back. Turning up the temperature in his veins.

This diamond thing, for instance.

He hasn't called a Saturday afternoon sauna meet, for what? Six months at least. But here he is slouched in an Astoria steam room, wrapped in white towels, sipping his day's first and only Scotch. He swirls the melting ice. In the warm, amniotic steam, the humid air, he's a creature from the Paleolithic. The heavy flesh rolling on his bones, a Sicilian pelt going gray across his back. Too old for the feint and jab, the juking and jiving, but also too old for anything else.

Whacking that little pissant Georgie...it had helped put him back on track somehow. Gave him the *taste* again. Some people wait their whole lives to find the one thing they're good at. Donnie's known it since he was a kid.

Things have changed, though. When he was first coming up into the life, pulling down his first scores, getting together a crew, you still had something to aspire toward. The goals came to you on a platter. Get made, work up to Capo, higher. But these days, all the old legends are in stir or dead, all the old schemes kaput. It's gotten to where just keeping your head above water is the best you can do. Staying out of prison has become a matter less of discretion and more of blind luck.

From the wall of steam in front of him, three pale, towel-wrapped forms emerge. They say his name, find seats on either side, slouching, closing their eyes. "You and your steam rooms, Donnie. Swear to Christ, I lose ten pounds every time we pull a score."

"No wires, no cameras."

"You always been smart that way."

"Get your nose outta my ass, Lukey."

A pause while the men settle into the heat.

"We got one more guy coming." Donnie dabs his bald head with a towel.

The three, trading glances. "Thought Tony was in Montana."

"He's someplace. Someplace that ain't here."

The fourth man arrives a few minutes later, unfamiliar. Younger. Mid-twenties. Fit. The tattoos: Christian crosses, Maltese crosses, a Madonna across his back, a string of inked rosary beads around his neck. He's got a thick, drooping mustache from a previous decade and Moretti's unfortunate recession of a chin. He sits across from Moretti. Says formally, "Buon giorno, il mio zio."

"Buon giorno, il mio nipote."

Moretti's face, its blunt nose and pinched eyes, is meant for sour expressions, for biting into rotten things. But now, goddamn, he grins fondly. "Boys, meet my nephew, Domenico."

"Nephew, boss?"

"Baby sister's baby son, fresh off the boat. Come to America to make his fortune. Ain't that right, Domenico?"

"America, you betcha."

"He don't speak much English. Tell 'em all your English that you know there, Domenico?"

"Non capisco..."

"Recite il vostro inglese."

"Motherfucker bastuhd cock-uh-sucker. Where's my money gimme my money. I put cock in your ass. What are you, sick mane-ee-ack? Where's my money, gimme my money."

"Domenico wants to see the world, don't you boy. Vedi l'america."

"Si! Si, si. Vedi l'america." The enthusiasm, however, is belied by his expression, or lack of it. The leaden eyes.

"Okay, here's what we got." Donnie sighs heavily, leans back, breathing through his thick lips. "Tony's gone off the reservation. His kid brother, too. Normally, you know, no big deal. He's off on a drunk or something. But the kind of coin we're talking here, these rocks, he knows the consequences he don't call in."

"You ain't heard from him?"

"Not since last night. He was talking about Russians.

Whatever. Fact is, he ain't called in. That means either, number one, he's dead, or B, he's found the rocks and he's taking them down to the nearest pawn shop, right? Have to be a gonzo fucking pawn shop, but still. Number C…okay, three possibilities. Number C, he's off with the Russians or maybe they've punched his ticket. Whatever. Anyway, I want all four of you on a plane to Montana. Lukey, you're watching Jake here. Jake, you're watching Mike. Delmonico here is watching all of you. First thing tomorrow or tonight, I want you a find that little fag Tony. You find his little pissant brother. Call me every six hours. You don't find those rocks by, what's today. Wednesday? You don't got good news by Friday, what time is it? You don't call me Friday two o'clock with good news, I'm coming out there myself. You'll be around long enough to see me deep fry your own nuts in garlic." Moretti eases back, scowling, flush.

Jesus, this is fun.

Donnie's nephew, having followed at least some part of this exchange, tries on a grin. Here's America. Che divertisi! The real thing. What he came to see. Wiseguys. From here, all he wants, the next big thing (maybe after the Empire State Building and Statue of Liberty), he wants to see somebody get whacked.

At sixteen, Sweeney had his height but not his weight. He was all Adam's apple and chin, elbows and knees. His ears flapped like awnings in a breeze. After the Nose had spotted his gym bag and boxing gloves in the corner—"Boxing gloves? You a fighter kid?"—he started feeding him some strong-arm work. "You look kind of, what's that word you like, *innocuous,* yeah. You can take folks by surprise, right?"

By the age of seventeen, Sweeney was the backup, the third of a trio, Eddie being the mouth, a thug named Jerry "Miracle Whip" Mayo the principal muscle, then Sweeney watching for shifty-eyed heroes, furtive 911 dialers. Slow work, for the most part, but he knew how to grab a fistful of shirt, knew how to draw blood from a nose.

Sweeney's father had been a boxer in the Navy, a speedy little welterweight with a glass chin. But when his father was feeling good at the start of a morning, he would stand before a steamy bathroom mirror in towel and shaving cream, shadow boxing in the loose-fisted, easy-limbed fashion of a man accustomed to five pound gloves.

A small man who compensated for his size by overdressing (fedora, tie, cufflinks), Davey Aniello was a second generation émigré who put a portion of every paycheck into a college fund for his kids. They were going to have all those American opportunities. The night after Sweeney's first arrest (a tag for scalping forged tickets outside Yankees stadium), Davey drove his son home in that particular kind of gelled silence reserved for fathers disappointed in their sons.

The cuffs had bruised Sweeney's wrists. He sat rubbing at the marks.

Pulling up to the house, wipers working against a light rain, Sweeney's father said, "Never thought I'd raise a criminal."

Sweeney took a sullen fifth.

"I won't raise a criminal."

Sweeney watched the wipers.

"You got three strikes, son. This is number one. Number three? You're out on your ear. Believe me that I'll do it. It'll break my heart, but I'll do it."

It would take another year to rack up strikes two and three. Four more years before Sweeney's father was found dead in his own backyard, barbeque spatula in hand and two bullet holes in his back. Some part of Sweeney had always felt that it was just a matter of time, that they would eventually look back on their years of not speaking as a lost opportunity. He'd catch himself thinking, "After Dad and me patch things up…" But now that opportunity was forever gone. Death seals every envelope. They never caught the fuckers who did it, and the cops wrote it off as a break-in robbery gone bad. A Mason jar full of loose change and small bills went missing. But Sweeney had more poisonous suspicions, believed somehow that it had something to do with him. One more straw to add to his camel's back of guilt.

Anyway, long story short, that year following his first tag, and in part to mitigate his father's disappointment, Sweeney began spending more time at Sparky's gym down by the docks. Three nights a week. The rich odors of saltwater and diesel exhaust and rotting fish, the sounds of seagulls and garbage scows. All of this mixed with gym-sweat and damp towels, liniment. Sparky's scornful Bronx rising up from behind the heavy bag. "Hit it, *hit* it, don't *kiss* it." Afterwards, the showers had a hard, painful spray that cut through his befuddlement. The sting of a solid right against a padded helmet, the water-bottle taste of a mouthpiece, blood in your mouth and the blinding, purging, satisfying loss of yourself in second or third round anger. This was manhood: Gulls and barges and blood.

Sweeney's problem? Rage. When he remembered his training ("Dance, kid, dance. Balance, keep moving, jab, watch that left, up on your toes, keep those legs moving.") he had potential. He was a workhorse. He had his father's speed and a good reach, and could dance away from the slower bulldogs in favor of quick combinations. But all it took was for some nickel-and-dime wannabe to tag him a couple times and he'd forget it all, wade in with blind abandon, windmilling through a red sea of repeated "fuck yous." From there, he'd either wake up flat on the canvas or standing over some other poor kid. Out on the streets, he was Shakespeare. In the gym, however, he was Jukebox. Plug in the right kind of quarter, you'd get a show.

We all choose those aspects of our lives to make sacred, and Sweeney came to hold nothing holier than the unfettered dance of two men set toe to toe.

~

Driving back from the hospital, down the east side of Bozeman pass, Sweeney turns on his cell phone, checks messages. With his own voice briefly in his ear, he punches buttons to hurry things along. He sounds wheedling, needy. Please, please, *please* leave a message, is the effect.

He thinks, I don't want to be this guy no more.

Two messages. A widow that hires him a few times a month to unplug toilets, clean gutters, carry dog food up to the pantry. She pays him by the resentful minute, counting out dimes from a jar. The second caller, a dairy farmer in Paradise Valley. "Yeah, I seen your ad. My kid's up to his mother's, so I need somebody a muck out my milking barns for me. Gimme a call."

This is what he's become. A peon, a serf, a nobody. A busker holding out his hat for pennies. A shit shoveler.

Next call is to Cal Merchant. "I got a hypothetical."

"Lay it on me." In the background, the splatter of skillets, the clank of cutlery. Cal making himself lunch.

"Let's say Great Aunt Sally died. Left you an uncut rock she smuggled out of, out of... *Romania*. During the war. Something like that. Who would you go to in town who's sharp enough to make an appraisal, tell you what it's worth, discrete enough to..."

"Julietta Siegal." Cal interrupts.

"Sure, okay." Of *course*. Kicking himself. "Thanks, man. All I needed."

"Now me, *I* got a hypothetical."

Sweeney gets a feeling. "Okay..."

"Guy from back east, *heavy* Brooklyn accent, shows up in downtown smalltown notown Montana for no very good reason. Ten years ago."

"Uh huh."

"Works hard to fit in. Volunteers like he's paying penance. Heavy bad Karma tonnage on this guy's shoulders."

Sweeney gives Cal his own line: "Farfetched, but okay."

"One day, after ten years of calm surf, six feet and glassy, he starts in with bodies on porches, uncut diamonds, that sort of shit." Cal's voice is light, but carefully so. "My hypothetical, what's a brother to think?"

Sweeney drives one handed, the phone going sweaty upside his ear.

Thirty seconds later, Cal says, "You there?"

"Yeah, but maybe we could pick this up again in a few days?"

"I'm just saying. Trust somebody. Maybe? I don't know."

"Appreciate it."

"Pas de problem."

On top of everything else, Cal Merchant, best friend he's got (cousin Eddie, Part II), is asking to be trusted. *Asking* for it. Implying, of course, that trust has previously been absent. Which isn't friendship at all. And which, when you close one eye and squint at it, is exactly right.

Shit.

~

The thing about Rockjaw? The mix of people. Any given afternoon, a switch operator for Burlington Northern will be drinking his suds beside a gimpy rancher who personally owns fifty-thousand acres of good graze along the Yellowstone. A medicinal marijuana caretaker will be hitting practice balls beside one of the early artists for Mad Magazine. A wolf biologist will be shooting stick with the bass player from Yeah! Yeah! Yeah! Sweeney's worked for them all one time or another.

His favorite clients? The disaffected rich. He's in the minority in this, but yeah. San Diego real estate sharks look-ing for distance from their ex-wives. Privileged sons from

Connecticut finding their identities as snowboarding pot-heads. B-list movie stars and Jesus freaks who built their nut wholesaling cocaine in Miami; gallery owners from SoHo and trucking magnates from Omaha. There are so many ways to make money in this world, and Sweeney's curious about them all.

Take Julietta Siegal. Pushing seventy now, diminished and hunched over a man's wooden cane, back in the late sixties and early seventies she'd been a bombshell. Broad shoulders, broad hips. A mezzo soprano, photos show her in an evening gown beside Jackie Kennedy. Old and having drinks with a young Marcello Viotti. A publicity shot of Julietta in Carnegie Hall, scowling mid-gesture halfway through Bizet. Sweeney's hip to opera, and, though she changed her last name with marriage, he finally put two and two together. This woman had been the shit, man.

Four years ago she hired Sweeney to put in a rail fence around the half acre pasture behind her new cabin, replacing a rusted tangle of barbed wire. A discrete little cabin with a distant view of the river. One of those idyllic little spots of which there seem to be an unlimited supply, so long as you've got, you know, *millions*.

She'd followed her husband (a fly fisherman) to Montana, but the grizzled old sonofabitch had a massive coronary three weeks after closing on the house. Lonelier than she deserved, she came out with a lawn chair to watch Sweeney work. Cane upright between her knees. He dug postholes, set rails. "What's your story, then?"

Sweeney sweated over his posthole digger, pried at rocks with a spud bar. "No story."

"*Every*body's got a story."

Sweeney, of course, diverted the conversation. "What's yours?"

Over the next week, he got it. Bits and pieces. By the time the job was done, Sweeney was half in love, Harold with his Maude. The highlight? He set the last post, pounded in the last nail. And to mark the occasion, Julietta stood up from her lawn chair, straightened her shoulders, and sang. A voice roughened by age, half an octave deeper, but *still*.

L'oiseau qu tu croyais surprendre
battit de l'aile et s'envola
l'amour est loin, tu peux l'attendre
tu ne l'attends plus, il est là!

She reached for her cane. "Come into the house. I have lemonade."

Turns out, her husband, Leonard Siegal, had been one of *those* Siegals. His name on jewelry stores scattered through half the malls in America. The third act of Julietta's life, she'd helped her husband build, manage, finally sell that business. "Had to learn it from the ground up, Ted. A bit of a trick, I'll tell you."

The cabin was a nice little post and beam number, tricked out craftsman style. Stickley chairs and tables. And those small paintings over the stone fireplace were Fechins, Sharps, Berninghauses. But the showpieces—what drew the eye—were the displays of jewelry, framed in shadow boxes. A diamond and sapphire necklace, set in platinum. "I wore *this* when I met Richard Nixon for the first time. Poor man." A ruby pendant surrounded by teardrop diamonds. "I wore this one to the Oscars when our friend Maximilian was nominated for that movie." A diamond and amethyst choker. "Leonard had his affair in 1989. This was how he *started* making it up."

The gangster in Sweeney briefly snorted awake, rolled over and cracked a yellow eye. "Hope you have a good alarm system, Mrs. Siegal."

"Alarms, yes. And guns. Lots of guns. Guns and guns and guns."

Charming old diva packing heat. Sweeney fell another notch in love.

But most interesting perhaps, in an office nook beside the kitchen—and where normally you might find a small curio desk, maybe a laptop, an answering machine—Julietta had set herself up with a jeweler's station. Magnifier light. Ionic cleaner. Gem tester. Diamond sieves, parcel papers. "I still do some work. Keep my hand in the business. If I left it up to those *kids*..."

Sweeney now dials her number from memory, pulling off the Interstate and turning south. "Mrs. Siegal? Hey, this is Ted Sweeney, not sure if you'd remember...well, thank you. Thanks. I'm good, good, thanks. Say, I have a question, maybe a favor..."

~

In the four years since Sweeney had built her fence, Julietta Siegal has installed herself into a small and fervent community of like-minded, formidably-outraged old women. A pack of bridge players and placard holders, liberal democrats with unlimited time and a surfeit of self-righteousness. You see these flocks of dames and dowagers in the affluent corners of America, marching on post offices and courthouses, fervent with the belief that they can change things. And by believing it, of course, make it so.

Pulling up to Julietta's cabin, Sweeney passes a retired movie star in a Grand Cherokee. Fifty years ago, she'd made a career out of a great set of tits and a passable scream. A slasher movie ingénue who had a brief run at the A-list when she starred next to Rock Hudson in a red-mesa oater. Rock had caressed her hand in an extended, minimally-outrageous way. The same hand now hangs loose over the top of her steering wheel, and waves energetically at Sweeney as they pass. He installed a trash disposal for her a few months ago.

He finds Julietta cleaning up the kitchen, rinsing tea cups. "Teddy. Dear." She tilts her check for him.

He kisses it. "You look fantastic," he says, and means it, though her glasses are heavier, her wrinkles thicker.

"So let's see it." All business, she throws off her apron.

Sweeney goes to his shirt pocket, drops the stone into her palm.

She hefts it in her hand. Raises her plucked eyebrows at him. "I love it."

"Love what."

"That someone whom I thought I knew still has the capacity to surprise me."

She puts a plug in the sink and holds the stone under hot water, rubbing it around with Joy dish soap. She dries it with a paper towel and produces a loupe from her junk drawer. A pair of tweezers. She steps over to the nearest window and starts with the squinting. A full minute later, she brings the stone up to her mouth, breathes a puff of hot air onto it. She glances at it again immediately. Nods.

She hefts it in her palm. Passes it back. "You get yourself in some kind of trouble, Mr. Sweeney?"

"Not that I know of."

"What you seem to have there is a slightly yellowed, near flawless dodecahedron glassy. Twenty-five to thirty carats. It's got those two very slight occlusions in the heart, but assuming no further flaws, if you brought this into my shop with documentation, I'd offer you thirty thousand dollars and feel guilty about it."

"Thirty grand."

"If it's cut well, and if it's as flawless as it looks, you've got a hundred thousand dollar rock in your hand. Inherited, you said."

"Yeah...."

"You don't see roughs this size out in the open. Ever."

He tucks it back into his shirt pocket. "Well. Thank you. That helps."

She touches his pocket with a crooked forefinger. "You *sure* you're not in any sort of trouble, Teddy?"

"Me, I'm golden."

She keeps her finger on his shirt. Presses it at him. "Glad to hear it."

~

Eddie used to point out, we're not criminals, we're competition. "Wiseguys used to have numbers? But what's Powerball if it ain't numbers? Tell me please why the U. S. of A. can run Lotto and we can't have numbers? And Shylocks? You ask me, Shys are the same as Chase credit cards. The Russians got their basement games over in Brighton Beach, which is like Atlantic City without the commute. No wonder RICO had to come along. Competition, man. And the Feds got the jails, they got the courts. What have we got? Nothing but each other, man. Nothing but each other."

Fifteen years later, Sweeney ushers Eddie's wife (his *wife*) into Sweeney's home. "It ain't much," Sweeney says, unlooping the black bungee cord he's been using for a lock, "but it's a calving shed."

"*Cozy.*" Tina's tentative coming through the door, clutching her elbows, trying not to brush up against anything contagious.

"Have a seat." Sweeney indicates a chair leaking the least amount of stuffing. "Want some water? Diet Coke? Beer?"

"Beer."

"I'll break out the fine crystal, that's how much you mean to me." He comes back with a can of Budweiser and a Flintstones glass. Dealing with Tina (it's coming back to him now), you got to mix your messages.

She ignores the glass and goes straight for the can. A good long healthy draw puts her in a better mood. She takes in the linoleum curling under the stove, the fern dropping leaves into the sink, Zeke lapping at his water bowl. Outside, the hot, bleached dust of the driveway. Inside, the residual odor of wet dog and bacon grease, a soupçon of engine oil.

Sweeney flicks on a window air conditioner. "Give it a few minutes, we'll be all right."

"You don't mind me saying...Jesus, Cosmo."

"It ain't Park Avenue."

"No shit."

"Maybe it's better."

"Get out."

"I like my life." He cracks a beer, lights a cigarette. "It just takes, you know, adjusting some expectations."

"Understatement of the year."

"Questions, Tina. I got questions."

"Sure you do."

He starts pleasantly enough: "Where'd your diamonds come from?"

"Like I said, Cosmo. Need to know basis."

"Yeah, I remember you said that. The thing is, though, you only got one option here, while you drink my beer in my kitchen. You got to answer my questions."

"Or what?"

"Or I'm sending you back to New York on the humble, hat in hand. I need reassurances. Otherwise, sweetheart, have a nice life."

"When'd you get so pissy?" She finishes off her beer, dimples the can meditatively with her thumb. "Anyway, you wouldn't do that. Just cut me loose like that."

From his hip pocket, he withdraws a laser-printed photo from the dead wop's briefcase. The one where Tina's sitting among wicker and water glasses, face lost behind sunglasses. "Look familiar?" He pushes it across the table.

She tilts it to the light. "That's *me*."

Sweeney notes that Tina's fingernails, holding the sheet, are a bright, fire-engine red. Last night, her nails had been bare. So. She helps him dump a body then goes back and paints her nails?

"I was wearing my Dulce's. So this was what, like, two weeks ago? That's Bryant Park." It starts to sink in. "Where'd this come from?"

"Short version? We got *two* corpses in the river. This first guy shows up in my chair a couple nights ago." Sweeney draws a finger across his throat. "Never seen him before in my life. I found his car, he had these photos. Then there's that guy from last night. Hyenas travel in pairs, right?"

"But, I mean."

"You been on somebody's radar for what, two weeks ago you said? They're following you, and now they know you're here. If you're still alive, maybe they're watching you. Which means you're valuable to them. I need to know who they are, where they come from. What they got to do with me."

She takes a breath. Considers her beer can. Finally says, "Right, okay. You're right. So. Yeah. Luccheses."

"No. No way. If this was 1980, *maybe*."

"Nah, there's still a few hanging on. Skin of their teeth kind of thing." Having decided to spill, she's already bored again. Staring at the window above his sink, tilting her head at a hummingbird suspended at his feeder. "That guy last night. Tony Castori. He's muscle for Donnie Moretti."

"Wait a minute. Wait a...Donnie *Moretti*? Those stones belong to Moretti?"

"Yeah no, not really. But Eddie was earning for Donnie when he grabbed them. Donnie probably wants his piece."

"So Eddie got sideways with Donnie Moretti?"

"Eddie said Moretti's washed up."

"Things change, but things don't change *that* much." Sweeney takes a moment to dig through a set of jumbled memories, comes up with Moretti in sweat pants, Walmart sneakers. Three chins shiny with chicken grease. Dark, glittering eyes. He's seen this face occasionally in his dreams, and never under pleasant circumstances. "That guy's Genghis Khan, he's thalidomide, he's DDT, he's..."

"Anyway, it wasn't Moretti. It was just that fag Tony. The other guy, probably his kid brother. They run together."

"Both of whom we tossed in the Yellowstone. Which

means Donnie's coming right behind, Donnie or somebody just as bad..." He briefly chews over possibilities. "The Luccheses. That's just great. I mean, yeah. I just want to take a second and say thanks. *Thank you* for bringing this to my door."

"Jesus, Cosmo." She slaps the table as she stands. Finds the fridge and another beer, popping it on her way back. "Grow a pair, right? I mean, I come to you with this *opportunity,* this chance where you might never have to work again, ever, and what do you do? You keep pissing and moaning about...what? Having to dump a couple bodies. Big deal." She tilts the beer back at a generous angle.

"You lied about knowing Tony."

"I knew you'd bitch and moan."

"You got that right." Sweeney thinks a minute. Says, "There's another player out here, too. Luccheses plus whoever's killing Luccheses. The guy who's messing with harmless old Ted Sweeney. Hey Tina? Who's messing with me?"

"No idea."

"Yeah right."

"Seriously. You think I'd hold something like that back?"

He waits her out.

"Here's all I know, Cosmo. Okay? I'll tell you what I got, then can we start figuring out how to move my rocks? Okay?" She sighs heavily. "*God.* So yeah. Okay. Eddie comes home about a week ago. And he's *freaking* out. Three in the morning and I mean, pale and trembly. He puts this bag in my hand, says to me, we got to hide this somewheres." She stares off. "So we find a place, right? Up in the attic. Eddie tells me, he says, any Russians come around, you take these rocks and go find Cosmo. He tells me, Rockjaw, Montana, he says. First time I'd ever heard of the place. Then he says, I'll catch up to you, he says."

"The Russians."

"The next night. I'm lying up in bed, I hear somebody downstairs taking an axe to the backdoor. An *axe*, Cosmo. They left it in splinters, pretty much."

Sweeney flashes briefly on the crowbar work done on his place. "So you're upstairs?"

"We had an attic door right over the bed. One of those fold down ladders. I crawled up, pulled the ladder behind me, laid there listening while they trashed our house. My mother's China, silverware, those nice clay pots I used to have? Gone. Just for the fun of it."

"Lucky they didn't set the place on fire."

"I don't…"

"Russians and arson? It's like bacon and eggs."

"Well, uh, yeah. So anyway." This hadn't occurred to her, and it takes her a moment to digest it. "So I, uh, I waited for a few hours. Got the rocks and got in my car. Hightailed it out to Montana. That was, what, five days ago now."

"Five days."

"Yeah."

Sweeney grabs another beer. Figuring his day's pretty much shot anyway. "Got any idea what Russians we're dealing with here?"

"Breetvah? That's a name I've heard. I've heard Breetvah."

The mouth of his beer foams, and he stares down into the boiling abyss of it. Breetvah. Donnie Moretti and now Breetvah.

Fuhhhuck. Fuck me running.

~

That cold spring when Sweeney was twenty-three, business was good enough he could afford the car of his wet dreams. A 1957 Eldorado Seville, lowered and chromed up, customized with a 454 Chevy. Even at idle, the compression ratio, the cam shaft rattle, they'd knock your fillings loose. A beautiful, lethal little rumble from the pipes. Some guys had posters of Farrah, he'd always had the '57 Eldorado. It was a car that started conversations, just garish enough to walk the line of irony. DeCicco himself had complimented his ride.

Eddie and Sweeney were full time partners, amigos, tres bon amis. They were Scorcese and De Niro. You got a gig? You got a score? It's both of us or neither of us. More rightly, come to think of it, they were Mister Miyagi and the Karate Kid. Wipe on, wipe off. Eddie saying, "See, one of these days, when you seen what I seen...." Half-smiling it into a joke, but you don't joke about shit like that. Eddie reminding Sweeney, constantly, who wore the pleated pants.

But Sweeney kept his mouth shut. Long as they were making money, he'd let Eddie have his attitude. Plus, they were family. You put up with a lot from family. Plus again, Eddie *did* know some moves.

That first Breetvah job, for instance. Eddie had an inside guy at a place called CorpCo Technologies. "So we jack the delivery van. Low risk, the driver knows we're coming. Sit on the cargo, chips or something, then sell it back to my guy for half the price. Company gets the insurance payoff, you and me, we get a thirty grand payday. Everybody comes out ahead."

The heist went off smooth. A parking lot in Williamsburg, the driver waiting with an elbow on the hood of his van, a twenty-year-old kid with an Adam's apple the size of your fist, a ponytail that didn't quite cover the Aryan Brotherhood swastika tattooed on his neck. He opened the double doors, giving them a look. The van packed floor to ceiling with bagel-sized boxes. "Computer processers. *Four* times faster than what's out there now." An Apple logo printed on the side of every small box. "Oh and hey, mind giving me a ride back to my place? I'm over in Coney Island."

"Coney Island?" Eddie considered it a second before punching the kid in the mouth. A straight jab to the teeth. "That's for the whatchamacallit. Hey Shakespeare, what do we call it?"

"Verisimilitude?"

"Yeah. Coney Island? My partner here can give you a ride. No problem."

Sweeney thinking: An hour's drive one way. Sure, no problem.

The guy reached in to wobble at a tooth. "Could have warned me."

Eddie stashed the van in a storage shed in Jamaica, Queens. Twelve days later, two o'clock in the morning, Sweeney and Eddie rode slow through empty streets in Sweeney's Caddy. The tires whispered against rain. Eddie said, "New interior?"

"Yeah. Nice, right?" Tan, calfskin upholstery. "Smells like a shoe store."

"*Niiiice.*" Eddie being grumpy and ironic.

"I like my car."

"It draws attention. I keep telling you, less attention the better. Yeah, stop here." A metal door covered with swirls and loops and angles of a fresh, artful graffiti.

Sweeney helped him scroll up the door. The van filled the

entirety of the shed. Eddie said, "Okay, right. Follow me up behind. We're going to Hoboken…"

"The fuck?"

"Yeah, what. I didn't set the meet. Follow me up behind. When you see me flash my brake lights five or six times quick, you find a place to park. We'll leave your car a few blocks away."

Forty-five minutes later, Sweeney climbed into the van beside Eddie. "Little cautious aren't we?"

"These guys are a taaaad unpredictable."

Eddie idled past chain link and razor wire into a building supply warehouse. To their left, stacks of plywood, two-by-fours, treated railroad ties. To their right, a series of bay doors. Eddie flashed his brights. "That look like a number ninety-nine to you?" He honked once. The noise was startling. Vapor lights for ambience and a mist off the Hudson.

Sweeney gave his two cents, "I got a bad feeling."

"Yeah, that fog. Gives you the heebie jeebies, don't it?" He hummed the theme from Jaws, then showed white teeth in the dim dark. "Lighten up, man. It's a done deal."

The door scrolled open, and a figure waved them into the bay. His other hand, the thumb was hooked under a shoulder strap for a rifle. He looked like ex-military. Haircut high and tight, fatigues tucked into boots. "Uh, Eddie…"

"Easy, cousin."

As the door scrolled down behind them, three heavies eased up from the shadows, two with repeaters (Sweeney, who had an eye for ordinance, recognized AK-74s), another with a Remington 12 gauge pump. A fourth stepped into the headlights wearing Gap khakis and a button-down Oxford. "Gentlemen!" he said pleasantly. "So glad a see you!" A smile polite as the Hamptons, but there was jailhouse ink on his knuckles.

Eddie exhaled soft, "We're gonna need a bigger boat." Added loud, "You Sergei?"

"I am Foma. I am taking the role of Sergei. He is sick." Foma's accent was guttural and phlegmy, full of the Ukraine, Chechnya, the Russian Tea Room.

"You got our money?"

"You have these chips?"

"In the back."

"Then yes, we have the money. It is not here, however."

"That's a problem."

"No, no, no problem, not at all. You leave now, you come back later. Sergei give you your money."

"We're gone. Cosmo, back in the van."

Foma said something in Russian, and the machine guns came alive. Rack, lock, load. "No. You leave now. You walk. Walk home." He waved his hands. Shoo.

"You're making a mistake, friend."

"I make no mistakes. Never, no. *Friend.*"

Eddie and Sweeney had put up their hands, but now Eddie made a move, attracting the guns. "Just finding my cell phone." He drew it slowly out of his overcoat. Dialed a number. Pressed send. "Bytchkov," he said. "Yeah, hey. It's me. No, Sergei's AWOL. Some guy here named Foma. *Foma*, I said. *I* don't know. What I *do* know though is, is he's stiffing us. Yeah, just a second." He walked toward Foma, holding the phone out before him "Bytchkov."

"Bytchkov." He spat to the side, cussing in Russia. "*Dolboeb*. Jerkoff. I no talk to him."

"Trust me, friend. Take this call."

"Fuck you. And Bytchkov too."

Eddie said, "Breetvah."

And like *that*…all the sound got sucked out of the room. This cavernous garage. Water dripping. The hollow ping of a radiator. It went quiet like the moment in outer space when the booster engines fall off. Sweeney's own heavy breath filled his ears. The Russian stood looking at the phone. "Breetvah." His voice flat, his accent filling the word full of new vowels. "You know Breetvah?"

"I work for him. Bytchkov does too."

"Pozdravlyayu." His tone dry.

"Spasiba."

Sweeney, speechless: When did Eddie learn *Russian*?

Eddie held out the phone.

The Russian spat again, ignoring the phone. "So yes then we give you your money."

"Good." Eddie put the phone to his ear. "We cool." Hung it up.

"You tell Breetvah, you tell him Foma from Chelyabinsk, you tell him that we are…" he clasped his hands together, "… we are brothers of the blood, yes?"

"Sure, yeah, I'll mention it."

Eddie and Sweeney walked back to the Caddy with Sweeney carrying a nylon grip full of non-sequential twenties and hundreds. He found himself wobbling with the knock-kneed gait that comes when a rifle scope may even *now* be zeroing in on the back of your head.

Eddie was unusually quiet. "You're pissed."

"Fucking-a."

Nothing more passed between them until they were in Sweeney's car. "Normally," Eddie said, "I like to see you pissed.

My cousin, I tell people, I say, he's got three gears. Reverse, neutral, and pissed. But you being pissed at *me*? Not so good."

"*My* cousin, I tell people, I say, I trust him. We got no secrets."

"Really?" Eddie was touched.

"Who the fuck is Breetvah, Eddie. For that matter, who the fuck's Bytchkov?"

"Bytchkov's the guy who turned us onto the deal. He gets a cut."

"You telling me we're paying up to Russians? *Russians*, Eddie?"

"Chill, man. Jesus. Take a breath. Look at your face. No, I'm just saying he turned me onto the deal. I'll show him gratitude, but we still earn for Anthony."

"The Russians, Eddie? I've heard stories."

"Yeah. They're true."

"You should have told me. That's all."

Eddie found a pack of smokes. "You mind?" He already had one lit. Kicked back in the seat and put a not-very-clean brogan up on the spotless dash. Took a moment to admire his smoke. "You play by the rules too much, Cosmo. Mostly, that's a good thing. You keep my ass in line. But if I'd told you we were playing with the Russians, you'd have bitched and moaned and backed out, and we'd be thirty grand poorer right now. Sometimes, my cousin, you just need to say fuck it. Roll the dice down the table. Am I right?"

"Who's Breetvah?" Sweeney could still taste his own outrage.

"Supposed to be this badass in Jersey City, running Brighton Beach from afar. Nobody *I* know's ever seen him, but they all toss his name around. Bytchkov told me to use it

I ever got in a pickle."

"They bought it pretty quick."

"They respect badasses. The *only* thing they respect. It's kind of refreshing, in a way, hanging out with the Russians. You always know where you stand."

Which was true, as far as it went. Where you stood, however, was usually knee deep in concrete above a rising tide of shit.

~

Most of us have an adolescence with at least a little romance, some teen years with a few memories of illicit love. A roll in the hay back when it felt like you were getting away with something. It's you and your love against the world. At the time, those days were incidental, but now, they prop up everything else.

Aggie never had that adolescence. And you know? Maybe she's stronger for it. By god, she is strong. Strong enough to make the necessary decisions.

Such as: This.

Trundling their slow way west, Aggie's about ready to strangle her daughter. "Get your feet off the dashboard."

Hair down in her face, concentrating on her cell phone, texting, Elizabeth sighs the heavy sigh of every teenage girl beset. Drops her feet off the dash.

"Who are you texting?"

A long, sullen moment. Then, "Dylan."

Her boyfriend of the moment. "Anything interesting?"

Elizabeth shows her the digital face of her phone: "Off 2 boring Fairmont with A. Gawd! Kill me now!"

"I don't know where you got all that meanness. It wasn't from me."

Aggie still thinks of herself as a ranch girl. No matter that from middle school onward she lived in a clapboard shack on the east side of town. A poor neighborhood with gravel streets. She had her daddy's love (all hugs and scratchy kisses) but he was a man who limped through life on a pair of matching Achilles' heels: Jim Beam and new John Deere machinery. Neither failure is healthy for a ranch, but together they are catastrophic. At age thirteen she stood watching a moving company wheel her piano out of the front door, jostling it hard enough to drop a side panel flat in the dust, revealing the hammers and strings. She went from having her own horse to not being able to afford a decent bike.

When she was a sophomore, Aggie and Henry Applebaum went to second, third, fourth base, all during one confused showing of *Gladiator*. Of course she caught pregnant, and two years later, his shrill, bird-beaked mother was standing in their doorway with Henry's luggage. "I knew you was like this. Trashy. *Knew* it. From the start. Trapping him like you done. Now the Army's got him, they've got..." she teared up, "they've got my boy."

Aggie was still in her waitress uniform, smelling like bacon grease, too tired to put up a fight. "The Army?" First she'd heard about it.

Her apartment was on the second floor, and in the days, weeks, months to come, she learned the lonely sound of tired heels on metal stairs, the painful ache in her shoulders of carrying a baby up to reheated meatloaf.

Husband number two, Neddie (ne, Nacho), drank Coors from the can and dropped five dollars a night into poker machines. A big tipper with all the right things to say, he had honey on his tongue and a condom in his wallet. He sweet talked her until she became Aggie Medina, which meant a whole new set of life experiences. Tortillas, pico de gallo, broken toes, a snapped collarbone.

The same week she walked out on Neddie, she found her job at the library. In the world she very much wants to inhabit, coincidence is just another name for answered prayers.

Enter Sweeney. How many potential husbands do you find volunteering at the soup kitchen? Sweeney in soiled jeans, a Mariners cap, sitting on his open tailgate, smoking. A cold day in October, and a fresh apple-crumble pie steamed at his hip. "Baked it myself." Lanky in a way you don't often see anymore. "Those guys over there," he twisted his head toward the homeless by the cinderblock wall. "Old coffee-grounds-beard and his buddy, Chief I-ain't-got-no-chin, they been looking at me like I owe them money, waiting on this pie."

"Well, I got the keys."

"I'm Ted."

"Aggie."

A comfortable handshake. Calluses and heavy skin. The hand of a man who *worked* for a living.

Things progressed until Aggie started trying on the last name, seeing how it fit. Aggie Sweeney. Heya Mrs. Sweeney, how are you. Make the reservation under Sweeney. Aggie Sweeney.

But then...

Then a month ago, a bookish eighth grader in a straw cowboy hat, a kid named Perry Gustafson, came up to the Information desk. "I'm, uh, doing a report on, like the Sopranos? Real life mobsters?"

She'd previously avoided the mobster shelf. Had maybe

been a little hoity-toity about her self-education. Somewhere between the impossible Kant and overrated McLuhan, between Dickens and Dick Hugo, that's where she'd staked out her territory. Gangsters? Not her bag.

But the kid had gotten her hooked. Books, websites, articles. Don't ask her why, she just became fascinated. All these oblivious, urban provincials, these wise guys, these arrogant schmucks who thought they were entitled to leech off hard-working Americans...Who were these people?

Then three weeks ago, here's a *New York Times* photo on microfiche. An FBI stakeout. A sidewalk, a restaurant, a cluster of Scorcese types on the alert for hidden cameras. And in the shadows, under an awning...

Couldn't be.

But it was. Stockier, younger, but there were those same scars around the eyes, the same crook to the nose. Teddy.

Teddy, the exception? No. Turns out he's every man in the world. Worse than most.

Coming into Bozeman, she puts her blinker on. Takes the first exit.

Elizabeth says, "You need gas or something?"

"I'm meeting somebody."

"Who?"

"Somebody."

She finds a spot on Main Street. Parks next to what used to be the Cowboy Café but is now a women's boutique. Hundred dollar bras. "By Appointment Only." On the street, young mothers with cell phones and strollers, businessmen in khakis and open collars, college kids emerging from coffee shops.

Aggie in Pamida sneakers and her daisy-patterned

Penny's bag. She is so tired of being broke. So tired of *envy*. She says to her daughter, "You wait here. I'll be back in a few minutes."

The girl shrugs, texting. *Whatever.*

Just down the block, at one of the benches in front of Daily Brew Coffee, a middle-aged man, middle-height, middle-everything, sits inconspicuously dressed in tan leather shoes and light summer pants, a suit jacket slung over the bench and a loosened tie. Legs stretched out, reading a newspaper. She'd wanted stereotypes. Slovenly and unbathed, a leer and gold chains. But instead he's got this *elegant* face, tidy eyebrows. Politely bemused. Hair swept back from the brow and a dusting of gray above the ears. Reading glasses on the end of his nose.

She is not treacherous, she is not unfaithful.

The man sees her, folds away his paper. Tucks the glasses into his shirt pocket.

He holds out his hand. "Aggie?"

~

He's *almost* to the point where he can look at his favorite chair and not see a body. As they move from the kitchen to the living room, Sweeney puts Tina in his recliner with a gesture. "Make yourself comfortable."

Sweeney, on the couch, snaps his fingers for Zeke. He plays with the dog's ears, guilty. He's been falling down on the job, dog-owner wise. Tina's been talking about everything she's going to do with her diamond money. Letting the fantasies just spin out of control. "Plus, not to mention, I've never been to Europe. Prague, Budapest. Turkish bathhouses. Maybe I'll buy a little island in Greece. Never drink a cheap beer again."

"And after that? After you're all done with your traveling. What's up then?"

"I'll figure something out. Go shopping."

"Shopping. That'll be fun for, what. A couple weeks?"

"I get it, yeah. Money can't buy happiness. Whatever."

"You can't live in New York. You know that, right?"

"Plenty of cities in the world."

"Well, the best of them is dead to you. So you and me, we're in the same boat." Sweeney looks pointedly around his living room. The dust motes suspended in beams of light. The cobwebs clotted with dog hair.

"Yeah, no. I'd shoot myself in the head."

Which is mean spirited enough to push him to his decision. Appreciate it but no, have a nice life, good luck, I'm not that guy anymore. This is my home. *Home.* He'll never fit in, he's always going to be the odd guy out, but it's what he's got. It's at once a revelation and a capitulation. Early in the fall, after the tourists flee ahead of winter, he recognizes at least one out of every three vehicles parked on Main Street. Faced with the potential loss of it, he feels an actual fondness for how the three hardware stores each sponsor a softball team. "Listen," he says, "I've been thinking maybe this isn't…."

She twists around in her chair. "Is that a car?"

Sweeney watches as the bubbles of Marilyn's prowler float above the waterline of his shrubbery.

In the time it takes for Sweeney to privately issue an unconditional surrender to the universe, to resign himself to the undertow of bad news pulling him down by the heels, Marilyn has parked and is knocking her knuckles against the door. Calls out a polite "Helloooo? Ted?" She lets herself in.

Materializes in the living room, big as life, staring across at Tina. "Oh, hello."

And now here's Sweeney, saying, with a final dose of despair, "Marilyn, this is Tina, old pal from Brooklyn. Tina, Marilyn."

~

Ex-wife on his left (the woman with whom he thought he'd grow old), ex-mistress on his right (the woman whom he thought would keep him young) and as far as Sweeney knows, they've never laid eyes on each other. Yet, look at them: Passing hard judgment, cheap shoes to tacky lipstick. Bristling. Hiding snarls.

"Anyway," Marilyn finally says, using the word as if she's clearing her throat. Sweeney notes a manila folder in her hand. "Ted. I brought this for you. We should, uh..." she waves toward her car.

"Yeah. Tina? You mind?"

Tina toasts with her beer can. Slumps back into the chair. Focuses on her phone. "Meetcha."

Leaving the house, Marilyn's says, "Classy."

"Eddie's wife." Which of course is only half the story.

Sweeney takes another two full steps down the path before he realizes that Marilyn's lagging behind.

Standing back there with the manila folder. "I thought... Shit."

"You okay?"

"Did she tell you about him?"

"Who? Eddie? Tell me what?"

Marilyn glances back. They hear the distant digital sound of Tina's cell phone. It trills out a high octave version of the theme from "Rawhide." At once oddly appropriate and utterly incongruous.

Maybe it's the proximity of Tina—another chicken in the rooster house—but Marilyn now does something so entirely out of character he's left speechless, mouth moving like a guppy's: She forces herself into his arms, nestles her check against his neck.

She's still familiar to him. All these years later, she's still as right as a seed in soil, a wrench over a bolt. Smooth and warm. Her hair smells like apple shampoo and sunlight and sweat, a hint of the industrial disinfectant they use to clean cop cars.

She lets herself linger for a few moments. When she pulls away, she's left the manilla envelope against his chest. "Eddie, sweetheart."

~

They sit in the cruiser, engine idling. Marilyn says, "Sheriff's office has that NCIC? That National Crime Information Center? Subscriber only type of thing." Even now she enjoys her privileges. "That's where I found the picture."

In his hands, a printout of a web page. A Department of Justice eagle seal in the upper left hand corner, then a block of text (continuing from a previous page) describing the more recent string of Eddie's exonerations. And then, taking up the entire bottom half of the page, and in the pale halftones of a printer losing its ink, a grainy photo of Eddie's corpse.

He's sitting in the front seat of an anonymous Buick sedan, wearing a blood-spattered white t-shirt, the left sleeve askew enough to reveal his age-blurred yin-yang tattoo. Temple propped against the wheel, eyes fixed, staring past the camera.

His throat's been cut.

Eddie used to be skinny, but in the photo he's put on some muscle. Joined a gym or something. He looks fit. He looks like he could live forever. If it weren't for the neat incision under his throat, the thin slit, sharp as a piece of paper, the lips of it pressed tight.

He wears a spattered bib of blood. The inside of the car has been washed in gore. Sweeney flashes to photos of old gangland hits, to Dillinger and Capone.

"I'm sorry," Marilyn says.

"Why...Jesus, why..." Sweeney rubs his face. "You'd think somebody would have said something."

"Too soon, I guess. This is only from ten days ago."

Sweeney stares at the photo. "Ten days?"

"Came in over the transom, apparently. Anonymous source, some guy bragging."

He considers Tina's timeline. She'd said that Eddie had brought her the rocks, what...? A week ago? He mumbles, "Same M.O. as those bodies I found."

"Yeah, sure. I thought of...*Bodies?* Plural?"

He considers Tina, kicking it back just a few feet away in his living room, sipping her beer.

"Ted? Bod*eez?*"

"Anybody have any thoughts about who did it?"

Marilyn's still digesting the pluralization. Her jaw sits askew, a cow caught mid cud. Finally says, "My other piece of news. That guy with the shotgun? A kid named Fontana Castori. Ring any bells?"

"Tony Castori's little brother. Yeah, works for Moretti."

Marilyn's face is a Venetian blind, and she's just twisted down a whole new look. Cop suspicion, tempered by reassessment. She'd expected him to be astonished, grateful for the information. "Yeah, so, uh. Kid got tagged for a dope possession last year, which was enough to put him in the system. Otherwise, he's clean."

Sweeney folds the snapshot of his dead cousin Eddie along its existing crease, then folds it again. Tucks it into a shirt pocket. Smooths it flat. "Thank you for this, sweetheart. I mean it."

She's still got the look. "You should talk to people, Ted. Open up a little. You got to trust somebody."

He stares off into the middle distance. "That's one theory, sure."

~

It's going to be a relief, in a way. To let this loose. He's been holding his thumb over this particular nozzle for so, so long.

He finds Tina kicked back crossways in his chair, ankles crossed. She says, "That was your ex? I saw her once in New York. I ever tell you? Tracked her down. I was jealous. She used to be a *hottie*. Kind of let herself go now, though."

Sweeney sits across from her. Elbows on his knees. "What."

He pulls the paper from his shirt pocket, smoothes it flat.

Tina can barely be bothered for a glance. "Uh huh."

Sweeney's right arm floats out, disembodied. It's *some*body's arm but maybe not his. He watches it grab a handful of Tina's black hair. His other hand comes around for a matching clump. "This happened ten days ago, Tina. *Ten days*. Look at it."

"Get the fuck *offa* me."

Which is when things go red for a while.

When he swims up out of it, Tina's got his handprint on her cheek and some blood welling out of one nostril, puddling over the rim of her upper lip.

So. Cosmo's back.

And it's like an alcoholic taking his first shot of booze in ten years. All that effort, all that time, all that *penance*...phhst. Gone. He feels the disappointment of it, and yes, what is this? What's this other thing? Anticipation, maybe.

He finds a box of Kleenex. Tosses it to her. "Here."

"Thanks. You dick."

She goes to work with the Kleenex, twisting one up a nostril. And it's not like it's the first time.

"Ten days ago."

She still hasn't looked at the printout. "If I came here, if I said, yeah, some guys took care of Eddie, but I need your help. Yeah, the last guy that tried to move these rocks, they still haven't found his body. Shit, Cosmo. What do you think would have happened? You'd disappear. You'd be that guy, what's his name, D. B. Cooper."

"Not true."

"I'm still bleeding."

"I'll get some ice."

He comes back with a dishtowel wrapped around cubes, his outrage balanced on a spoon. "So were you guys even married? Or was that a lie, too?"

"Sure, yeah, of course we were married." She glances at him. "Why would you even think such a thing?"

"You don't seem too broken up about it is all. Eddie being dead."

"Let's just say, Eddie changed." She holds the cold towel first to one nostril, then pulls it away to study the pink in the dampness. "Let's just say, compared to what he's been putting me through? This bloody nose is a kiss on the cheek."

"Where'd he get the rocks?"

"I don't know."

"How'd you get them?"

"Pretty much like I said. Black bag, Eddie, Russians chopping at the back door."

"When'd you find out that Eddie was dead?"

"He didn't come home for a while. No big deal, right? There's a girlfriend over in Redhook. He doesn't know I know. Anyway, then I get that picture in the mail." Her eyes go to the coffee table where the printout is rebounding toward its former folds. "Same picture."

"The Russians?"

"Trashed our house that same night. That's when I took off."

"Where are they now?"

"The rocks? Safe deposit box in Brooklyn."

"The fuck."

"Eddie said you'd have to go to New York for a decent fence. And you *know* I'm not driving across country with however-many-millions in my glovebox."

"Where'd he get the rocks, Tina?"

She inspects the damp knot of towel in her hand. That outer layer of disdain she's been carrying around, the heavy coat of contemptuousness, it's gone. She sighs heavily, surrendering. "Breetvah. He said he, quote, lifted them off Breetvah, unquote."

Sweeney goes to the window. Outside, a Montana late afternoon. Hazy in the distance. Maybe a forest fire somewhere. He's had this view for seven years now. The ranch house quartering away. Paint peeling on the south faces. A loose gutter knocking in the wind. Distant black specks of slow-grazing Angus. The smell of cow shit and hay and his own unwashed shirts. Seven years inside a Hank Williams song.

Behind him, she says, "I got the impression Breetvah was working some kind of middle man deal."

The old folks could dog sit for him. And Aggie's safe enough for a couple of days. And the kind of money we're talking about? He pulls it off, he could take Aggie for a slow cruise around the world.

Sweeney picks up the photo of Eddie. Consider the toner-gray splatters of blood. The fixed eyes. "And Moretti?"

"He was the cleaner. I don't know the details, but Eddie was complaining about how big a cut he was taking. I mean, like, half?"

"Breetvah needed Moretti to clean the diamonds? That don't make sense."

"I'm just telling you what I heard."

Breetvah and the Russians. Moretti and the Luccheses. That's on one end of the scale.

And on the other? His outrage on Eddie's behalf. A life cut short, *stolen*.

Also, diamonds.

Sweeney pays attention to a new pulse in his throat. Years ago he'd compared it to sex, this same kind of feeling. He'd told Eddie, building up to a good score, it's like getting wood. You can't argue with it.

"All right," he says.

"All right what."

"New York is what. Get your credit cards."

~

Sweeney and Eddie did three jobs with Bytchkov. The computer chip gig that almost went south. That was first. Then a shared investment in high quality Rolex Submariners out of Beijing. Such a beautiful weight and heft, those watches. Silky-smooth second hands. "Niiice." Sweeney's first exposure to the lucrative world of knockoffs, and he *liked* it. Dig the return on investment. Eighty bucks a watch, sold for five hundred per over the course of a summer. Bytchkov set the price point.

Eddie said, "Five hundred bucks, or Bytchkov backs out of the deal." And while Sweeney resented being told what to do, he came to admire the foresight. These babies went for thirty-five hundred bucks straight retail. If they'd sold them for anything less than $500, the scam would have fallen apart. But any *more* than that? You might as well go buy the real thing. It became a rolling bazaar out of the trunk of his Caddy. Sweeney flipped through a thick roll of hundreds. "I ever get to meet this Bytchkov guy, I'm shaking his hand. Goddamn genius is what he is."

"I been telling you."

The third gig put Sweeney on the road to Montana.

Saturday afternoon in December, one week before Christmas, Eddie and Sweeney drove in slush through the decrepit ghettos of broke-down Brooklyn. Sad strings of Christmas lights hung from the limbs of bare trees. The homes of plumbers and electricians fallen on hard times. Eddie said, "Take a left up here."

"You tell him when we'd be showing up?"

"He just said show up." Eddie unwrapped a mint

toothpick, rolled it back and forth in his mouth. "I told you about him, right? How he's kind of crazy?"

"Yeah, you mentioned it."

Eddie had been squatting in a basement off Dyker Beach. A Murphy bed, mini fridge, two bar stools, and an old coin-operated pool table with the coin mechanism ripped out. A sheet of plywood could turn it into a dining table, but who's got time for that. Three nights a week they'd drink beer and shoot stick. Nine ball, eight ball, straight pool.

Eddie bent to break a full rack. "When these guys came over," he sent the cue ball careening, "these Russians from the late seventies, early eighties, they emptied out the prisons." The nine ball dropped in the side. "I'm stripes, I guess. Okay, ten ball, corner." He dropped it. "Those prisons, they'd have forty, fifty guys in a cell with ten beds. Lice, bedbugs, oatmeal three times a day. Teeth coming out from scurvy. Nothing we could ever do to them here over that's worse than where they came from. Twelve ball, side." He shot and missed. "Shit."

"Bytchkov. How'd you hook up?" Sweeney dropped the two ball.

"He came to *me*, man. Had this idea he'd, you know, unite the tribes or something. Italians and Russians. *That's* how crazy."

"Three in the corner."

"Nice shot. *But* he's got good ideas, too. That gasoline tax scam, right? Everybody was into it, but he's the one come up with it."

"Five over here."

"But. But I mean, these guys, there's honor, then everything else. Step on their toes, insult them, they'll do anything. *Anything*, Cosmo. Kill your mother, crucify your dog, burn your house down."

"Crucify your *dog*?"

"Seriously crazy …"

Twelve hours later, Eddie said, "Okay, this is it. This is Bytchkov's place."

A narrow plank house on Sheepshead Bay. East 24th Street. A flimsy white metal fence crooked around a patchy square of lawn. Cracked concrete and an old Ford Econoline with dark windows. A puddle of oil, bald tires.

"Gee, this is a real shithole."

"His palace, he calls it."

Bytchkov came to the door himself. Chewing and wiping grease on a sleeveless t-shirt. "My friend Eddie! So good always a see you. And you, you are Coseemo."

"Cosmo, yeah."

Six inches shorter than Sweeney, Bytchkov had issues with his neck. It didn't swivel too good. His dark eyes darted to compensate. The skin of his chest, his arms, hung off him in a sheet. Under his shirt, an intricate crucifix. The five domes of an orthodox church. Jesus weeping tears of blood. "You are the badass that Eddie tells me about? The Shakespeare? The one without the mercy?"

Sweeney glanced at Eddie. "Uh."

"He looks meek and mild," Eddie said, "just don't get him mad."

"Like the Hulk, yes? Grrrr." Bytchkov showed his teeth. Heavy on the stained enamel, short on gum. "Bruce Banner. American comic books. I love them."

From the bowels of the house, they heard children running up wooden stairs. A giggle, and a young girl shouting in Russian. Bytchkov scowled fondly at the noise. "We go down to my office now, okay? Okay. Less crazy. More privacy."

Bytchkov led them down a narrow staircase, damp and carpeted, away from the smell of boiled cabbage and into an odor of mice and wet newspapers. Sweeney touched dark paneling for his balance. Bad juju down here, man. "Appreciate you putting us onto those Rolexes. Made *my* Christmas merrier."

"Yes, yes, yes." At the bottom of the stairs, a heavy door painted black. And instead of a knob, a plug of fiberboard and a padlock. Bytchkov pressed the door open with his flat palm. "My office, welcome."

To the extent that there was a desk (one leg broken off short and shimmed up with romance novels), a metal file cabinet, a floor lamp, Sweeney supposed that yes, this was an office. But every other detail suggested a deranged lunatic trying desperately to pass as sane and industrious. The iron gray shelves were filled with folders bleeding paper and an old dot matrix printer wrapped in its own wires, a pewter bowl full of...what. Were those *teeth*? Some with mercury fillings. A matched pair of lime-green armchairs leaked stuffing. A deal coffee table held, centered like a floral arrangement, a specimen jar full of milky formaldehyde and the decomposing threads of a human hand.

Off his elbow, Bytchkov said, "Cozy, yes?"

No dummy, Sweeney was hip to the test. Reaction? He opted for bland and ironic. "Cozy, yeah. Nice. *Warm.*"

"Thanks, yes."

But then, because he was a little irked, a little pissed—who did this guy think he was, testing *him*—added, "Kind of like Breetvah's pad. Smaller, but you know, *tasteful.*" Here's Sweeney swinging dicks in some abattoir of a basement with a Russian psychopath.

A long, long moment later, the lower half of Bytchkov's bucket-sized head split into a halitosis-clouded grin. His fist sledgehammered into Sweeney's arm. To Eddie, he said gleefully, "You were right my friend. One crazy motherfuck. Am I right? Yes, I am right. Bytchkov is right. I like you, my friend. *Breetvah!*"

Eddie: "Yeah, crazy." And handed Sweeney his most unreadable glance.

~

Ten years since Sweeney's been on a plane, and flying's a novelty again. Bozeman to Denver, he's got his forehead against the plexiglass, naming landmarks. Paradise Valley, Hellroaring Plateau, Yellowstone Lake. Eight hours later, coasting into LaGuardia, it's Dyker Heights, Greenwood Cemetery, Prospect Park. "I played little league on those fields."

Tina pops gum over a fashion magazine. "Uh huh."

It's all down there, all of it, the whole world. Neighborhoods appearing ex nihilo at the top of their subway stairs. West 14th with its fake bohemianism, the gaggles of NYU students lining up for cheap pizza. The financial district with its high-priced lunches, its silk-tied aficionados of good Scotch and bad business. SoHo street vendors and Upper East Side Jewish housewives walking terriers. The angry and muttering homeless; tourists standing befuddled on street corners. The endless recycling of subway trains twenty feet beneath the city, the dark, stale air and rancid odors of urine and garbage, dimly lit concrete pylons scrawled with graffiti. Chinese couples in identical black polyester pants and secondhand dress shirts, arguing incomprehensibly. The Yemeni clerks at corner bodegas, working when you pick up your paper in the morning and still there at ten that night when you buy your beer. The Great Wall of China may be filled with the corpses of its workers but the buildings of New York are kept level by the sleepless bones of immigrants.

God, he's missed it.

But coming off the plane, he's the only guy in a baseball cap, hiking boots. His jeans are the wrong shade of blue and his shirt only acceptable if it were ironic, if it were vintage, if he were fifteen years younger. Standing in the cab line, Sweeney says, "I need a suit. I know a place."

"Tre Fretelli on Madison? Yeah they're gone. They got a Duane Reade there now."

"Well. I need a suit. I *need* a suit."

"You always was a clothes horse, Cosmo." She gives a genuine smile. Her first one. "There's a place in Atlantic Center. Eddie used to shop there."

They're not going back to Tina's place. The Russians might be watching. *Certainly* the Russians would be watching. Instead, they've booked rooms off Park Slope. Close to her bank, Tina says.

This being Sunday, though, the banks are closed. "Haven't had good Thai in a while," Sweeney says. "I read about this place on the web. You mind?"

Tina's okay with it, and they end up out on the sidewalk at Fifth Avenue and Ninth Street. A bright Sunday evening in Brooklyn. The shadows going long and the heat leaving the streets in a faint fog of body odor and exhaust, an undercurrent of dog shit and melting ice cream. Kids on razor scooters trundling down the sidewalk, bumping seam to seam. Cadres of Park Slope parents behind baby carriages. The too-slim trust fund hipsters suckling at their ATM tits. Sweeney, half to himself: "This used to be all crack houses and hookers."

Tina has her chopsticks and she's not bad with them, shoveling up Pad Thai. "What's across the street?"

"Eh ...?"

"You keep staring at that brownstone."

First lie that comes to mind? "I used to live over there."

"Yeah? Which one?"

"Place with the awning. I was what, twelve years old?"

"I never knew you were in this neighborhood. Park Slope? Fancy."

"Not back then."

Sweeney convinces her to linger. "What's waiting for us back at the hotel?" They order a couple more beers. And just before dusk, just before the street lights come on, he sees her.

His sister's still in the same apartment. He knows this from the web. Rent stabilized, two bedrooms, you don't give that up. When Berenice and her husband first moved here, it was all they could afford. A Brooklyn dive in a bad neighborhood. But the affluence grew up around them, as it is wont to do. Her husband, Louis? Little weasel of a guy. More nose and less chin. He'd scorned his legacy, his father's hardware store up on Flatbush—"What, you think I'm gonna be selling house paint my whole life?"—until the world bit him in the ass a few times. Now, check out his website photo. Jowly and gray above a red hardware apron. Santa without the beard. Grinning like he's three beers into the night. Just another Brooklyn blowhard.

But Bernie? A high school chemistry teacher. Classy and too smart for her husband, she'd squirmed against the apparent dead end of her aspirations. "I walk through *metal* detectors going to work, Cosmo. But after I go back to school, get a master's. I could be vice principal inside a year." They were in the playground off Third Street, Bernie's little girl, Clara, giggling in the toddler swing. Uncle Cosmo coming close, then going away again. She reached for his mustache. Over by the tire swings, Bernie's four-year-old, Marco (Cosmo's godson), was climbing the chain, reaching toward the cedar crossbar. "Kid's gonna hurt himself."

"Long as he doesn't break his neck, he'll be better for it." His sister the world-weary cynic.

During Montana's longest winters, snow blowing under the door and the windows gathering feathers of ice, when recently-divorced Sweeney was exploring the philosophical depths of cheap vodka and a spinning cylinder, it was the thought of Bernie and Clara and Marco that kept him out of the ground. Three good lives still being lived back home.

Later, after everybody got online, he kept track long distance. By Marco's blog, he's a basketball player, and mad about the Lakers. And even little Clara—she'd be in what, sixth grade now?—has a Facebook page maintained by her mother. Photos of Clara at soccer practice, at the petting zoo, in school plays. Sweeney keeps wanting to drop his sister an anonymous e-mail. "Change your privacy settings, woman."

And now here she is, his own flesh and blood, trudging up the street, pulling a rolling cart filled with orange juice, milk; one arm hung over with co-op grocery bags. She's always had a good strong stride. A woman who might have played college basketball. And she's aged gracefully. He'd have picked her out of a crowd. It's like looking in a funhouse mirror. Sweeney with longer hair, breasts, wider hips.

His heart squeezes out a few dusty, self-pitying notes. His *sister*. There's someone in this world who would still love him. If only.

Approaching the stoop, she produces a phone. Even across the street, he hears her imperious tone, calling up for help.

Sweeney's famished for detail, knowing how he'll spend the next few years picking through the bones of this moment.

The door opens while she's still digging for keys. A teenage Marco—he'd be fifteen by now (fifteen, Jesus)—holds the door open with one heel while leaning forward for the bags. In the glimpse Sweeney snatches, he's a lanky, clean-faced kid. Strong cheekbones. The curly crop of mouse-colored Einstein hair he'd had as a toddler has straightened out and gone black, draped down over his eyes. How they're wearing it these days. A Lakers jersey and jeans down on his ass. Flip flops. Grabbing for the groceries, he's already going through one of the bags, digging for cookies, donuts, chips. He grins at his mother and just like *that* Sweeney can see the charmer he'll become. Yeah, Sweeney thinks fondly, kid's gonna be a cad. A good kid. Sweeney can tell. His godson.

And in a second story window, Sweeney catches a glimpse of pigtails, a pink dress. Clara. Little Clara.

His sister herself, upon closer inspection, looks tired, unkempt. Jeans loose in the seat and her blouse untucked in the back. Maybe like the rest of us, she's been having a hard time of it. There's no doubt a story back there somewhere. But he's no part of it. Not now, not ever.

Sweeney rises from the table, hitting a knee, tipping water glasses. He tosses a handful of crumpled twenties on the table. Dead man's cash. He's *got* to get out of here. Now. Now. Now. "You good? I'm good. Let's go."

~

"You liked the Rolexes, yes? What I have next, the Rolexes is nothing we compare them to it. *Nothing*."

Turn on a couple more floor lamps, and if it weren't for the smells of gunpowder and formaldehyde, Bytchkov's office looked less like a mausoleum and more like a down-on-its-heels men's club.

Sweeney and Eddie got comfortable in armchairs while Bytchkov's little snake of a brother tottered on a stool off his left elbow. Jasha, they said his name was. An emaciated lizard of a guy. Long torso and short legs. A flyweight in the ring, but put that .44 in his belt, he's a heavyweight to the ears. A shaved head and a pimp's tattoos. Pierced lower lip, silver rings in one nostril. The kind of kid, if he listened to music, it was loud techno; if he read anything apart from cereal boxes, it was *Penthouse*. Bytchkov introduced him as a brother, but the accent was all Long Island.

This afternoon was already giving Sweeney a headache.

Bytchkov leaned forward and whispered, "Kidnaps." Then sat back, satisfied.

"Eh now?"

"Kidnaps!" Bytchkov slapped his hands flat on his desk. "Sons and daughters of rich men."

Sweeney's first thought? Get me the *fuck* out of here. And as soon as possible.

Second thought? This was going to be touchy.

It wasn't the, you know, moral *delicacies* of kidnapping. This point in his life, halfway down the slippery slope of a lifetime's worth of compromise, equivocation, and rational-ization, it would have been almost impossible to take any kind of a stand, moral-outrage wise. I mean, sure, Italianos did *not* mess with a guy's family. What're we, Irish? Running those Westy snatch rackets? Fuck that. We're Italian, we got standards.

But even more? Getting away with it. *That* was the problem.

Eddie read his mind. "I don't know, man. There's problems with kidnapping."

"What problems."

"Getting hold of the money, making the drop, *cleaning* the money. Then the Feds. Feds always get involved. You say, don't call the cops. What do they do? They always call the cops.

"My cousin," Jasha twisted a little on his stool. Kicked his heels like a toddler. "*Genius* by the way. He's been collecting names, social security numbers."

Cousin? Ten seconds ago it was brother. Sweeney said, "Identity theft kind of thing?"

"*Identity* theft?" Jasha was scornful. "What do we look like?"

Shakespeare leveled a look, thinking. One of these days, kid.

"Jasha, Jasha, Jasha," Bytchkov made a calming motion with his fingers. "These men are not amateurs. These men, we could learn something from them."

Turns out, Bytchkov had been sitting on this gig for months, years. "One of my girlfriends, sweetness that she is, yes, she is expert at, at..." Bytchkov mimed typing, "at this hospital. She works the...*computer,* and sometimes women arrive to have babies and she writes their names and numbers. And when a baby dies, she gives me those names and numbers. I wait, and then I apply for documents, yes? I create bank accounts. You see?"

An old scam, it wasn't rocket science. Sweeney had read articles. *Newsweek* had a thing.

"These babies, poor little dead children, each of them now have bank accounts in Cooks Islands, in Liechtenstein, Niue. You see?"

"What'd I tell you. Fucking genius." Jasha stared back at Sweeney, at Eddie.

"We need four of us to do the kidnaps safely. We do the kidnaps, then they put money in the accounts of the dead babies. And then my dear one my Jasha, he's good with, with... computers, too, he transfers money here and there and then there again, and poof. It's gone. In our pockets, only better."

Eddie had another toothpick, and was slowly, meticulously unwrapping it. Giving it all his attention.

Sweeney cleared his throat. "Who're we kidnapping?"

"This is pretty part." Bytchkov found a sheet of yellow legal paper. Blue writing in a language of reversed letters and accented swirls. "Pavel Asimov, shipping. Coffee, also heroine. Abdul Zakayev, professor, lawyer. Drives different Mercedes every day of the week. Mirali Tuycheiv. Big football player, good, but now too old to play. Famous ten years ago. Owns Park Avenue apartments. Also, prostitutes. Many, many womens. These three men, they all have children, yes. Children they love."

Sweeney kept hoping Eddie would chime in. Make the point that yeah, this wasn't Columbia, Equador, Nigeria. This was America, bub. Land of the free and home of the we-don't-fucking-kidnap-people.

But Sweeney had the silence to himself. After a while, he said, "What makes that part pretty?"

"Uzbek. Chechin. Tajik. These who have betrayed mother Russia. These with questionable...ped-uh-grees? Is that the word, yes. As with dogs, eh? Peddygrees. They do not deserve America. They do not deserve..."

"Yeah, right, so here's the deal," Jasha interrupted, cutting short the familiar diatribe. "We grab their kids, right? Bam." He clapped. "On their way to school, whatever. We drop a note to the dads, half a mill in each of those bank accounts or we start sending you fingers. Bam. Each one of these guys, they've got twice that much in cash sitting around. Three times, who the fuck knows. It won't be hard for them. It's done. I make the wire transfers. Bam. It's perfect."

Sweeney shifted. The smart money would say agree to everything, nod and say yes. Then get the fuck out of here. Split. Change your name. Get a job waiting tables in California. But Sweeney could never hold his tongue. Never, not once. "Yeah, no. It's not. It's a long way from perfect."

"What do you mean by this?" Bytchkov's tone was tepid as tapwater.

"All these babies, they died at the same hospital, right?"

"Yes."

"So you think they're not going to put that together? Trace it back? Who could have had access to all that information? That's going to be a short list. Maybe one name long."

Bytchkov could have been watching sprinklers go around for all his expression.

"So yeah, they're going to put it together. They'll collar your girlfriend, make her sing. The first kidnapping? You might get away with it. Second one, by the end of the day they'll be coming through your door with battering rams."

Jasha was on his stool, puffing up like microwave popcorn.

"Who the *fuck* ..."

"Jasha." Bytchkov patted the air. He stared at Sweeney. Then pushed slowly back from his desk. When he stood, the angle of the lamps—was it intentional?— cut hard, foreboding angles into his cheeks.

He came around the desk. Agile for an otherwise awkward man.

Sweeney braced a heel. He should have been packing. You're an idiot for not packing. His first move would be toward Jasha. Quick punch to the throat while Sweeney grabbed for the gun. Sixty seconds from now, even odds, him and Eddie would be lunging out the front door like Butch and Sundance.

Instead, Bytchkov reached for Sweeney's head (and Sweeney was this close to knocking those ugly hands away) and kissed him hard on both cheeks. Mwah! Mwah! Odd sensation, the unshaven, sweaty chin of a middle-aged man scrubbing up against Sweeney's baby-smoothness.

"You were right, Eddie. Yes, you were right. Shakespeare! One smart motherfuck. Jasha, see, yes this is what I mean, this is how we could learn from these two."

Everybody took a breath.

"Okay," Bytchkov said, sitting back down. "Okay, yes. Of course. You are right. So she is my girlfriend. She is too close to me. You must do it.'

"Sorry. Do what now?"

"You kill her, yes? But quick. For me? Painless. Yes?"

This was how Russians did business. Killed their own girlfriends.

Ergo, ipso-facto, if things didn't work out with Sweeney and Eddie...what's a couple more stiffs?

Sweeney glanced discretely at his knockoff Rolex. Forty-eight minutes after shaking Bytchkov's hand, Sweeney had two choices. He could paste on a smile and go along with the program, or, or, *or* . . . kill these two soulless Russian psychopaths where they stood. No third option.

Shit, Eddie. Shit. Sweeney glanced at his cousin, tearing him apart with his eyes. Eddie studied a hangnail.

Stalling, Sweeney said, sweet as sugar, "How much we talking about here?"

~

Sweeney's position on kidnapping? Worse than murder, really. Murder is bad juju, sure. But it's over in a wink. *Bang*, somebody's gone. Negated. But kidnapping, the extended and ongoing *preemption* of a human being, is to his tastes much worse. You *own* them, man. And not only them, but everybody that loves them. Here's your puppet strings, let me grab them for a while. Twist them all up in knots.

Sleepless at two in the morning, Sweeney's gone melancholy, staring out over Union Street. Scratching around in his boxers. Three stories above a muggy Brooklyn night, he's got a half pint of Jim Beam and a head full of memories. Water towers on the horizon and sea-salt smells from Gowanus.

The window's cracked, and it's like performance art, listening to the sidewalk conversations. A black kid, fourteen or fifteen years old, says into his phone, "...so I tol' her I said, that's my money!" Then he's gone again. Out of Sweeney's life forever. To be replaced by a gaggle of Hispanic chicas, walking along in a pack, huddled close. "You is so *much* better than him, so *much* better, and he don't *even* know what he's missing…" They fade away. Then a set of expensive, angry heels, a metronome of Manhattan ire. "Troy listen, listen, *listen* to me, will you just listen? I don't mind it that you had to leave early. Okay, well yeah, clearly I *do* mind. But what I mind most is you didn't…." And she fades out again.

The room has a thirty-eight inch flat screen with HBO, but he hasn't even turned it on; the real show's down there, man.

His cell phone buzzes, dances around on the dresser.

He's been meaning to upgrade, maybe get an iPhone; And yeah, if he spent more than a day or two in Brooklyn, he'd have to take the plunge. *Every*body's got those smart phones. Used to be, people avoided eye contact out of fear or arrogance or courtesy. Now they're just checking e-mail.

He flips his old clamshell open, figuring it's Aggie. "Yeah, Sweeney."

"Ted Sweeney." A voice disguised through a cheap digital distorter. You can pick one up at Radio Shack. Basso as Darth Vader, twisted on the higher notes like guitar feedback.

"Yeaaah?"

"Also, Cosimo Aniello." The distorter blurs the verbs. CosmAnllo.

"Never heard of him."

Digital silence.

Sweeney: "Who's this?"

"Breetvah. My name is Breetvah. You've heard of me, yes?"

Sweeney waits long enough to make sure the question isn't rhetorical. "I've heard of you."

"Good. That is good. Things will go easier. So, yes. I'm sending you a photo." Ahm sendng y'a pht.

Then nothing. Dead air.

Sweeney sits on the edge of his bed, phone in his hands. Finishes off the little half pint in two hard swallows. This guy. *This* motherfucker. He's the one. The *guy*. The one who arranged the body in his favorite chair. Who sent out those envelopes. *Not* incidentally? The guy who likely killed Eddie. Breetvah.

Even clouded by booze, the anger arouses something in Sweeney. The things he'd like to do to this guy.

His phones gives off a short buzz.

He flips it open.

To see a photo of Aggie, blurry on the saltine-sized screen. Curled fetal on cheap carpet, wrists duct-taped to her ankles. Duct tape over her mouth and eyes. Half a roll's worth of tape spent trussing her up.

Aggie. Who tends horses. Who works at the library.

His phone buzzes again. Another photo arrives. This one of Elizabeth, in almost precisely the same posture. Aggie's nose on the left of screen has them facing each other.

Elizabeth. Who loves her stuffed animals but hides it. Who goes through boyfriends the way the rest of us fold shirts.

Sweeney's eyes go disjointed. They roll off each into separate orbits. The hemispheres of his brain spit grease, flare into flames. Anger tightens into a coil under his sternum, rears a swaying head.

His phone buzzes again. This time it's a text. "Get the diamonds. Lose your whore. I call you. No cops."

No need to mention, "Else they die." You send a photo of two women duct taped fetal, "else they die," is a given.

Aggie and Elizabeth, else they die.

~

Seventy-eight organs in the human body. Maybe six-and-a-half quarts of blood in Sweeney's larger-than-average corpus. Twenty-five square feet of skin were it stretched out flat. Toenails growing slow, fingernails fast. The hypothalamus, the pituitary, the thyroid. A head full of hair pushing out nine inches a year. This complicated engine called Ted Sweeney. And now every inch of it, every pulsing, restless ounce…it all wants to cut out this cocksucker's liver and feel the hot blood around his fingers. From hell's heart, I'm stabbing at you, fucker.

The last time he felt like this—and memory skips around a bit here—it was Philadelphia. A leather daypack spilling out five pounds of China, the slick black fabric stained with the blood of some Muje in a Mets cap. More bodies in a back room. Silk drapes hanging heavy with rain. And Sweeney with a 9 mm Beretta not his own, unsure how it came to be in his hand.

The salient points? Rage, memory loss, blood.

And now? All his concern about life in Montana, about the hot air of his various deceits…phssst. It's gone, burned away by the image of Aggie, lingering in his eye like a flashbulb echo. Her jaw wrenched half-open under the tape. Maybe a racquetball stuffed in there. Racquetballs work good.

But after the first rush of adrenaline, as implacable and inarguable as fluid pushed from a hypodermic, after this high tide pulls back, he's left only with the effluvial muck of his despair.

Posture all you want, Sweeney. This guy's got you over a barrel. Breetvah. How do you strike back against a ghost? How do you maneuver here, what's your play?

Assuming you're willing to sacrifice Montana—which he

is, okay? move on—and even in the context of that grand gesture, what carrot do you have to bargain with? What stick could you use to coerce?

He's got nothing. As of this instant, nothing but his own tit in the wringer.

From what he knows about the Russians? They're going to see no percentage in keeping Aggie alive. They're predictable in their ferocity, their pragmatic heartlessness. If he ever gets to the point where he can actually trade the stones for Aggie? It'll be like cashing in for a corpse.

Maybe he goes to the cops. He considers this for a moment...for about as long as it takes him not to be a moron. It would go against every instinct. And anyway, from what he's seen, cops don't know how to take care of a kidnapping. They always screw up the end game.

Despair, fatigue, melancholy. Eskimos have ten thousand kinds of snow, Sweeney has sadness. And what's this now? A despair that arises from impotence and outrage, tempered by a soupcon of cynical calculation. There's always a move you can make. Somewhere.

He flips at the phone. Stares at Aggie's photo. Again, and again. Flip, flip. From this time forth my thoughts be bloody, or be nothing worth.

Big words, Sweeney. Big words.

Catering to the disaffected rich, turns out, is one of Montana's principal industries. Wheat, cattle, tourism, sure, you bet. But *dig* the coin generated by second homes, the thousands of log mansions tucked away in darling little stands of aspens. Remington rip-offs and trout ponds out back. Bierstadt through each window and a nice wrap-around porch.

God bless the faceless out-of-staters. How they support an entire subculture of antler chandelier artisans and fireplace masons, snow plowers and gardeners. Not to mention, a good portion of these homes—empty nine, ten months out of the year—the owners aren't as wealthy as they'd like you to think. They sublet, thus making their private paradises available for a rate. They rely on property management firms to take care of the details.

Take this place on Jack Creek, for instance. Rented sight unseen with a Visa card in the name of an infant dead these last twelve years. Fed-ex the keys, see you next week. Ten miles south of Rockjaw, it's forty acres backed up against National Forest. End of the road, with a view. Three stories. Front yard is asphalt driveway. Backyard is all flagstone and hot tub. By rumor, the owners are third generation Pfizers. Or maybe Waltons. Or Krogers.

Marble countertop and flagstone floors in the kitchen. An eight burner stove with an exhaust hood that'll suck the gravel right off your palm. Down a short hallway, past framed photos of soft white men on yachts (victims of too much too early, beached now in middle age, simmering in the juices of myopic self-interest), a half dozen bedrooms. And down a spiral staircase (constructed from kiln-dried teak shipped up from Costa Rica), a wet bar and liquor cabinet, snooker table and…Jesus, is that a bocci ball court? Anyway, the middle of the room, two log pillars. Old growth white pine, thick as Ionic columns.

With loops of heavy rope stretched around their bases. And handcuffed to the ropes, a pair of women, legs out-stretched.

Aggie. Unconscious, or nearly so. Bruised at the eyes and blistered at the mouth, lips cracking. Duct tape gum still visible on her cheeks.

And Elizabeth. Eyes swollen from weeping, sure, but otherwise unharmed. Cramped, stretched out in an awkward parody of a yoga pose, arms twisted back. She straightens her legs, working to nudge her mother, to touch her with her toes. "Mom?" she whispers, stretching out another hard-earned inch, squirming. "Mommy?" Then louder, frustrated: "Mom!"

Which awakens the sound she's been dreading, the noise that will (assuming she makes it out of this alive) jerk her awake at all our hours for months to come. The slow, muted scuff of sneakers descending the stairs. Then a voice. Lighthearted, conversational: "Elizabeth? What did I say about talking?"

She closes her eyes. Senses, despite herself, the change in light, gray to black, as his shadow falls over her.

She tilts her head further away, fighting against tears, against giving him any sort of satisfaction.

Eddie and Sweeney sat in a rental car, a little compact Honda, across from the NYU hospital on First Avenue. Hazard lights on and windows cracked for their smokes, air conditioner running full blast. Half an hour now they'd been watching taxis and Lincoln town cars cycle through the hospital's courtesy lane.

Eddie, behind the wheel, was coked-up and nervous. Twiiitch*ee*. The last six months he'd been running his own distribution thing up in White Plains. Far enough away he wasn't edging in on the Gambinos but close enough he could make supply runs on the weekends. Good money, good hours, good benefits. Downside? An Achilles heel for his own product. Eddie and self-control? Forget about it.

Eddie ground his teeth, danced his fingers around the dash like Chopin. "I'm just saying, they shoulda given us the full size sedan. Did you see that chick at the counter? Looking down her nose. I told her I wanted a full sized sedan. They give us this little crackerbox piece of shit. I find out where she lives? Forget about it."

"Eaaasy, cousin."

"Fuck easy." Eddie reached for another beer. Cracked it and slid it into a foam Yankees sleeve. His idea of a stakeout: eight ball and a twelve pack of Coors. "Easy don't get you rich, it don't get you laid, it don't get you respect."

"Will you quit with the dash at least? Jesus."

Eddie glanced at his own fingers. "Yeah, shit. Sorry."

Sweeney had just lately been preoccupied with the notion of empathy. The equation of it. Intelligence plus self awareness divided by a certain kind of guilt equals empathy. Sweeney had it in spades. A curse in this business. Cousin Eddie? With Eddie it came and went. More often than not, halfway through a strong arm gig (some guy bleeding on the floor) Sweeney would glance up at Eddie and see how he was off someplace else, as cold and distant as a housecat.

Eddie said, "Bytchkov's gal gets off her shift at 6:30. He said Friday nights she goes out to eat. Her and her two nursing pals. We follow behind, catch her in an alley, go for her purse. She fights. Boom, it's done. Easy peasy."

This whole thing's been giving Sweeney indigestion. One thing to whack a guy that deserves it, to respond to violence with violence. But this woman? Her only sin was bad taste in boyfriends.

"You were born in this hospital," Eddie said. "You know that, right?"

"Yeah, I heard."

"We paid a visit. I was like four years old? We come in here, I seen this little red-faced turnip of a kid all swaddled up. Crying. Jesus you could cry. Even then you couldn't stop crying. I thought, if that's what babies are, I ain't never having one. My bachelorhood comes thanks to you, Cosmo."

"Four years old."

"Your old man gave me this bubble gum cigar. Remember those? Big pink Cohiba. I bit the end off, spit it out. They all thought that was the funniest goddamn thing."

"Well."

Eddie's mention of Sweeney's old man? Payback, maybe,

for not collaborating on Eddie's rental car umbrage.

"How is your dad, by the way."

"I hear he's all right."

"You two still ain't talking?" Eddie could fake sympathy the way Sweeney could play the piano. And Sweeney couldn't play the fucking piano.

Sweeney changed the subject. "I been thinking about Breetvah."

"Oh?"

"Bytchkov pays him up the ladder?"

"If the guy exists."

"But Bytchkov's paying up to *some*body."

"That's a fact."

"So he exists."

"My opinion? Yeah. But, something else is going on, too. Maybe he's a midget. Short guys, you know, they don't command no respect. So he hides out. Maybe he's a woman, right? A vampire, can't come out during the day. Whatever. But Bytchkov, whenever he talks about Breetvah? He's *terrified*, man. Think about that for a second. Bytchkov. Terrified."

"We go through with these kidnappings, Bytchkov's not letting those kids go."

Eddie found a cigarette. Tapped it on its filter. "No."

"So we take out his girlfriend, then we, what, we murder three kids?"

"Well, not personally."

"Jesus, Eddie. I mean, Jesus..."

Eddie sat up in his seat. "That's her."

The snapshot from Bytchkov had Helena Glinka as late twenties. A thin, pretty smile and red hair going prematurely grey. It was hard to picture a woman even so moderately attractive pairing up with a schlub like Bytchkov. But seeing the woman in the flesh, it made more sense. Narrow shoulders, heavy breasts, big hips. Everything went progressively thicker to her shins. Mismatched hospital scrubs, heavy handbag, and a weak-ankled limp. She stood on the corner with two other nurses, all of them exhausted but trying for smiles. The end of their shifts.

Sweeney's first thought: Poor woman. His second? A freeze-frame image of himself putting a bullet through her terrified face. He considered his own inward recoil, the flinch and start, and how these two reactions would proceed to haunt him. He glanced at Eddie, hoping for commiseration; instead, he found only calculation.

Sweeney said quickly, like pulling off a band aid, "Count me out."

"What?"

"Can't do it. Count me out."

Eddie smirked. Sweeney and cold feet? They weren't strangers. "In for a penny, in for a pound, cousin."

"*Look* at her. Seriously. Look at her."

"What I got going on with Bytchkov, you need to know, this is only the first move. We do this right, there's no stopping us. Me and you." Eddie put his hand on Sweeney's arm. "Me and *you*."

"But we got to kill that woman."

"First step."

"Can't do it."

Eddie took a breath, priming the pump on his next round of arguments. Sweeney had a weakness with regard to Eddie's cajoling. He knew this about himself. Safest play would be to just leave.

Sweeney stepped out onto the sidewalk. Stood there, considering his history with Eddie, their future. The dilemma of alienating a Russian psychopath. He put his head back into the car. "Best I can do, Eddie? I'll keep my mouth shut. I'll do that for you."

And as ugly as it is to admit, Sweeney might have kept that promise, allowed the woman, those children, to be murdered for the benefit of Eddie's bank account, allowed his own secondhand guilt to be swept under his Freudian carpet…had he not himself been collared eight days later.

~

Check out Sweeney in the hotel room mirror, modeling his new suit. Lookin good, man. Off-the-rack Armani, dark blue. Work that summer wool. His pants hemmed quick, greased by an extra fifty. *Thank you*, dead wop with cash in a briefcase. He lifts his chin, knotting a Hermes tie the color of tarnished silver. Double Windsor, *bien sur*. Dimpling it with that certain kind of je ne sais *kwah*. Funny how it all comes back to you.

Tina had said, "Big spender."

"However this goes down, money's the least of my problems."

He's hoping now that the fancy threads will distract from the smears of sleepless lampblack under his eyes. The tremble in his hands. Eight in the morning, he's already running on fumes.

Turning in the mirror—slender Sweeney in a decent suit—he *likes* it. The Montana tan speaks of ruddy health and the weight in his shoulders reads like gym time. The dress shirt's half an inch smaller at the collar than what he used to buy. And the jacket has a nice pleat in the back. Good for covering up some kind of pistol.

For instance: From the Fed-Ex box he'd shipped to himself from Montana, unzipped beside the TV, the dead wop's .357.

He spins the cylinder. Holds it up to the mirror.

The stainless steel matches his tie. Nice.

He tucks it under his belt in the small of his back. *Almost* unnoticeable. He pulls his belt a notch too tight. Jumps up and down a few times. The gun stays put.

Okay. Before heading out the door, he calls Marilyn. Six thirty in Montana, it's understandable that her phone would be off. He says to her voicemail. "Call me. It's an emergency."

Out in the hall, he knocks on Tina's door. "Banks open in half an hour." Above all else, he needs to hide his anxiety from Tina. Right now, all the leverage is his. She needs him more than he needs her. But if that changes, if she understands his dilemma, no *way* he's getting his hands on those stones.

Meanwhile, and until he gets the next call from Breetvah, he's got some room to maneuver. Not *much*, but some.

And after he gets the call, after he gets his marching orders? Maybe he'll be able to stonewall the guy. (Keep your head, Sweeney. Play it smart.) He'll do the predictable bluff and bluster: "Harm one hair on her head. Let me talk to her." Yadayadayada. And if he can elbow out a few extra hours, maybe something will occur to him. Some new angle. Please let something occur to him.

Sweeney knocks again. "Tina?"

A muffled assent from inside.

Something in her tone drops a quarter. A rustling, then she has unlatched the door. Leaving it for Sweeney to open.

"Tina?"

Her room is a mirrored repeat of his. Cramped floor plan dominated by a queen-sized bed. Wall-mounted flatscreen. Worktable with a phone. But Tina's room has been overturned by…what. Grief? Anger? Exhilaration? Some tectonic sort of emotion.

She sits in the chair by the window, ignoring him, chewing on a knuckle.

"Tina?"

She looks up.

She's been crying. And how. The bedspread, the dresser, the work table, they're all covered with a garden of crumpled Kleenexes. The empty box sits discarded on the floor, eviscerated. A roll of toilet paper from the bathroom has taken up second-string service. Same clothes as yesterday. "Tina?"

"Georgie's gone."

"Georgie…"

"My kid brother. He's missing. They got him. I know they got him. That's how come they knu-knu-knew about Muh-Muh-Montana." Hitches and sobs.

Old news to Sweeney. Should he have mentioned it? It would have complicated things. And even now, his first thought: Here's yet *another* goddamned thing. "Did you tell Georgie you were going to Montana?"

"Maybe. I don't know. I can't ruh-ruh-member."

"Sweetheart," He sits on the edge of the bed facing her. Takes her clammy hand. "Sweetheart, best thing we can do is we get the rocks. Once we've got some leverage, we can make them pay. Whoever did this to you, to Georgie? They'll pay."

Revenge, that's what he has to offer. A thin soup, of course. But it's something.

~

When wiseguys start getting some scratch together, first thing they do is imitate their betters. The boss invests in a house in the Hamptons? The capo shops Brentwood. Capo buys an Escalade? His soldier gets a Four Runner. These are gestures that show both loyalty and admiration.

Which is why, when Sweeney got called to an informal sit down with Anthony Acerbi, he had to drive out to Staten Island. To the guy's home. Which was yeah, an honor and kind of creepy at the same time. Am I walking down into a basement lined with plastic, or what?

If he ever found the place. The streets all ran together like noodles in a pot. North, south, up, down. Sweeney'd been out to Staten Island maybe five, six times his entire life. And never up to Todt Hill. I mean, if you've got the bank to live up here, why not buy an apartment in Midtown? It don't make sense.

Anthony was a Castellano protégé. They practically went to grade school together. So after Castellano moved into the white house, it only took Anthony about six months before he'd found his four bedroom rancher at the bottom of the hill. A swimming pool ringed by lounge chairs and flowers in pots. By the time Castellano got his ticket punched by Fat Sal and them, Anthony had gotten used to the burbs, acquired a taste for the slow life. He stuck it out.

Sweeney wasn't *obliged* toward Anthony Acerbi. Showing up wasn't required of him in the way that say, if an envelope was missing he'd get a visit. But him and Eddie *aspired*, right? And with that kind of aspiration, when you get called into a meeting, you go. You kidding me? You go. You got to be there yesterday.

If he could ever find the place.

Five left turns later, Sweeney pulled into a likely-looking cul de sac. Parked on the street and walked toward the sound of a lawn mower.

There was about a half-acre of grass in the backyard, and Anthony was working it over with a push mower. Shirtless in Bermuda shorts and sneakers, the old man still had some meat in his shoulders, even if the belly skin hung loose and the hair on his back had gone gray.

A pitcher of iced tea had been set out on a glass table. Anthony saw Sweeney and made a gesture. Help yourself.

So Sweeney sat there drinking lukewarm tea, sole audience as one of the five or six biggest names in the Gambinos wrestled a mower around brick planters.

Sweeney was overdressed. He took off his tie. Hung his suit jacket off the back of a lawn chair.

Odd to be sitting there without Eddie. But the invitation had said come alone.

Anthony finally shut down his mower, mopped his bald head with a towel, limped on skinny, old man legs over toward Sweeney. In the silence, Sweeney could hear the sounds of a barbeque across the way. He stood to shake hands. "Anthony."

Sweeney loomed over this old man. Four inches taller, forty years younger, fifty pounds heavier. You'd think, then, that Sweeney would have some advantage. But you'd be wrong, wrong, wrong.

"Thanks for coming on short notice, Cosimo. Appreciate it."

One of the things Sweeney's always liked about Anthony? Politeness. We should all judge a man by how he treats his employees. He had a little Bronx in his accent, but none of the attitude.

"Goddamn crab grass," he said, settling back, looking fondly at his lawn. "And dandelions. My whole life, I can't get rid of crab grass and dandelions."

"Looks good to me." In fact, it was a putting green.

"You're a good kid." Anthony drank deep from his tea. Held the glass to his forehead. "I'll say this quick, then we can catch up. I want to hear about your family. But first thing? We got a problem with Eddie." The words seemed to pain him.

Sweeney flashed to any one of Eddie's half-dozen ongoing sins that the families might object to. "Problem?"

"He got permission for that thing up in White Plains, so that's okay. But we hear he's using too much of his own product. We've all seen it, Cosmo. Italians and that cocaine. It's red Indians and whiskey. Never turns out well."

"I'll *talk* to him."

Anthony nodded soberly. "I know you two are a pair. Everybody knows it. Eddie being strung out hurts nobody like it hurts you."

"I'll talk to him."

"You're a good kid, Cosmo."

"Thanks."

Anthony reached over and covered Sweeney's hand with his own. Sweaty, calloused, but a paternal gesture all the same. Paternal first and then, as the hand lingered, disturbing. The pressure of the fingers spoke volumes of mixed messages. "I didn't just toss that off. I mean it. You're a good kid. You know how rare that is these days? The business we're in? You do good work for us, tough work. You do it quick and you don't make a mess and you keep your mouth shut."

"Thanks, Anthony. Appreciate it."

"Quick, clean, mouth shut. That's your secret, Cosmo.

That's why everybody likes you, why everybody gives you work. Eddie, though. Eddie's in White Plains this afternoon, right?"

"That's what I hear." In fact, it was news.

"Go on up there. Do him the favor of talking some sense into him. Make him see the big picture."

"Okay."

"Now. How's your papa doing? Your mother? They're well?"

"Me and Dad, you know about that. But otherwise, not bad, yeah, everybody's good..."

Never having gone to trial, Sweeney never had the satisfaction of due diligence. Never got to learn exactly how the cops knew what they knew. But it surely started at Anthony's. Of course they'd have Acerbi under surveillance.

Sweeney's a small timer, but you show up at Anthony's and leave in a hurry, you're drawing *some* kind of attention. Anybody with half a brain should have realized that Sweeney would be picking up a tail, wiretaps, e-mail hacks. Sweeney should have known (of course, of course) that various crime units were already pinning his photo to their corkboards.

~

"I'll get us an Uber," Sweeney has his cell phone. Glances at the readout. "Oh *man*. Battery." The dissembling feels false, his voice inflectionless in the wrong way. He ain't no kind of actor, but Tina's oblivious.

"We can walk." She touches an eye with a fingertip. Now that they're out on the street, a sense of propriety has outmaneuvered her grief. Sorry, Georgie. Life goes on.

"Cobble Hill?"

"Back up Park Slope."

"After you." He's managing to maintain a superficial kind of calm, but inside he's screaming: *Go*. Get a move on, move your ass, go, go, go.

Ten minutes of brisk walking, they're on 5th and Garfield. Sweeney holds the door open for her. Nine o'clock in the morning and the air-conditioned bank's already a relief. "Boxes are downstairs." Past a couple tellers and an ATM, a long flight of stairs.

Sweeney watches Tina sign her name to two different ledgers. A rent-a-cop in the corner digs a fingernail into his teeth.

Three minutes later, two sets of keys hang off the box's silver door. Tina hooks her fingers through the wire handle. "You ready?"

"Just get the stones. Jesus."

Tina's inclined to pout, but then yeah, she agrees. Not the time nor the place. She extracts the box and sets it on the bank's gray marble table. Opens the lid.

Inside, a black velvet bag, cinched tight. A cheap bag, like something that might come with a board game to hold the pieces.

Tina's fingers fumble at the string. Then she tips the bag gently toward the marble. Shakes it. Shakes it again.

~

What Sweeney don't know about diamonds is a lot. But he *knows* that he don't know, which, as they say, is the beginning of wisdom.

Mostly he knows what you pick up off the street, the lingo of the part time larcenist. You walk into a pawnshop with rocks pried out of a setting, they'll talk about cut, clarity, color, carats. They'll mention moissanite and heat conductivity. How the value in a stone comes from the purity of color, the flawlessness. If there are enough inclusions in the meat, it's the difference between gem quality and that Nigerian bort shit they put on drill bits. On the other hand, if it's too pure, too perfect, that means it's fake. The trick with gems, you've got to walk that line between perfect and not *too* perfect.

Most of all, though, Sweeney knows that diamonds are better than cash. Untraceable and unaccountable. They leave hoof prints filled with blood and tears (a pile of loose stones like this would have come into the moment pulling contrails of violence, regret, retribution), but they're *diamonds*. Antwerp, De Beers, Israel, New York on West 47th between 5th and 6th.

That's what he knows.

What he *don't* know, but might have read online, is that the state-sponsored diamond company in Russia, Alrosa (and like every other diamond company in the world), has had problems with overproduction. Diamonds are only worth a shit because people *think* they're worth a shit. Rarity is essential to the perception of value. And rarity, for a number of years, has been an artificial condition. De Beers started it, Australia did a riff on it, Russia followed the leaders. They've all been overproducing then hoarding.

A good business plan. Until.

Until the bottom drops out. And then, when a lack of demand collides with oversupply? It's like Wile E. Coyote spinning his legs off a cliff. Everybody starts waiting for that moment when the mutt glances down, for him to zip toward his inevitable coyote-shaped crater.

So let's say you're Vladimir Putin, with some national pride built into two big diamond mines, Mirny and Udachnaya, and let's say you've got Alrosa with a couple acres worth of good rough catalogued in file cabinets (*billions* of dollars worth of stone, just sitting there chilled). Given that you're always open to some collegial bribing, when they come to you hat in hand and with some good solid grease under the table, you do the right thing. You keep Alrosa solvent. You buy $1 billion worth of rough.

That's all public knowledge. What's not public (but available between the lines), is what happened on the predictable QT. A mid-level Moscow bureaucrat defects to the states. He's got one eye on Cape Cod and another on Palm Beach. Tied up with the Solntsevskaya Bratva, two years out of Butyrka, he steps off the plane with a bag full of rocks and a list of American contacts who might help a *bratan* out. A short list of wiseguys with the juice to not only move this kind of ice but the connections to make it worthwhile.

Next thing, a body's bumping up between the piers. Tattoos and powder burns on the temple. It's CSI time, albeit with less photogenic lab rats.

After cutting off the shirt, scoping out the domes of Annunciation in chromium and cobalt, they could give exactly less than one shit about the body. What's another gangbanger, more or less? Granted, more exotic than most, but a gangbanger nonetheless.

Next case.

This is all good theory.

What's *not* theory is the tumbling cascade of stones just now under Sweeney's nose.

Focusing on them, it's like looking through a child's

kaleidoscope, a cardboard tube pointed to the light, twisted and twisted again. Octahedrons and dodecahedrons, high quality roughs polished along the flat faces. *Glassies.*

Jesus, though, the way his mind works? First thing that pops into his head is a strip club. *Girls, girls, girl.* A beautiful woman rotating around a bronze pole, just out of reach. Also, cocaine. His old Caddy. Springsteen and a Colt .44 cold between his legs. Next, he winces at the thought of the chintzy-ass stone he just bought Aggie. A fragment of a fragment, a shard of a shard. Compared to this.

This is like. It's like. Jesus. It's like standing in a long line for the water fountain when you're ten years old, then that first, cold, impossibly sweet rush of water down your tiny little parched throat. It's like stepping out of the car after fourteen hours on the Interstate, that delicious stretch of your legs. It's like seeing your whole life spread out on a table, steaming on silver platters, dripping grease. His *life*, man. Right here.

He does a quick count while Tina watches, waiting for a reaction. Mentally divides the pile into quarters. Maybe fifteen or sixteen stones per quarter. Maybe another half dozen in the thicker cluster in the middle. Call it seventy uncut diamonds, each one fifteen to twenty carats. The biggest, maybe thirty.

On the low end of blackmarket wholesale, he's looking at two and a half million dollars. High end, maybe four million. Average it out: Three million.

Much less, of course, than rumor and wishful thinking might have had it. But still. Three million dollars.

What Sweeney needs right now is a certain kind of certainty of purpose, a daunting professionalism. For Aggie. For Elizabeth.

He takes the edge of one hand and pushes the stones into

a pile. Feeds them back into the bag. Quickly.

"Cosmoo…" Tina draws it out like she's dangerous.

He twists the string tight around the bag. Drops it into the inside pocket of his suit jacket. "Let's get out of here."

"No, no, no way, no…" Tina claws for his jacket.

"Scene," he hisses, jerking his head toward the guard.

"Cosmo…" Plaintive now.

"We'll call us a car. We're going to Midtown."

His certainty minimally reassures her. "Midtown?"

"Fifty-seventh and Lex."

"Your fence?"

He half nods.

"Ohhhkay…." She keeps her eyes on his jacket. "I guess that's okay."

~

He's rehearsed the next stage in his head. After that he'll go by instinct. He used to be good at instinct.

Step one: Out on the street, he produces his cell phone. Pretends to be frustrated (again) by the dead battery. "Borrow your phone?"

Tina hands it over without a second. An older model iPhone. Sweeney slips it into his hip pocket.

And yeah, that's pretty much the end of his plan.

Here's Tina for you. Dumb enough to give him her phone, smart enough to natch immediately to her situation. According to the strictures of this particular game, she's already a pawn to the disadvantage. Nine thirty in the morning on a Brooklyn sidewalk, they're facing off. Three million dollars is the board.

"Cosmo…"

"My fence, this guy, he's nuts." Sweeney plays it calm and reasonable. "I can't have you tagging along in the back seat. You understand, right?"

"No, yeah. Give me my phone, Cosmo. For that matter, give me my god*damned* diamonds."

"This goes wrong, it goes *waay* wrong." He turns a hip towards her, lets her glimpse the bulge in the small of his back. "You want to be an accessory?"

"So you drop me off at the corner." Tina's starting to sweat it, begging. "I'll watch from half a block away."

"We're not playing here, Tina. This ain't amateur hour."

"I'll scream. Right here. I'll scream my goddamn lungs out."

"Okay. Listen. You go find you a burner phone." Maybe he's conceding something. "Call your cell. I'll call you back, give you updates. Where I am, what I'm up to. Every ten minutes, twenty minutes."

"You won't fuck me over, Cosmo?" Pleading now. "You're going to fuck me over, aren't you. Just say it. Let me hear the words. Say you're going to fuck me over."

"Tina. I'm doing this for *you*, Eddie, for all of us." The thought of his cousin puts a genuine mist in his eyes. "It's just, I need to do it solo."

Necessity provides the tipping point. She wants to believe. "Swear?"

Jesus, she's buying it. "Swear. On...everything. I swear on those two good years we had together. By how much we used to love each other."

It's all too much for her. Georgie and her own grief. The tensions of the last two weeks. Now Sweeney playing an unpredicted ace. Did he say *love*? She visibly wilts, settles back on her heels. "You swear?"

"Swear."

And this is how, five minutes later, he's sitting alone in the backseat of a Lincoln town car, three million dollars in his jacket pocket. Couple days ago he was digging around for the last fry in the bag, wearing seventeen dollar Carhartts. Now he's in Armani and burping Brooklyn Thai, the price of a Montana ranch trembling next to his heart. He says to Ahmad, his new driver, "Find me a place where I can rent a car. Hertz, Alamo, whatever."

"National?"

"National." Sweeney puts his hand patriotically over the smooth lump of diamonds. Feels them pulse in three-quarter time. Lacri*mo*so. "National."

~

By Sweeney's read, the only way Aggie and Elizabeth have a shot? He's got to find a way to put Breetvah's balls in a vice. Maybe he kidnaps somebody near and dear. A wife, a daughter? They'll do an equitable exchange. Two warm bodies for two warm bodies.

Problem is: What's he know about Breetvah? Nada, buptkus, zippo. Does the guy even have a wife, a daughter? His only connection to Breetvah was Bytchkov. And that bridge, for obvious reasons, is burnt. But there's another connection as well. Tina.

Even odds? The men who trashed Tina's house are the same bastards who killed Eddie. Breetvah and his crew.

Maybe Sweeney pays a visit to Tina's house. Takes a look. Sees if it offers some insight, some *clues*.

Thinking that word, Sweeney gets punched in the gut by

his own impotence. What is this, the fucking Hardy boys?

Still, he's got to do something. Until he gets the next phone call, until he is specifically held accountable for the rocks in his jacket, he's got to make some kind of play.

Bensonhurst, she'd said. Seventy-second. Nice little red brick townhouse. Big windows on the second floor. Good parking.

National had given him a Honda CRV. Little four-cylinder with the zero-to-sixty pick-me-up of a hamster wheel, a smell inside like cat piss and mildew. But it's anonymous, which he likes. Driving through Brooklyn, Sweeney lights a smoke. Rolls down all four windows.

Twenty minutes later: You know how many red brick townhouses there are on Seventy-second? A *lot*. Why couldn't she have given him a cross street. Seventy-second and…?

Sweeney pulls off to the curb to start up Tina's iPhone. She'll have her appointment book in there, maybe some addresses. Confirmation e-mails from Amazon.

But, no. The first screen is the four-digit pass code. Which is disappointing though not a catastrophe. Nothing's ever easy.

Just for shits and giggles, not expecting much, he punches in Tina's birthday. She was born in August eighth, so he tries 0808. No. Too much to hope for. The year was 1978, so next he tries 0878. Of course this doesn't do it, either. How about Eddie. Born on…what. March 15? So 0315. And, nope. Sweeney? Hell, why not. For nostalgia's sake, he punches in his own numbers. September 12 makes for 0912. Of course, no.

Okay, think.

There was a pizza joint a few blocks back. Eddie'd always

had an appreciation for good pie. Sweeney pulls a U-turn and finds the storefront. Calls the number on the awning. It's early, but not so early that they shouldn't be gearing up for lunch.

"Yeah, Dave's."

Sweeney puts on a not-bad cousin Eddie impersonation. A nasal twang, a hoarse undercurrent of ready-to-be-pissed. "Yeah, hey, this is Eddie Adamo, and I..."

"Eddie! Jesus, man. I heard, we heard, well, Jesus, man. How you been? You doing okay?"

Taken aback, Sweeney wings it. "Yeah, yeah. Those rumors, right?"

"Man, I can't even...wow."

"Yeah, so I need a pie. I got people, they're gonna be here inside of ten minutes. Hungry after an all nighter, yeah?"

"I gotcha. What kinda pie?"

"One of those supremo ones. All the shit. Just drag it through the garden. No hot peppers." Sweeney remembers this about Eddie—no jalapenos. "Big as they come. You get it here inside fifteen minutes, I'll tip an extra twenty."

"You got it."

"You got my address, right?"

"You still at...?" A brief rustle of paper. He reads an address. Another two blocks east.

"That's it"

Five minutes later, Sweeney's idling slow past Eddie and Tina's little house, keeping an eye out for surveillance.

Red brick, right. Otherwise, Tina was full of shit. Two stories, narrow as a ladder, cornice bricks crumbling like cake. Fifty years ago it might have been picturesque. Maybe the front yard used to be filled with roses, peonies, violets. Now it's bean trellises and corn stalks. Broken gutters staining the walls like hair gel melting out of a hat.

From the west, he sees nothing suspicious. The house comes up on his right...then it's gone. Still nothing.

Feds would be hardest to spot. They'd have a room rented with a sightline to the front door. Wire taps, shotgun mikes, cameras. But if this place is hot to the Feds, Sweeney's fucked no matter what. It's therefore an unproductive worry, the Feds.

If it's Moretti, he'd have assigned a couple soldiers. But your typical wiseguy lasts about five minutes on a stakeout. They get bored, ask what their bosses ever did for *them*, go buy each other drinks at the nearest bar.

Russians, though? They'd monitor a place for weeks if there was a buck in it.

And yeah. No shit. Half a block later—past a long row of middle-American Toyota Tercels and Honda Civics and Chevy Malibus of older vintage—two goons sit horizoned in the front seat of a Grand Marquis. Windows down, elbows out the window, cigarettes smoldering.

They're eyeing the front door, but they don't have visual access to the back. Russians. *Not* the sharpest tools in the shed.

Sweeney ducks lower and, once he's well past, takes a right turn, then another. Slips into the alley.

There's no surveillance, but...

The back door—the same door that Tina said had been trashed with an axe (nice narrative touch...*visual*)—stands in one piece. Unscratched. Two locks. Solid oak, stained dark, weathered.

Sweeney parks and walks to the door. Under his feet, on

the concrete stoop, a rope welcome mat crumbling with mold and moisture. A kitchen window beside the door, protected by security bars, has lace drapes and a forgotten houseplant on the sill. Sweeney puts his nose as close to the window as the bars will allow. A cheap fridge, humming. Cabinets closed and intact. Couple dishes stacked in the drain tray. On the wall, a "Fuck the Cook" needlework that Sweeney remembers from Tina's apartment.

Okay.

Okay.

Okay, Sweeney.

This changes…everything.

You're a fool.

Consider how much of this mess, this whole house of cards, how many of his preconceptions, have been built on the words of a woman whom he already knows to be a liar.

Russians. Breetvah. Moretti. All of it. Bullshit. Probably.

So, okay. Take a step back. Reevaluate. What does he know for sure?

He's got three million dollars in his pocket. That's one thing.

And the guy who's been trying to fuck up his life in Montana has kidnapped Aggie.

But that's all. That's it.

And Eddie's death is such common knowledge that even the pizza guy has heard about it.

Plus…*plus*, there's two assholes in a Grand Marquis out front.

Which is a start.

The thing with cell phones, Marilyn's opinion, they're like snowmobiles. They die on you at the *worst* times. Twenty miles up the trail in waist-deep snow. Right when you need them the most.

Seven thirty in the morning, Marilyn plugs her phone into the prowler's charger, starts the car and turns on NPR. She's not on duty until eight, so there's no guilt about the distraction. Good coffee between her legs and a bagel with cream cheese beside her.

She orders her beans online from a roaster in Brooklyn, buys her bagels in Bozeman. Going to bed at night, she's already looking forward to breakfast. Her Sunday *Times* is delivered by mail on Tuesdays. Her *New Yorker* on Thursdays. She has her routine, her tiny pleasures, the comfortable fluff that, in aggregate, constitutes a life.

She's smart enough to see it for what it is, the fluff. And console herself with the thought that it's this same awareness that makes for a good cop. She's perceptive. Consider this twenty minute drive from her front door to the courthouse. A drive she's made, what...Five days a week, times fifty-two weeks, for three years now. She still finds it fascinating, her own transition.

Six a.m., swinging her legs out of bed, she's an old biddy. Cat curled on the next pillow, dog off her hip. Down comforter coated with pet hair. She stumbles to the shower, glances reluctantly at the mirror (her ass…bigger) and, after the shower, steps into her uniform. Buckling up her utility belt, she's already somebody else. By the time she slips a key into the prowler, Marilyn Sweeney is more than halfway buried, replaced by this jaded ball buster of a cop.

She eases out onto the frontage road and sets the cruise control five miles below the speed limit. Gets a grim pleasure from seeing the traffic stack up behind her. Morning commuters.

Even as she drives, she starts seeing the world with a new eye. Everything's a crime. Cow dogs running loose in a field? Biters. A rancher burning trash? Permit violation. Brand new Mustang parked up next to a ramshackle trailer? Meth dealer. Throw in some spousal abuse, drunk drivers, serving civil papers and busting medical marijuana providers, that's pretty much her job in Montana.

A kid in a three-quarter ton Ford diesel comes fast around the corner, sixty-one in a forty-five. She flicks her lights at him. As they pass, he gives her a pale, wide-eyed stare, mortified.

"Asshole," she says happily.

Coming through the canyon, she turns on her radio. "Dispatch, Charlie 313, I'm ten-eight."

"Roger that, Marilyn. Just in time. Over."

"Oh?"

The dispatcher, Patricia Mulligan, becomes more officious the more serious the crime. "Car 313, proceed to I-90 eastbound, mile marker 384, we have a possible 10-54."

It takes Marilyn a second. Then: Dead body.

Sweeney's bridge buddy.

"Roger. On my way. Over."

Rather than going to the courthouse, she pulls onto the Interstate, hits her lights, accelerates hard.

She's wondered often: How is it in New York? Beating the pavement, working a crime scene, filing paperwork. *Procedures.* Because however they do it, it ain't like Montana.

Interstate 90 between Rockjaw and Big Timber follows the Yellowstone River. At her mile marker, she takes the exit and pulls into a fishing access. Wedged between the highway and the river, there's room for a dozen or so cars and a toilet. Paths in the weeds where fishermen have tramped up and down.

The only vehicle is an old Chevy Suburban. Muddy blue, dented rocker panels, cracked windshield. She recognizes it as belonging to a retired Amherst English professor, Peter Hadden. Rumpled linen kind of guy. A pipe smoker with family money. Privileged, but he doesn't flaunt it.

He's in patched, down-market waders, leaning on his bumper. Slouch hat and sunglasses, age spots and the befuddled expression of an old man ambushed by late-life fatherhood. Stranger to this gawky, petulant creature beside him. His teenage son, six inches taller and ten pounds skinnier. Hair in his eyes and a cigarette in his lips. Kid's eighteen, so the cigarette is legit. But she finds it offensive. Cigarettes in the morning, no doubt medical marijuana after lunch. The kid's name is…Drew, yeah.

"Deputy Sweeney." The kid speaks up first. "Nice to see you again."

Smooth talker, this kid. She remembers that about him.

"Drew. Dr. Hadden. You called in an incident?"

Hadden's paler than usual. "Over here. Darnedest thing."

She follows him down one of the paths beaten into the

grass by fishermen. Couple hundred feet away, his fly rod lies flat in the brown grass, tip pointed to the river, green arc of line still wafting in the water. "We were stripping streamers, like this." Hadden mimes jerking his rod back. "And darnedest thing, I cast into the corner, get hung up. And I started trying to, well…Here." He picks up the rod, strips line until he meets resistance. Pulls hard.

And twenty yards downriver, a dark piece of fabric rises to the surface from amid the tangle. Fabric, and then beneath it—limp, dainty, loose as a conductor waiting for the beat—a pale human hand.

Sweeney left a message on Eddie's cell. Waited around for an hour, then decided, sheeyit. Looks like he has to drive up to White Plains. Eddie had given him an address on Midchester Avenue. "Got an empty rental house where we cut the coke, me and these kids I got working for me, mix it up with baking soda and lactose." But the address was an empty lot. A square full of weeds and rusting metal. An old swing set, a mound of tires.

Sweeney sat in his Caddy, considering. A small thing, maybe, for Eddie to lie to him about the address. But why would he? Sweeney stepped out for a smoke. Maybe Eddie wasn't limiting his operation to White Plains at all, in which case he'd have to lie to everyone to keep the Gambinos happy. Maybe he was protecting Sweeney, keeping him out of the loop. But what kind of favor was that? Sweeney was going to get blamed no matter what.

Eddie, man. Just like the guy. Give you a present with one hand, sucker punch you in the kidneys with his other.

Sweeney was grinding the cigarette under his toe when an old Chevy station wagon, crooked on weak springs, pulled up next to him. Eddie rolled down the window. "Cousin," he said. "Brings you to White Plains?"

Sweeney hadn't seen Eddie since the Bytchkov job. Eight days ago now. Long time, given how tight they were. How tight they *used* to be. You want to think there are friendships in the world that might last, you know…for*ever*. That the human animal is capable of forming those bonds. Ten thousand beers you buy for each other, you save each others' lives, *kill* for each other…You'd like to think that some things wouldn't change. But they do. They *do*. Maybe you forget Christmas one year. Maybe you neglect a phone call. Maybe you leave your partner to clean up his own mess. Nothing hurts like the demonstration of a previously-hidden disdain. Nothing poisons like a lack of respect.

Sweeney was reasonably sure that Eddie would cover for him with Bytchkov. It was in Eddie's best interest, after all. Stonewall, make excuses. But no doubt *that* clock was ticking. The dilemma Sweeney had seen in Bytchkov's basement was essentially unchanged. Sweeney was either with them or against them. Being now against them, he needed to make some kind of move. But not yet.

Eddie said, "Get in. Let's take a drive."

The station wagon had a cracked dash, and bare metal under his feet instead of automotive carpet. Sweeney sank low in the seat. "You got my message?"

"Yeah."

The blinker was going, but Eddie let the wagon idle at the curb. He stared at Sweeney. A minute, maybe two. A good long time. Finally, he hit the steering wheel with his palm. Frustration, real or dissembled. "Goddamnit, Cosmo. What are we going to do? What's our play here"

Sweeney breathed easier. Finally. "We take out Bytchkov."

"Simple to say." Eddie pulled away from the curb. "But, yeah."

"How you want to do it?"

Eddie ignored the question. "So what's this about Anthony?"

"He wants you to lay off the blow."

"Asshole."

"The old guy sounded pretty serious."

"I'll talk to him, smooth it out."

"You do that."

"Meantime, you and me, we need to get to know each other again, spend some quality time." He tossed a leather envelope in Sweeney's lap. "Peace pipe?"

Unzipped in his lap, a womb-full of drugs. Codeine in a prescription bottle, a plastic vial packed tight with coke, a Ziploc full of X. An invitation to the kind of night that would either put you in a coma or send you to Mexico. Intensive care or Cancun.

Eddie said, "You been to the Cherry Pit?"

"Heard about it." A strip club in Yonkers.

"They got these dancers, man. Top notch talent."

Sweeney was only human. "I'd like to see that." Opened the vial of coke and rubbed a fingertip across his gums.

Eddie reached across to knead Sweeney's shoulder. "My man."

Through the blur of that evening, the visual smears of red and blue neon, house music insistent enough to bring Sweeney's own pulse into its orbit, the slow-rotating ceiling with Sweeney spinning at the axle, Eddie kept setting off alarms. The way he kept staring past Sweeney, not meeting his eyes. Sweeney finally said, yelling over the music, "What *is* it with you."

"What?"

"What is it! With you!"

Eddie frowned at his drink. Made a decision. Drank hard and chewed at his ice, staring directly at Sweeney for the first time all night. "We went ahead. Without you."

"What?" Sweeney heard only half of it but could read lips for the rest.

Eddie cocked a discrete finger toward his own temple.

They'd been tipping the help like rock stars, and a topless waitress hovered close, playing with Sweeney's hair.

"Who did it?"

"Does it matter?"

Sweeney leveled a gaze. "Maybe."

"B himself. He wasn't happy."

Sweeney was relieved, at least, that Eddie had avoided this particular stain. But inside, even past his glorious, bemused haze, Sweeney still balked. That poor, poor woman. And if she was dead, then those poor, innocent kids. And poor Eddie, too, having that on his conscience. Because surely he'd wake up one day with regrets.

And Sweeney? Here's a question. You take a guy who can't swim and shove him in a pool. That's murder, right? But take that same guy and somebody *else* shoves him in the pool. He's drowning, but you only stand there and watch. Is that still murder? And if it's not, then what is it?

Sweeney gave the night an extra ten minutes, said, "I gotta go."

Eddie didn't even try for surprised. He stared off, interested in the wallpaper. Tossed Sweeney his car keys. "Take the wagon. I'll catch a ride later."

"I'll leave it at your, you know, your *head*quarters."

Eddie was a thousand miles away. "Do that."

~

Half a block later, Sweeney's rearview mirror lit up with a red strobe, a rolling dashboard light. It had been raining, and the lights fractured against wet pavement.

There's that *oh shit* moment. Stretched out and distended in memory.

They'd been waiting.

Sweeney with his elbow out the window, his other hand loose on the staring wheel (keep your hands out where they can see them), stared into a flashlight. "What's the problem, officer?" He quailed, hearing his own sibilant slur. Offisher.

Two of them, in suits. "Mr. Aniello," a voice, cordial enough, but with a barely disguised delight. "Please step out of the car."

"Problem?"

"Hands against the vehicle please. Feet out. You know the drill."

"The problem, man?"

"Stolen vehicle? For a start."

Turns out, Eddie's wagon was hot. Lifted from a mall parking lot in Hicksville. And, oh yeah—while Sweeney sat on the curb, watching them search the vehicle, hands cuffed behind him, hunkered in the rain—Eddie had six ounces of uncut coke in the glove compartment, packaged in vials. Not to mention a pistol under his seat, a .38 with the registration numbers filed off deep.

They were Feds. Not bad guys, it turns out. Sweeney might have had a beer with them, under different circumstances. The older of the two, a guy in his sixties (gray, poorly-trimmed mustache and a few yards of extra skin hanging down under his eyes), came to sit beside Sweeney on the curb. "The drugs say intent, Mr. Aniello. Seven years. The stolen vehicle, that's four. But that pistol? That's a class-C felony, my friend. That's fifteen years."

Put it all together, tack on another year for the drunk driving, even if the judge was sympathetic, Sweeney was looking at twenty-plus years, maybe paroled in ten. If he was lucky.

They threw those numbers at him again in the interrogation room, his future spread out across the metal table like cards..

"Yeah," Sweeney said three hours later and still not even close to sober, "we can talk deals. But I'm not giving up Anthony. Or Eddie. Or anybody else close like that. My family, those guys, they're off limits."

"You're breaking my heart."

"What it is."

"It doesn't leave us much."

"Yeah, though," Sweeney said, thinking of Bytchkov's basement, considering the hand in a jar, the bowl full of teeth. "Yeah, it does."

"Talk to me."

"Russians? You guys like the Russians, yeah? Sexy. Newspaper headlines. I can give you a Russian. Murder, kidnapping. Maybe a gasoline scam." The nurse girlfriend, murder one if the body turned up, if the Feds got lucky with the forensics. And the kidnappings? Maybe the Feds could set up surveillance. Catch Bytchkov right after he takes the kids. Turn the snatcher into a snatchee. Sweeney would get all kinds of satisfaction out of that.

A poker player, Sweeney caught the glances between the Feds.

"One thing, though…" Sweeney shifted on the hard metal chair, cleared his throat. "You got to keep my cousin out of it. Eddie stays out of jail. We clear?"

~

Sweeney's off his game. The spirit is willing but the chutzpah's...meh.

He leaves his rental in the alley. Strolls up behind the Grand Marquis, playing it pedestrian casual. There's no movement inside the car. Just two shadows with smoldering smokes. Sweeney thinks of his own cigarettes and gets a nicotine itch. Save it for later.

He has the .357 in the small of his back. And coming closer—five steps away—he reaches around. Dig the feel of a good pistol, the potential of it. Right on. In New York, just *carrying* this piece could get him a mandatory three-and-a-half.

He pulls it out smooth with his right hand. Be quick, Sweeney, be brutal. Reach in through the open window and punish the passenger (a quick couple raps to the temple), open the door and dump him out onto the sidewalk. Point the pistol. "Drive." On the way to wherever, make the driver spill what he knows.

Pray he can speak English.

Sweeney's three steps away, now two. Breathing harder. Feeling the plunger behind his adrenal gland punch a few CCs into his bloodstream.

Which is when the pizza arrives.

Some kid's ancient little Ford Fiesta, rusted out on the rocker panels and dragging sparks, pizza sign strapped to the roof, hauls ass into Eddie's little driveway. Thinking about his tip, he runs to the front door, manhole-sized pie balanced on the flat of his hand.

The goons in the car sit upright. All attention focused on the door, on the pizza.

Nice.

Nicer still, The Marquis's backdoor chrome lock buttons are clearly popped up, conveniently unlocked.

So no whipping necessary. Easier just to open the back door, slip in behind. Cock the pistol and shove the barrel hard up against the nearest ear, which happens to be the passenger's.

All of this Sweeney does in a trice. Says pleasantly, "Howdy fellers."

First surprise? The passenger isn't Russian but Hispanic. A green do-rag and earrings up and down, all the usual tattoos, knuckles to nape. Considerately, he's already placing his hands on the dashboard. A Hispanic gangbanger in his early thirties. *Ancient* for the gangs. That green belongs to the Trinitarios. A reputation for machetes. A thirty-year-old Trinitario? We're talking a mean, sword-wielding motherfucker.

But Sweeney's got the gun. So, you know, we're even.

The driver, by the fact that he doesn't have a gun directly in his ear, he's got some latitude for some *attitude* (an Eddie saying). He twists around all of a piece, like his neck is fused. He's jowly, florid. A white guy in khakis and a polo, sweated through at the armpits. An accountant on the back nine. Sweeney's hit first by the incongruity of it all—Hispanic gangbanger on a stakeout with Greg Norman—but then he recognizes the driver.

The guy's eyes protrude like a thyroid case, Marty Feldman on a bad day. He whispers, a tremble in his voice, "Shakespeare?"

Fuck me. Fuck, fuck, *fuck* me. "Heya Jimmy."

"Shakespeare!" Louder.

Sweeney lowers the pistol. "Jimmy Rug."

~

Sweeney and Jimmy Ruggino go back. Not as far back as Sweeney and Eddie, understand, but *back*.

During Sweeney's matriculations in the tire shop—bag runner to driver to trigger—Jimmy had been two years behind, the next little grommet in the chain. Some part of Sweeney always wanted to be a mentor, so he took an interest.

Good kid, Jimmy. Jug-eared and anxious, crooked teeth and a rotating series of bruises (his old man was a *mean* drunk), but between those unfortunate ears, the kid had a head for numbers. And thanks to growing up in Corona, he could speak Spanish. Not many people remember how Corona used to be Italian before it went Dominican. Anyway, Nose liked kids with a brain.

The first few days, Sweeney pegged Jimmy for slow. He spoke with the rhythm of a guy who's overcome a stutter. "That hatchback iinnn pod three. We rohhhtating the tires, too?" He had a hard time looking anyone in the eye, and when he drew any sort of inadvertent attention—when the Nose called out his name across the bays—he froze like he'd just stepped in dog shit. His expression one of resigned fatalism.

Three days into it, Sweeney took him aside, said, "Hey kid, you drink beer?"

Sure he did. Fourteen years old, hundred and twenty pounds if you put your thumb on the scale, but Jimmy could down Budweiser like a meatpacker.

Sweeney and Eddie were sharing a basement apartment over in Midwood. One of Sweeney's paternal uncles kept these row houses. No love lost between Dad and brother—blood feud kind of thing—so Sweeney got a rate, just to piss off the old man. Couple mattresses on the floor, some

Penthouse centerfolds, a PVC bong in the corner. A not-bad shelf of vinyl, Sherwood receiver, Akai speakers, turntable. First generation Nintendo. A thirty-two inch color TV rough on the corners where it fell off the truck. "You guys live *here?*" Jimmy, awed. "And these're your books?" Ignoring the video games in favor of Sweeney's paperbacks.

This was Sweeney's Russian phase. Six months ago he'd read *Notes from Underground*. A book that made you sit and blink at the wall for a while. Dostoyevsky. In the biopic of his life, this page of the script would read, "Sweeney Gets Smart: Montage." A series of fade-tos. Sweeney in the library slipping a hardbound Turgenev under his jacket. Sweeney at home, dropping Anna Karenina flat on the kitchen table. Sweeney under a tree in Prospect Park, eating a slice over *Brothers Karamazov.*

Jimmy Rug tilted his head sideways to read the spines, "No *Crime and Punishment?*"

"Not yet."

"Youuuu haven't…? I mean, that's the best one. Raskolnikov, hey."

Knock on a guy's melon with curiosity but little hope, sometimes you get surprised.

A few months later, trying to do the kid a favor, Sweeney brought him to his gym, put him in a boxing ring. Pipe cleaner arms swinging heavy gloves, a pale, concave stomach and ugly, marbled pox of cigar burns on his back. An hour later, and by way of consolation, Sweeney said, "Some guys, they're born to use their heads instead of their hands."

Jimmy had paper towels twisted up both nostrils. "I think he punched a few points offff my I.Q., too."

When Eddie and Sweeney started messing around

with Bytchkov, Sweeney put some distance between him and Jimmy. For Jimmy's own good. As a consequence, the friendship never went south, never got contaminated by the paranoia endemic to this thing of ours, never got smeared with the monkey feces of friends fucking over friends.

And now Jimmy Rug is beside himself. Half climbs over the front seat to hug Sweeney around the neck. "Cosmo? But you're dead, man! I went to your fuuuneral, man. Those fucking Russians, I mean, Russians right? Cosmo, Jesus."

Sweeney finds himself awkwardly patting Jimmy's fat back, cheek to sweaty, unshaven cheek. He smells body odor and farts and lunch meats. Last week's spilled beer.

When Jimmy pulls away, he's touching the back of his hand to his eyes. "Cosmo. Jesus."

The Hispanic gangbanger has eased his hands off the dashboard. To Jimmy, says, "Quien es tu güey?"

Sweeney has enough Spanish to catch the ambiguous subtext. "Me and Jimmy go back."

"Until the Russians ran you off the fucking road."

"Russians." Studying Jimmy, Sweeney sees a tremor. A slight, Katherine Hepburn quaver in the cheeks. "You okay Rug? What's with the…?" Sweeney raises his hand, lets it shake.

"My Parkinson's? Yeah, my damn Parkinson's."

"Ah, shit. Jimmy."

"What it is." He shrugs it off. "Now whhaat about the Russians?"

So Sweeney gives him the sixty second soap opera of Bytchkov. Has the minimal caution to replace Rockjaw with, what? "So yeah, now I'm in Cheyenne, Wyoming. Out in the middle of nowhere."

Jimmy flickers commiseration and indignation. "Sounds like you did the ruhhight thing though, dawg."

Even while he's been talking, Sweeney's been going through a reluctant calculus. Cover's blown. Cosmo's done a Lazarus. Inside twenty-four hours, the news is all through Brooklyn. Thirty-six hours, Bytchkov gets a phone call. Forty-eight hours, Bytchkov and his murderous sense of justice are deciding the fate of Sweeney's extended family.

Or he could kill these two where they sit. Put a bullet in Jimmy Rug.

But that's not possible for any number of reasons, the condition of Sweeney's own soul first among them.

Okay, Sweeney. One catastrophe at a time. "I heard about Eddie." Nods toward the house.

"Yeah, ain't that the shit. Poor guy. Never thought I'd say that about Eddie, but yeah, poor guy."

"Anybody know who did it?"

Jimmy opens his mouth with a pleasurable anticipation, the delight of unlikely gossip. Then remembers Sweeney's piece of ass on the side. Closes his mouth with an audible click. "Maybe somebody's got some ideas somewhere."

"His wife, right? Tina."

"Yeah, well, she took off quick, man. Like that." Jimmy snaps his fingers.

"Which is why you guys are, I mean, you're waiting for Tina a show up?"

"She took suhhomething belonged to Donnie, is why." Jimmy makes a regretful, what-can-you-do expression. "Business."

"I saw you guys, I thought you might be Russian. That's why the pistol."

"Russians?" Jimmy blinks. "No, yeah, Donnie, he just said, guuhho find Eddie's wife. Couple hundred bucks a day to sit in a car. Two hundred a *day*. Man."

"Hard to pass that up." Rugg working for the Luccheses?

"You ain't kidding."

"So, Jimmy. Jesus. How you been? You're still in the life?" Sweeney's interested. Enough to give it five minutes of increasingly precious time.

Turns out Jimmy got clipped for dealing not long after Cosmo died, spent his time in County. "Which is where me and Lucho met up."

"Who's Lucho?"

"I'm Lucho, dawg." The gangbanger giving Sweeney attitude, a mix of bored-and-pissed.

Turns out, Lucho's married to Jimmy's baby sister, Julietta. They got kids. Everybody goes to the same church. Jimmy works night security, picks up freelance jobs. "And I'm making it, ain't we making it, dawg?" Fist bump. "Just doing whatever we can. I mean, this? It's a whole new world is what I'm saying. Everybody doing what they can. I'm still beholding to the Gambinos. Officially. But unofficially, here I am on the clock for Moretti. Whole new world, Shakespeare."

"Gambinos know about you freelancing?"

Jimmy ignores the question. "Used to be five families? Now there's six. Think about that for a suhhhecond. And nobody's got the weight they used to. Everybody's just trying to do what they can."

The gangbanger swats Jimmy on the shoulder. "Repartidor de pizza."

Balancing the pie in one hand, the delivery kid's walking back to his sad little Fiesta, lifting the lid of the box, considering his useless pie.

Sweeney checks his watch. "Listen, hey, I'm gonna go ahead and pay this kid. But give me your number, yeah? We'll grab lunch."

The Park County undersheriff is a guy named Gary Kertan (pronounced Curtain). A military haircut and aviator sunglasses hanging out of his shirt pocket. One of those cops who you suspect of manufactured evidence and spousal abuse. A secret drinking problem. Arrogant enough, you keep looking for mistakes, hope he'll slam his own fingers in a car door. He swaggers toward Marilyn through the takeout lot. "What we got? A floater?" Maybe he heard the word on "CSI Miami" once.

She gestures toward the river, a search and rescue diver in tanks and mask, a scuba suit, duckwalking toward the water. "Yeah, we…"

"I'll take it from here." Kertan puts his glasses on, tilts the mirrors her way. "Why don't you work crowd control." Kertan's done the contextual math. Drowning vic? They haven't seen any reports for a few months weeks. Missing persons? Ditto, not much. Possible murder then. And they only get one or two of those a year. Make the most of it.

This is the downside of her job. She's got to bite her tongue. Chauvinistic cocksucker. When she makes sheriff, you're back to bagging groceries, asshole. But for now, he's senior. She turns away from the diver (already up to his knees) to eye the small crowd gathering.

It's turned into quite a day for the Rockjaw gossips and gawkers, the police-scanner junkies. In the barrow ditch of the Interstate, a small flock of magpies bicker over recent roadkill. Given the proximity, perhaps Marilyn can be forgiven for drawing a parallel: squawking magpies and John Q. Public. The retiree with a digital camera and two-foot lens; the young couple in shorts and flipflops; a family with dad holding up his kid for a better look. Thank you, Apple, for police scanner apps. Half the time, these people arrive at a crime scene before she does.

She considers her own cell phone, still picking up a charge. Maybe it's time to check messages.

She's turning back to her cruiser just as another sedan pulls into the lot. Spotlessly clean four-door Taurus. Rental car from a mile away. Passengers in all four seats. Four white males. Maybe it's a return-to-the-scene scenarios you read about. Unlikely, but.

The Taurus parks close to the water, just far enough away not to be hassled by Kertan. The heads inside tilt toward each other, conferring. She walks toward them.

Twenty steps away, fifteen, ten. The driver catches movement, glances up with a double take. Attention from the local fuzz, not something he digs.

She's up on the balls of her feet, getting ready to speed up to a quick jog, when she recognizes the driver. Pulls a name out from under the neglected couch of her subconscious. Among the dust bunnies of New York, the forgotten quarters of Brooklyn: Lukey Ray.

He's still got that little mustache he was always playing with. Ten years ago, it was blond and meager, thin like lint from a clothes dryer. Her husband, with the carnivore's instinct for a soft spot, had teased him: "Be sure not to get any cream on that, Lukey. Cat might lick it off." Now the mustache is thicker but still blond. This guy's been in her home. Sat at her table. She cooked chicken tetrazzini.

In the half second it takes her to put on the brakes, turn on her heel…does he recognize her? His eyes go first to the badge, then the pistol. Then they're on the way to her face.

She turns quick, feigning forgetfulness. Walks back to her cruiser.

Lukey Ray. Is this the guy dumping bodies on Sweeney? Involved somehow. But to her memory, he was an awkward thug, smart like a door mat. He just did his job. Sending those photos around? Too subtle. He wouldn't see the point in it. There'd have to be somebody else offering the orders. Somebody up the ladder, somebody who wouldn't be seen dead in a rental sedan with three soldiers.

Plus, Lukey answers to the Luccheses. What kind of beef would the Luccheses have with Sweeney?

Thinkaboutitlater,Marilyn.Fileitaway,compartmentalize.

Right, okay. Where was she? Cell phone. Messages. Pick up your messages.

And then, off her right shoulder, a shout. "Hey, Marilyn!" The scuba diver, Jay Sutton, whom she knows from CPR certification, stands hip deep in the river, leaning against the current, holding his mouthpiece away from his face. "We got another one down here."

"What's that?" Marilyn walks toward the river, keeping her face tilted away from the rental car. Kertan stands, hands on hips, staring down at the river. With not a little satisfaction, Marilyn pushes past him. "Say again?"

"Yeah, no shit, we got *two* bodies down here."

Sweeney's alone in the alley, forehead on the steering wheel, door open, leg out on the street. Reassessing. His conclusions? It's shit. *All* of it.

Aggie and Elizabeth kidnapped.

Bernie, Marco, Clara, maybe they're already being discussed. Should he call them? He can't imagine that conversation. "Yeah, hey, this is Cosmo your dead brother. Sorry about the funeral thing. And uh yeah, you guys need to move down to Florida for, like, the rest of your *lives*."

Eddie's dead and buried. Or at least dead. Jimmy Rug's gotten fat, and picked up a pretty good case of Parkinson's. And Sweeney? What's he got? A pizza box taking up half the back seat. And self-pity. Loads of *that* shit.

What's his next move? What does he do now?

The sound of an engine rumbles at him down the alley. Sweeney opens his eyes. Sees an early model Crown Vic, tricked out with spinners and a lift kit, coming up fast then breaking hard off Sweeney's bumper, skidding enough to leave rubber. A bare arm emerges, waving a finger. "Close a *fuckin'* door man."

Not the right time, *man*.

Sweeney's rages have rarely been blind, though it's true things go dim for a while. And they're not *senseless*, though they never ask much permission. Rather, they're more like nausea. Pushing up from the gut. Sepia and slow-mo. Amygdala to the hypothalamus to the adrenal gland. Cortisol spritzed through his carburetor. There's something called the Intermittent Explosive Disorder. Anger arises from pain, they say.

No shit, Sweeney says.

He's already up close and personal. The kid in a black leather vest over a bare torso. And Jesus, the smell out the window. Body odor and bong water. Kid's Caucasian but going for black. Wearing a spotless Yankees cap, the brim flat and unbent, price tag dangling and stickers still in place. Under the cap, a mat of pale dreadlocks.

"What a fuck you staring at, old man?"

Last week's Sweeney, version 2.0, would have felt a paralyzing sympathy. This poor, lost soul. We're all of us searching. But for what? A tribe. Love. Companionship. And nobody's finding them. Nobody. Saddest thing in the world.

But this most recent Sweeney? The one at the end of his rope and the bottom of the barrel, sleepless and frantic? This Sweeney? Well, here…

There's a reason Roman generals, when Rome was in its ascent, cropped their hair short. If you're in combat, you don't want to give your enemy something else to hold onto.

Case in point: Sweeney's already got his fingers wrapped through the guy's dreads.

The kid doesn't weigh much. It's no great effort to drag him out through the window. Five frames a second, the only punch the kid manages to throw, Sweeney slips it easily. Lets it float right on past.

Sweeney steps away from himself, glances at his watch, considers the weather. Meanwhile, Shakespeare is punching the kid into the ground. Breaking the greasy nose at the bridge, cracking the skin like cheap binding, knocking teeth loose. Blood trickles down the corners of the kid's mouth.

Shakespeare breathes deep, and straightens. Cracks at his neck. Glances down.

Poor kid, Sweeney thinks. Scorn always camouflages insecurity. *Always*.

Sweeney takes a toe and turns the kid's mouth to one side. Don't puke while you're unconscious there, buddy.

The Crown Vic idles away, rudderless, open door waving. Fifty yards down the alley, it eases with a soft crunch into a phone pole.

First rage, then regret. This endless ocean of regret.

~

From what Sweeney knows about the universe, his phone call's coming any second now. Before he can compose himself, before he can find his breath. Just give it a second to catch up.

In the front seat, he works to find a Zen place. Studies the blood trickling between his fingers, the according scroll of skin on his first two knuckles. He flexes the fingers. Rookie mistake. Punching with his fist. All these little finger bones, fragile as Crayons. Better to use your elbow, your knee, your boot.

And yeah, sonofabitch. Here's his phone with the vibration and chirp, startling him.

Sweeney flips it open. "Yeah."

"You have the diamonds?" That voice again, run through a digital blender.

"Yeah."

"Okay, yes, good, now here is what you must do, yes, you go…"

"No."

"What?"

"No. Go fuck yourself."

Nothing but a digital void by way of reply.

Sweeney waits him out.

"No," the voice finally says, patient through the distortion. "You do not understand. Your little farm woman, she will die, you do not do what I say."

"See, now, I figure she's dead already. Even if I give you the stones, what reason you got to let her live? So what I'm saying is, fuck you. I'm keeping the rocks."

"So you have kill your woman. Her girl whore too."

"Give me a reason not to."

"I'm giving you an address. My fence. You give the stones to him. He calls me, I release your woman."

One thing: This guy's not Russian. The jumbled syntax comes and goes. "Who's your fence?"

The voice gives it to him. A name: Abdul Zakayev. And an address: Upper East Side, fifteenth floor, which is a problem. Surveillance cameras, doormen, guest lists. *Would* be a problem. "Yeah," Sweeney says, "it's still fuck you."

"They are dead, your woman. Dead in big way. In big pain. Maybe I fuck them first, yes? Up the ass."

"Fuck you, and you know what? Tell Tina I said fuck you too. How's about that? Do that for me yeah? Tell that lying bitch I said fuck you, too." Sweeney shuts his clamshell with a quaver, a tremor, an internal quail.

Aggie, oh no, oh Aggie.

It's the only play. The only play. Sweeney repeats it until he believes it. As long as Sweeney's got the rocks, Aggie's more use to this guy alive than dead. But if the guy ever gets his hands on these stones, there's no reason to keep her alive. Perforce, the only play.

On Sweeney's passenger seat, Tina's smart phone. Not *quite* the latest in technology. 4G this and that. E-mail and internet, a quick and easy conduit to the world. A Cadillac to his Pontiac. A flat gray screen opaque, unreadable. Waiting for a friend a family member, a "favorite," to dial her ten unique numbers.

Sweeney counts down. One Mississippi, two Mississippi…

Eight Mississippi, and it rings.

The theme from Rawhide. *Rolling, rolling, rolling.*

And on the flat face of the phone, alive now with lights and digital detritus, another ten digit number. Area code 917. New York.

Tina and Breetvah. They have a thing.

Eddie and Breetvah worked together. Tina bumps into Breetvah. They hit it off. Eddie comes home with diamonds, Tina seizes an opportunity and lets Breetvah cut Eddie's throat. Or does it herself. But then…lack of foresight, *maybe* they have a problem moving the diamonds.

But why would Breetvah have a problem moving rocks? He's *Breetvah*.

In any case, Tina remembers Eddie mentioning Sweeney in Rockjaw. Her and her squeeze, they drive across America. On the way, talking it over…how do we make sure Sweeney helps us? We shove him out of his nest. Put him in a place where he'll *have* to go for the money.

And now Breetvah's cutting Tina out of the loop.

But if he's already got a fence in New York, why the hell did they drive to Montana?

Sweeney has a ballpoint from his shirt pocket. Before the

phone dies, he jots the number down on his palm.

Abdul Zakayev. The name rings a bell. Somewhere, Zakayev, Zakayev, Zakayev....

He picks up his own phone. Dials a number. "Cal? Hey man. I got a hypothetical, my friend. Biggest hypothetical of my life."

Cal Merchant's posture says ex-military. The heavy, lightning-bolt ring on his right hand says Army Rangers. And despite the tangled threads of his more recent work (bodyguard, surveillance, computer tech) he's *still* a Ranger. Routine and regiment, they're in his blood.

He needs six hours of sleep a night. Five, he can function, but six lets him hit on all cylinders. Eleven-thirty, lights out. Five-thirty the next morning, he rolls off onto the floor and gives up forty pushups. Hard on his sex life—one of the reasons why he's still single (one of them)—but you can't think without blood flowing to the head. Breakfast is oats and brown sugar, raisins. Then his run. And unless it's a blizzard, he takes it outside. Much the poorer option, he'll hit the treadmill in the basement.

He runs up Windmill Road. Headphones and an iPod, funk and soul, ZZ Top and Bon Scott AC/DC. Merchant *needs* this private hour. Granite cliffs to the north, tumbling stream to the south. After eight years of these early-morning runs, he's *seen* some things. Bull elk, black bears in raspberry patches. Three grizzlies, a few dozen coyotes. And last year, wolves. Two quicksilver ribbons slipping through roadside brush, matching his pace. His balls sucked *right* up into his chest.

Given how he makes his living, the smart money would put him in Denver, Seattle, close to a decent airport. Better yet, he'd be offshore, a friendly coast with no extradition. The Maldives or Madagascar. But no. He needs this run, man.

How does he make his living? Short answer: Information tech. What he tells people, anyway, which is usually enough. Closer answer: Information retrieval. Closer answer still: I get you answers. Any answers. Leveraging a messianic skill with his satellite broadband and Rolodex of contacts (it is, in fact, a Rolodex; he wouldn't trust a digital file), and his informal post-doc, private contractor work in various sandboxes and third world shitholes, dictatorships built on foundations of coke, Russian repeaters, slave-based resource extraction. Merchant's a rare talent in today's world.

Top of his resume? He's got a ready-made hack into not one but two private surveillance satellites. He also built his own piggyback on Facebook's facial recognition software and can readily troll through the 1.2 trillion photos on the web, looking for a given alignment of eyes, a certain twist of the lips. He has cell phones for three black-listed FBI agents with grudges and two corrupt, active agents on the dole. More than once he's Fed-Exed thick envelopes of Euros to bureaucrats in Beijing. Give him a question and a contract, within a few days, he'll get you some kind of answer. He's a bureau chief without the bureau, he's research librarian for government-sanctioned psychotics, he's Jeeves and James Bond and Encyclopedia Brown. Has five or six steady clients with the scratch to pay his hourly (don't even ask), but Homeland's his steady date. They got the budget, and not much oversight, no accountability. They're liquid, and paranoid.

If he took these skills to Malé, hung out his shingle for reals? He'd clear a couple million a year, easy.

Instead, he stays in Montana. Blame it on his morning run

and Ted Sweeney. Alias Cosimo Aniello. Alias, Shakespeare. Alias, Mobbed-up-Maniac-Making-Good. Ask anybody: You only get so many decent friendships in a given life. When a good one comes along, you take care of it, water it like a houseplant, feed it like a goldfish. And in any case, tortured penance is always compelling. Merchant wants to see how this all plays out.

Seven years ago, the second time Merchant ran into Sweeney, he'd invited him up for some trap shooting. A couple conversations over the pool table made him curious, and the anomalies in Sweeney's story swiveled his ears forward. Sweeney, a guy who clearly didn't give a shit about the things that drew people to Montana, was drinking hard in the manner of adjusting to a shattered heart. But a guy could drink hard anywhere. Why Rockjaw? The accent was Brooklyn, but the athleticism, the easy way with a pool cue, the flat-gazed confidence...there was more here than city kid gone country.

Shooting trap, Sweeney dusted 78 out of 100, though it was clear he'd never been around a clay pigeon before. He knew shotguns, but had to be told when to say pull.

They had a beer. Afterwards, Merchant pulled a perfectly acceptable thumbprint off Sweeney's glass. And ten minutes after that, after a quick tap dance around inside the IAFIS database, it was just...holy *shit*. Aniello, Cosimo. See also: Badass trigger. Baaaad*ass*, man.

Merchant's been reluctant to parse through his own admiration. I mean, what kind of guy admires a murderer? But at the root of it? Curiosity, plus a search for the company of men, a peer. Gradually, over the last seven years, a few thousand bottles of beer, couple hundred days fly fishing the

Yellowstone, curiosity has segued to comfort. They're an old married couple. And while Sweeney, like all those old school Italians, is an unashamed racist cracker, he's *aware* of it, which makes him a new animal entirely. It's a joke between them. Sweeney's racist non-racism.

Long and short of it, all these years later? Cal would happily lay down on the tracks for the guy.

Which is all just a way of providing context for Cal's behavior, when, eight o'clock in the morning, he gets Sweeney's phone call.

~

On his deck in running shorts, stretching his calves, cooling off after a run. Eighty-five degrees already. On his hip, his cell phone buzzes.

Cal's is the kind of business, you always look at the number. It's also the kind of business, he rarely picks up.

This is Sweeney, though. "My brother."

The familiar voice, harried, exhausted. Traffic noise in the background. Someplace not Montana. Which is, yeah, interesting. Merchant just saw Sweeney two days ago. Sweeney says, "A theoretical, man."

"Go for it."

"So I got a theoretical idea that I haven't been the only one keeping some major-ass secrets. Is that a fair statement?"

"Fair enough."

"I got an idea you're in with law enforcement, yeah."

Cautious: "I know some people."

"The kind of people, maybe, that can track a cell phone from its number?"

Deep hesitation: "Maybe yeah, maybe no. I don't know."

"Can you help me, man?"

There's a tone in Sweeney's voice that Merchant never thought he'd hear. Pleading.

Merchant takes a long moment, considering implications. "Maybe you could tell me why you need it?"

Merchant hears him out. Takes about five minutes of Sweeney talking, uninterrupted. Finally, Merchant says, "You got the number?" Merchant repeats it back to him. Then, "You talked to Marilyn yet? Okay, yeah. I might know somebody that knows somebody. Let me find some people, see what they say."

"Cal, man. I just…thank you."

"Meantime, what else can I do?"

Sweeney laughs. And it's one of those nervous half snorts that manages to compress, between its pages, dried flowers of relief, debt, gratitude. Merchant's considered it before, how hard it must be for Sweeney to keep his secrets to himself. Jesus, it must feel good, letting them finally squirm loose. "You're saving my life, Cal. Thank you."

Out on the concrete, Mr. Crown Vic is up on hands and knees, spitting out ropey strands of blood. Sweeney rolls down the window. "Need a hand?"

The kid wipes a finger across his lips. Flings blood. "Gone fuck yourself."

"That's the spirit." Sweeney puts it into gear.

What's this thing that Sweeney's feeling now? Buoyancy? Cal Merchant, man. Guys that'll stick by you? Worth their weight.

He parks up close to Jimmy Rug's Grand Marquis. Knocks a knuckle on the window, leaving a smear. Jimmy rolls down his window. Checks out Sweeney's bloody knuckles. "Five minutes it's been, Cosmo," he says with some admiration. "Five minutes."

"I need to talk to Moretti. Can you set that up?"

Jimmy's head quavers. He might be thinking. "Yeah, I can set that up."

"Maybe soon? Maybe like this afternoon?"

"What, am I his secretary?"

"Yeah, well. Anyway. Here's my number." Sweeney hands him a corner torn off his rental car agreement, number scribbled along the margin. "And Tina. I need some friends of hers. You got any names?"

"Nah, man. I never knew that woman. She was some kind of mystery to me."

"You got to know *some*body."

"There was that one guy, what was that guy's name. Hey Lucho, that guy said he was Russian? Anyway, he was into online porn. Greasy, slimy sort of turd. Kid with the chains?"

Lucho plays it cool, studies a hangnail. Not his business.

"Jasha," Sweeney says.

"Yeah, that's it. Jasha." Rugg gives Sweeney his admiration.

And seeing that look, it's like hearing *Auld Lang Syne*, how it puts a fishhook under Sweeney's sternum. That painful little tug. "Where's my man Jasha hanging his hat these days?"

"Wherever porn guys hang out. I don't know. Corner of slimeball and jerkoff. But then yeah, he's also got this little warehouse over in Red Hook. Commerce, and what, Van Brunt maybe? Single story, white brick, Got a couple garage door bays. No windows. Can't miss it." Jimmy Rugg briefly assesses Sweeney. White shirt spotted with blood. Slick hair gone tousled. "Careful, though. That guy ain't all there."

"I know what you mean."

"Seriously. The man is whaacko."

"I knew him before."

"Don't get killed again, is all I'm saying."

~

Sweeney has a history with Red Hook. He's always appreciated the...what's that word. *Gumption*, maybe. Old-fashioned word for an old-fashioned place. If Manhattan's a martini in crystal, Red Hook's domestic beer in a can. If Park Slope's a Weimaraner on the couch, Red Hook's a grizzled mutt, slobbering at chain link. It's getting gentrified, like everything else New York, but still. When the wind is right you can still smell fish guts from previous centuries, the rotting nets, the pleasant tar-and-oak smell of barrels rolling off docks. In Montana, when Sweeney lifts one of his own t-shirts off the floor and holds it to his nose, he thinks of Red Hook.

So despite the fact that, at the end of this drive, he's going to have to brace a guy who no doubt wants to see him swinging from a rope, eviscerated on an autopsy slab, Sweeney's not necessarily dreading the trip.

Coming from Bay Ridge, he takes 4th Ave to 9th Street, then across Gowanus, following a blue and yellow Ikea shuttlebus belching exhaust. Broken concrete and crumbling brick, glass on the street and graffiti on the walls. By the time he's somewhere around Jasha's warehouse, smelling the hot asphalt and the burnt garbage, it's like coming home.

Take that guy there, doing a sidewalk strut to a private beat, one heavy arm over the shoulders of his emaciated girlfriend. The kind of fat man that collects all his flab around his waist. Skinny legs shaded by a shelf of blubber. A ribbed tank top to show off his ink. At a glance: Guy gives a shit what *any*body thinks. Screw anybody who don't think I'm pretty.

And his girlfriend? A prostitute, sure, but who's Sweeney to judge. Mid-twenties by her legs and ass. Pleather skirt and heels. Fishnets and Juice Newton hair. Sweeney's already past, and can't help glancing back. By her face? Late forties. The cheeks already deep as divots. Heroin, maybe, or meth.

Three or four paces behind them (and *break* Sweeney's heart a little) the prostitute's daughter, ten or twelve years old, hopscotching around with a Justin Bieber backpack, bowing to it like a dance partner, bringing it close to her lips, swinging it away again.

Okay, Sweeney. Task at hand. Rugg said the warehouse

was Van Brunt and…

Sweeney eases his foot off the pedal. The fat man.

Gold chain, and the letter J coated in glass bling. A pencil-line sketch of a beard around the bottom of his jaw. Hair buzzed down close.

Take away fifty pounds… sonofabitch looks like… Yeah. *That's* him. Force-feed a starving weasel nothing but cheeseburgers and beer for ten years? You could come up with a creature not unlike this. Thin and lethal Jasha gone fat.

Sweeney coasts to the end of the block, takes a right and parks. Twists his rearview to watch Jasha pull out a ring of keys, step up to the last warehouse on the corner. One of three identical buildings set in a row. Single story, yeah, but otherwise Rugg's description was bunko. It's got piss yellow bricks, with one garage bay, not two. And a pair of small barred windows on either side of the door.

Catching Jasha out on the street like this? Maybe Sweeney's luck's starting to change.

His phone rings. A New York cell number. Tina with her burner. He lets it go to voicemail. A second later, Tina's phone rings from the same number.

Okay, Sweeney. Where were we?

You got to get into the warehouse. Bars on the windows. Padlocked garage bay. A heavy metal door protected by a second, swinging set of jailhouse bars.

Think, man.

Another half block up the corner, there's one of those small, neighborhood bistros. The kind of joint that sells umbrellas and Funyuns, sliced meat from a cold case and organic milk. Maybe baseball caps. Maybe, if he's lucky, hoodies.

Just under the Continental Divide, the city of Butte, Montana, is a ghost town of abandoned mine shafts and sagging tenements, beneficiary of the kind of fierce, defensive pride that arises mostly from fear. On the ridge immediately above town, a statue of Mary smiles benignly down over an open pit copper mine, a superfund site gradually filling with rainbow-skinned groundwater the acidity of vinegar.

A century ago, Butte was a melting pot of Irishmen and Slavs, Poles and Russians. Any given day, you'd see women and children outside in the sun—hanging laundry, cooking cabbage, playing stickball in alleys—while their men worked in funereal darkness below, swinging picks, pushing carts, coughing under carbide headlamps hissing hot. These days, though, the ten thousand miles of underground tunnels are filled with black water and the only steady work goes to bartenders and cops.

Cal Merchant finds Johnny Counts Enemies asleep on the sidewalk outside the M&M bar. Budweiser forty in a brown bag by his left hand, cheek propped up on his right fist. Long black braids pooled around his head and his t-shirt hiked up to show a slice of hairless stomach. Open mouthed, snoring lightly. Another drunk Indian, immediately dismissed by every Butte eye passing over him.

Merchant unfolds a state road map. Squats and punches a forefinger into Counts Enemies's chest. "Hey buddy, hey pal."

Counts Enemies smacks his lips. Opens one skeptical eye. Closes it again. "Piss off."

Merchant lowers his voice. "How do you get to the alley behind the bar, I'm wondering?"

"Piss off, I said."

"Ten spot in it for you."

"Sleeping, here." Counts Enemies stretches his heels out on the sidewalk, rolls over to face the wall, showing Merchant his back.

Merchant folds up his road map and takes it back to his pickup. Drives around behind the M&M. Sits and listens to AM country radio, checks e-mail on his phone.

Ten minutes later, the truck door opens and Counts Enemies slips in next to him. Glances up and back, and slouches low in the seat. "Drive up toward Homestake." A voice soft as cotton, cultivated, southern accent. "And you *owe* me, man."

"Yup."

A Modoc out of Miami, Oklahoma, Johnny Counts Enemies is still one of only a handful of full blood Native Americans to graduate from the FBI academy, and the only one (to Merchant's knowledge) to graduate at the top of his class. Guy's got an I.Q. of 180 or something. Spanish, French, a smattering of Farsi. He stares out at this lamentable white man's world with the opaque pupils of his ancestors, the same glittering shards of coal that happily witnessed the scalping, emasculation, and evisceration of our own great- great-grandparents.

"You been good? How goes undercover?" Merchant pulls onto the Interstate back toward Rockjaw, climbing toward the Divide. "Still working the local cops?" Merchant has heard rumors of a prostitution ring involved the city police. And when he learned that Counts Enemies moved to Butte six months ago, it was no big jump to make the connection.

Counts Enemies squints at Merchant, considering him. "It's undercover, you know. Slow, boring. *Careful.*"

Merchant hears the reprimand. "I wouldn't ask, but I'm on a clock. A kidnapping."

Counts Enemies absorbs this. Considers the various scenarios that would compel Merchant to cash in one of his FBI chits, to risk an ongoing investigation. Ten minutes later, approaching an Interstate rest stop, he says, "Pull off here. That silver Hyundai." He hands Merchant a set of keys. "Gym bag in the trunk."

Merchant finds a black canvas gym bag between the lug wrench and spare tire. Hefting it in his hands, it's lighter than you might think.

Last time he saw a Stingray, it was housed in an aluminum casing the size of a desktop computer. Lights and knobs and handles, cable ports, a cumbersome AC power hookup. But when Counts Enemies unzips the bag, what he pulls out is the size and shape of a bag of Starbucks coffee beans, sleek in black molded plastic, rounded on the corners. He unwinds a magnetized antenna and sticks it to Merchant's roof. Produces an iPhone from his hip pocket and plugs it in. "What's the phone number?"

Merchant's got a thing for sexy hardware. He recites the number from memory, then watches as Counts Enemy plugs the digits into his iPhone. "They got Stingray apps now?"

Counts Enemies shakes his head. "You didn't see it from me."

"Yeah, sure. It's just, *damn.* That's slick."

The screen blinks, digesting digits. After a moment, a map of Montana pops up, complete with a light blue circle superimposed over Paradise Valley, south of Rockjaw. "We'll get the nearest tower first, then once we're within range, it'll triangulate with two other towers, give us an address." He sits back. "Looks like we're headed to Rockjaw."

"You don't need to get involved."

"Mr. Stingray stays with me." Counts Enemies sits back, unplugs his phone. "'Sides. I need a break. I'm beat." He kicks back, tilts his baseball cap over his eyes. "Wake me when we get there."

The question: Do you go in strong or weak? Do you appeal to vanity and ego or terror and self-preservation?

Sweeney's washed the blood from his knuckles and pulled off his necktie, folded his dress shirt neat in the back seat of the Honda. Now he's got a black Yanks cap pulled down low and some wraparound shades off the rack. No hoodie, but a yellow raincoat, flimsy as a cheap garbage bag. And *piéce de resistance*, the pizza box. Balanced flat over a fist that's gripping the Smith, the perfect little embodiment of wrath and retribution.

Sweeney glances up and down the street. Empty sidewalks, and no banks that might have cameras pointed at the street. No ATMs. No nearby stoplights with traffic surveillance. So far, so good. He uses an unbloody knuckle to press the doorbell. Hears a distant and harsh metallic buzz.

He stands there. Three minutes. Four. Presses the buzzer again. Leans on it.

The door past the bars cracks opens six inches.

Two feet away, there it is: A face that's haunted a good number of Sweeney's sleepless nights. "The fuck you want?"

"Supreme pie, extra pepperoni." Sweeney drops his head so the cap brim covers him to the nose. Keeps his eyes slightly averted. Bored with the day. Just another delivery kid with attitude.

Jasha looks Sweeney up and down. Maybe there's a flicker.

But: "I didn't order no pie." And shuts the door.

Sweeney gives it half a minute. Leans on the buzzer again. When the door opens, Sweeney's checking his rental car receipt. "This is Van Brunt, yeah?"

"Yeah, but I didn't order no pizza."

"Well, shit." Sweeney, frustrated. Stares off at the horizon. "This is the address they gave me."

"Not my problem."

Sweeney gives it a beat, then: "Wanna buy a super-sized pepperoni for five bucks?"

"Five bucks?"

"Man, how about four. I'm just throwing it away otherwise."

Jasha studies the box. "Hold on." And shuts the door.

~

The inside door opens, then the security door. Then here's Jasha, offering up a small bloom of bills.

Sweeney wedges in a heel and pushes forward with his knee. Dumps the pizza to one side. Punches into Jasha with the flat of the pistol. He's not aiming for the nose but that's what he hits. A crack of breaking bone, and Jasha's flat on the ground, undone by his appetites.

Sweeney steps into the dim odor of strip clubs (sweat, cigarettes, cheap perfume). Kicks the door shut behind him. Then stands a moment, letting his eyes adjust to the gloom.

The warehouse has been hollowed out to the exterior walls. Loose carpet scraps on the floor and a few bars of fluorescents overhead. Most of the light in the room comes from a filming studio set up at the far end of the space. Between here and there, metal utility shelves filled with DVD jewel cases and blank disks. Priority mail envelopes. And the studio? Three separate light stands, glowing behind silver umbrellas. A pair of palm-sized digital video cameras on tripods. Under the lights, a fake living room. A couch, a chair, a rug. A cheap seascape on the wall. And this: Scrambling for her clothes, the twelve-year-old girl, naked.

Sweeney, catching a glimpse of bare torso, tries to find someplace else to look.

To one side, the mother. Smoking a cigarette, lost in a private, drug-induced tour of her own bleak interior. Not even blinking at this guy who's suddenly appeared in the room, gun in hand.

Sweeney says, "Kiddie porn? Mother*fucker*."

"I remember that voice." Jasha sits up. Pinches at his nose. "You're supposed to be dead."

Sweeney takes a step and kicks Jasha hard in the ribs. "The fuck down."

Jasha grunts. "Yeah, Shakespeare. I remember you."

Sweeney gestures to the zonked-out hooker. "*You*, come here. Bring the girl. Come here. Come *here*."

Even through the heroin haze, the woman understands gestures. She staggers toward Sweeney. The girl comes along behind, buttoning her little blouse. Sweeney says to the woman, "How much is he paying you?"

"English, not so good." A thick Russian accent.

He says to the girl, "You speak English?"

The girl's fixated on Sweeney's gun. Can't take her eyes off it.

"I'm not going to hurt you. Do you speak English?"

Fragile, she nods.

"What's your name?"

"Alena." A tiny voice.

"Alena. That's a nice name. How well do you know this guy, Alena? Do you know him? How long have you known him?"

She covers her lips with her fingertips.

"Alena?"

"Momma brought him home. He's going to make me famous. Like Lady Gaga."

"Is he paying you? What's he paying you?"

The little girl proudly produces a damp square of currency, folded with the care of a doll's dress. She opens the folds and displays it for him. A ten dollar bill.

The final, largest fragments of Sweeney's well-broken heart tense and tremble and shatter.

What's Sweeney got, cash-wise? The remnants from the dead wop's stash. He switches hands with the gun, digs at his wallet. Three hundred and...ninety-five dollars. "Here." Returns the ninety-five to his wallet (cab fare) and hands the three to the girl. Says to the mother, "Those are hers. Not yours."

"Yessir."

"I mean it. Don't spend it on smack. No smack."

"Nosir."

"You do, I'll find out. I'll find *you*."

"Yessir."

"What am I doing. You don't even speak fucking English. Okay. Go." He steps to one side, gesturing toward the door. "Leave. Don't come back. Ever. Alena? Don't ever ever *ever* come back, okay?"

The little girl takes this all in as a matter of course. No theatrics, no screaming or tears. She finds her mother's hand and leads her through the open door. The mother stumbles slightly, glancing back at Jasha.

"Don't look at him. Go."

After they're gone, Sweeney pulls the door closed. Locks it. Turns back. "Jasha," he says, "How you been?"

~

Jasha, on the couch, under the lights, works hard at playing it cool. And he's got a talent for it. Spreading both arms out wide and slouching deep. A bubble of blood hangs on one nostril. "You're looking good for a corpse, Shakespeare."

"I been getting that a lot lately."

"Not the way I mean it."

A pair of rotating fans have been set up on either side of the lights, moving the stale air. Under their oscillating whirr, caught in the current of their breeze, Sweeney narrows his eyes. "You the one who killed Eddie?"

"Is that what you're here for? Payback?" Jasha manufactures his own little squint. "Nah. Wish I'd been. That sick fuck? Only a matter of time. Somebody somewhere got wise."

"What about Eddie's wife. You kill her too?"

"Tina? Did she get whacked?" He touches fingertips to his nostrils. Pulls them away to inspect the fresh dimes of blood. "Shame."

"Her and her boyfriend."

Sweeney pauses, leaving him an opening. One which, ideally, Jasha would fill with the name of Tina's boyfriend, a street address, place of employment. Instead, Jasha snorts derision.

"What's his name again? The boyfriend?" This is as subtle as Sweeney's inclined to get, all he's got time for. Aggie curled fetal on concrete.

"I didn't even know she was fucking around."

"What about that guy, what's his name...Breetvah. Yeah, her and Breetvah."

Jasha flashes surprise. Then laughs. A brief, I looked upon the face of God kind of laugh, caught between a giggle and a gulp.

"Jasha."

"You know, I never trusted you. First time I met you, back in the day, everybody's like all, *Ohhhh*, Shakespeare. Bad ass motherfucker. Smartest guy in the room. All that shit. But me, I'm like, uh uh. Guy's got narc written all over him. What do you know. I was right, they were wrong."

A small square of chamois cloth on a table behind the lights. Something to wipe off the lenses, maybe; or soak up the bitter tears of children. Sweeney wraps it around his left fist, steps forward. And: Punches Jasha in the nose. Not hard enough to push bone shards back into the sinuses but hard enough to knock him flat onto the couch.

It takes a minute, Jasha snuffling hard, wheezing, coughing, before he has the wherewithal for another empty threat. "You know who you're fucking with here? The people I know? You're dead, motherfucker. Again."

"So you got nothing to lose." Sweeney plays with the wrap of chamois. Twists it tighter around his fingers. "I need to find Breetvah."

"Dumbass."

"Breetvah, I said."

"Breetvah's dead."

"Bullshit. I know he's alive."

"*Eddie's* dead."

"Yeah, I know that much"

"Eddie *was* Breetvah, asshole."

"Bull*shit*."

"Like I said…" Jasha leans forward to blow a clot of blood out of one nostril. "Dumbass."

Sweeney stands stymied. But if that's…I don't see…Huh?

To fill the space, he says, "So was I the only one in the dark or was this common knowledge or what?"

"Me and Bytchkov knew. Always thought you did, too." Jasha wipes his nose with his forearm. Stares at the broad swath of red on his pale skin. "Eddie was Bruce Wayne, Breetvah was Batman. If Batman was, you know, a crazy-ass serial killer."

"Who killed him?"

"Donnie Moretti probably."

"Wasn't Moretti."

"Zakayev, then."

"Who?"

"Abdul Zakayev. I *know* you know that name."

The fence from his phone call. Fifty-seventh and Lex.

"One of those guys whose ass you saved when you ratted out Bytchkov. Zakayev knows it, too. What I hear, even now he's still all about Shakespeare this and that. They don't make em like that guy Shakespeare no more."

"What'd he have against Eddie?"

Jasha's eye goes to the gun, then back to Sweeney. Up to the ceiling. He sucks on a tooth. Spits blood. Says, "Zakayev's connected. Turns out, he's co-*neck*-tud. Eddie…*Breetvah*, he was in the midst of taking over territory. That's all."

"Eddie and Breetvah."

"Sick guy, man."

"Well." Sweeney finds a director's chair, fills it up with

puddled defeat.

"Not what you wanted to hear, eh?" Jasha shows bloody teeth.

Sweeney, alone. Without a plan. There is a wisdom that is woe, there is a woe that's madness, and there's a madness that's...

"But me?" Jasha says, "I'm glad to see you, Shakespeare. Means I get to tell Bytchkov we can kill you all over again."

By way of retort (but with little conviction), Sweeney shows him the pistol, one side then the other.

"That day you died? Bytchkov still lights a candle, praying your soul into hell. Now he gets to light a whole new candle. Day you died *again*. After you leave here, the clock's ticking. Think about that. You, your family, everybody you ever even *smiled* at, everybody's dead. Like grass under a mower, man." Jasha makes a horizontal gesture with his hand.

"And yet." The pistol, higher.

Scorn bleeds from the valve of his lips. "Yeah, well. People talk about Shakespeare and his hits? I heard it's all bullshit. What I heard, it was all Eddie. What I heard, you never actually had the balls to..."

Sweeney shoots Jasha not *quite* between the eyes. A little high, half-an-inch to the right. But it's enough to freeze the look of derision on the man's face. Kick his body back into the sofa. Enough to paint a Jackson Pollock, scrambled egg masterpiece on the wall behind. Maybe Sweeney's found his calling. The medium? Blood, Brain, and Bone on Brick. He considers his slow-dripping handiwork.

Meanwhile, the 250-pound slab of meat previously known as Jasha Somebody-or-other goes twitchy with its new condition. A jerk here, a shiver and a shake there. The stress of a soul leaving its body.

Sweeney waits for remorse, regret.

Nope. Nothing. Nada.

But no. Yeah, here's something.

Silence. Peace.

Past the ringing in his ears, there's a comfortable, soothing quiet. He might be standing in the only entirely-quiet corner of the five boroughs. He might be staring up through dripping trees after a hard rain. He might have just closed his eyes against a saltwater breeze and the sound of waves.

Okay, snap out of it, Sweeney. Go through the checklist. What have you touched since you walked through the door? Chamois cloth, door knob, pizza box. Put the cloth in your pocket (toss it later), wipe the knob before you leave, take the box with you.

One of the many virtues of a six shooter? No empties ejected to skitter along and lodge between floorboards.

He's good.

Homestake Pass to Rockjaw, then south. Counts Enemies pretends exhaustion. Kicked back, foot on the dash, trucker cap low. You don't see a guy in what, three years? You want to catch up a bit. But maybe Counts Enemies is pissed at him for cashing in the favor.

Eleven, twelve years ago, at a strip club in Puerto Vallarta, amid a circus of whooping, half-literate college kids from USC, Merchant and Counts Enemies were each the only representatives of their respective ethnicities. Drawn together by this slimmest of commonalities, they ended up buying each other beers, shots, lap dances. Before the night was done, they'd each spilled some personal revelations and made surfing plans for the next day. Counts Enemies knew about this little town up the beach. A good break, and off the beaten path.

Floating out on their boards, waiting in a meager lineup before dropping in, at a glance they had some shared attitude. Counts Enemies with a bloody dagger tattooed on his right forearm and on his left a tangle of hair meant to be a blond scalp. Along his back, in fierce red ink, the stylized fist of the American Indian Movement. And Merchant? He was Merchant. A black man surfing alone in Mexico. Speaks for itself.

Turning south off the Interstate, Counts Enemies pretends to jostle awake. Reaches blindly for the Stingray.

Yawns, punches up his phone. "It'll take a few seconds to triangulate."

"Okay."

"Meantime. Fill me in."

"On…?"

Counts Enemies works his lips sourly, as if he's anticipating tooth decay.

Right. Dumb question. "I got a friend, turns out, he's in WITSEC…"

"Friend or client?"

Fair question. "Friend. This is gratis."

"Okay."

"Somebody's fucking with him."

"Ah."

"*Extensively.* Up to and including the kidnapping of his woman and her daughter."

"And he didn't go to the cops because…?"

"Because the best solution might end up being a solution the cops can't abide."

Counts Enemies glances at his phone. "Where's Jack Creek?"

"Ten minutes."

"Your phone's at the head end of it. Who's your pal?"

"Not sure it's my place, man."

Counts Enemies touches Merchant on the arm. Points two fingers at his own eyes. An opaque, unreadable gesture. By the friendliest interpretation? "Hey pal, it's me. You can tell me anything." But the more likely version? "Drop me off the side of the road, then, and fuck you."

Merchant says. "Ted Sweeney. Ten years ago, he was mobbed up back in Brooklyn."

"Sweeney? No shit."

"You know him?"

"Hell yeah. He installed a sprinkler system for my cousin a few years ago. Nice guy."

"Nicest guy. Used to be a trigger for the Gambinos."

"Jesus."

"Yeah, so now it's all catching up."

"His girlfriend got snatched?"

"Aggie. Her teenage daughter as well."

"So the kidnapper's phone is up Jack Creek?"

"Yeah."

Counts Enemies reaches into the black gym bag between his feet, pulls out an FBI standard Glock 22, .40 caliber, 15 rounds. Releases the magazine to check the load. Opens the slide and blows air theatrically through the mechanism. And for the first time since he's known him, Merchant sees the man smile. A brilliant, beatific, sunshine-through-clouds kind of grin. You can't help but return it. "Well, oh*kay* then."

Here's the thing about Eddie Adamo.

Jealousy.

That's it, what you need to know. His whole life, the guy's one jealous sonofabitch.

Take cousin Cosmo, for instance. Cosmo had *stability*. Born with a silver spoon full of it. Mother, father, sister, they all sat down to dinner. Cosmo's old man was a little hardnosed, sure. But he was *there*.

The flip side? Eddie's dad split early, fleeing in fits and starts. He was a weekend dad, then Christmas and Easter. An address and a phone number in the Bronx. The smell of bourbon and Old Spice equals, to this day, childhood nostalgia. Ten, eleven years old, Eddie'd see small families at street fairs, parades. Mom and Dad swinging a toddler up by the hands. "*Whooops*ie daisy." And his first thought? "T'hell with *all* you people."

An only child, Eddie suffered from an ailment common to that species, the arrogance that arises from being the sole and unwilling, helplessly-addicted recipient of his mother's affections. An Italian of that postwar generation, a woman whose formative years were defined by want, by need, Zita Adamo saw heftiness as virtuous, as something to *achieve*. The woman waddled through her late thirties and early forties, a gradually ballooning Zeppelin of closely-held tomato sauce recipes, strong opinions about the second Vatican council, and an infatuation with all things Kennedy. There were two men in Zita's life: young Jack-Jack and her son Eddie.

From thirteen, fourteen, Eddie hit the streets. What's school got to teach him? Algebra, biology, Hemingway. The fuck *ever*, man. I'll be over here. He was the ghost in his mother's apartment, leaving before breakfast, home after dark. A presence that shut doors soft behind him. Lingering only long enough to recharge the batteries of his ego, depleted by an uncaring world. A pinch of a cheek. And, "You so bello, intelligente. You got a girlfriend yet? No? Kay. No one in this America good enough for bello."

Eddie on the street. He's got the mullet and the comb, a heart on his thigh tattooed with a needle and Bic ink. Here's a kid who never let nothing show. He's got more layers than geology. He's got rings like an oak tree. Instead of sap he bleeds scorn. How'd he get this way? Nature or nurture or what?

Take a moment, any moment. Pick one. The March he turned eighteen. A Pisces, sure, but that whole fish and water thing? Passive and sensitive? Bullshit. Kid was a bull, maybe a crab, singlehandedly turning the astrology racket up on its ear. A day with a late spring snowstorm. Heavy, wet flakes, hitting hard, and Eddie had his jacket tented up over his head, running for the tire shop.

Ten minutes late, he grabbed his overalls off a hanger, tried to make himself inconspicuous as he hopped on one foot, pulling them on. Then, yeah, there was that knock of metal against glass, the Nose in his office. Waving Eddie up.

So. The tire job? Good while it lasted.

Eddie passed Cosmo with his broom. Gives him a shrug. What're-you-gonna-do.

"Boss, hey, this snowstorm, I just…"

"Sit down. Shut up. You want coffee?"

"Sure, uh yeah. Boss."

They kicked back with Styrofoam cups. Nose considered his philosophically. "You're a good kid."

Eddie double clutched. Getting fired to maybe getting promoted. "Thanks, boss."

"You got ambition, yeah? You want a go places, work your way up the ladder, am I wrong?"

"You ain't wrong, boss."

"You know how to keep your mouth shut."

"You ain't wrong again."

"Yeah, uh huh. So I got me a…*delicate* kind of situation over by Coney Island." He sipped his horrible coffee. Made a face at it.

"What's that, boss?"

"Gimme a second, Jesus. I'm thinking how to put it into words."

"Sorry, boss."

Turns out, the Nose was Shylocking. Small timing it with some micro loans. "What a pain in the ass." A pain compounded by the restrictions of turf. How he couldn't step on nobody's toes. "Everybody and their brother's already got their territory, yeah? So if I want to get into this particular business, I got to go where nobody else wants to go. Brighton Beach."

"The Russians, boss?"

"Just one so far, but yeah."

Turns out, he had this barber with a mysterious debt, some yid from eastern Yovakiastan. "The guy's stiffing me. Not even returning my calls." But the Nose couldn't let loose his usual apes. "The Russians, is why. They have their own thing. Somebody's cousin'd be burning down my tire shop."

Long story short, he wanted unintimidating Eddie to go put some pressure on the guy. Classic Nose kind of move. Subtle. A couple different agendas. Test Eddie, get the money, send a message. "You're shaving already, yeah? Go get a hot towel treatment. Maybe you talk to him about paying his bills, maybe you don't. You're a kid. He ain't going to feel like I'm threatening him or nothing. Then you come back, tell me what you seen. We're moving in slow on this one."

Eddie had been to Brighton Beach one other time, when he was maybe eight or nine. There was some kind of hazy memory. A Coney Island day that got rained out. Couple hours spent looking for a candy store from his dad's own youth. "They got a fountain of chocolate. A *fountain*."

Anyway, he heard the place had changed. One thing to *hear* about it, though, another thing to see it firsthand. Jesus, man. Look at the signs. Gorbachev, cold war, Reagan. Good-will Games. But these commies still had the balls to put up store awnings in Cyrillic? Thirty-three odd letters each one like a phlegmy commie flag, waving out over Eddie's beloved Brooklyn.

Nose gave him a Neptune Avenue address. Hoodie up tight, boombox under one arm, Eddie ambled past a wedge of narrow storefront, squeezed between a deli and a dry cleaners. No awning, but a crude paper sign taped across the window, blocking most of the glass. Half a dozen Russian letters in Sharpy scrawl. A crude pair of scissors drawn as if by a sixth grader. One o'clock in the afternoon, the lights were on inside, and shadows move past. Off the bottom edge of the paper, Eddie glimpsed wingtips.

Eddie squatted on a square of sidewalk across the street. Tipped an old man's fedora up beside his boombox and dropped his forehead on his knees. Punched play on a tape of Rachmaninoff. A ray of sun spotlighted just another junky kid angling for change.

Over the course of the next five hours, Eddie earned twenty-three dollars in nickels and dimes, and counted thirteen Russian soldiers rotating through the barbershop. Six of them wore track suits, lemon yellow to blood orange. You can't buy taste, and it don't take a genius to spot a racket. Nobody was getting haircuts. Nobody was coming out preening, touching their new dos. They were all younger men, mid-level and lower. Most with the heavy lips and prominent brows of eastern Europe. It wasn't Christie Tick's over across from Dyker Park, that's for sure. Bush league, is what it was. The Nose didn't have nothing to worry about, was Eddie's opinion.

But then this last guy? A garish, rust-red sport coat that matched his pants. A flash of gold watch. Twenty pounds overweight, and he took his time with an affected cane. Enjoying the day. He paused at the storefront, glanced at the time, stepped down inside. By Eddie's own Timex, thirty-two seconds passed before he was back out on the street, making an envelope disappear.

The barber was either paying up the ladder or paying off debts. Given the day's rotating thugs, Eddie's bet was that he was paying up. So Nose *might* have a problem. Competition for the yid's wad from some well-connected pinko.

Eddie pulled himself off the pavement, pocketed his loose change, set the fedora firm on his head. Gave it a tilt. Ambled across the street and pushed into the barbershop like he owned the place.

Confidence, kid.

In coming years, elder Eddie, the blood-smeared creature with a rap sheet ten yards long and enough chutzpah to flood the streets of New York, to soak the city like Sandy, he'll look back on this moment with a nostalgia typically reserved for puppies and babies, weddings and graduations, beautiful moments long, long gone.

Ten minutes since the Russian capo left with his cut, Eddie found the barber still collapsed in a swivel chair. Head in his hands. Red hair gone gray in a greasy combover. He looked up at Eddie with red-rimmed eyes. "What you want?" A thin man, short, but with a voice deep enough to startle.

"I'm here from the Nose. We need our money." Nothing subtle or artful. Gimme money.

The barber was unsurprised. The world kicks you when you're down. "I no got it." He dropped his head into his hands.

Eddie felt dismissed. "That don't matter. We need it."

Without looking up, the man made a gesture with one hand. "Shoo. Leave. Little boy, go home."

Little boy? Yeah, no. Not the right thing to say.

Eddie glanced around for a handy bludgeon, too flustered to see much past his own umbrage. Decided on a simple smack up the head. "Old man. Money?"

But then…just like *that*, the spritely old turd had Eddie's wrist and had him twirled (with a clatter of combs and scissors) up against the mirror. Fingers wrapped around Eddie's windpipe.

"All you people. All, all the same." Despite the strength of his grip, the old man started to tear up. "Take a man who works his whole lifetime and…suck him dry…tear him *apart*. Apart!"

Eddie's left hand pried helplessly at the old man's fingers. He couldn't breathe. His lungs started to burn and his tongue grew thick. His right hand played a frantic piano riff down the shelf, searching. Came up with a straight razor resting in soapy water. He brought the blade around with a warm splash, a seminal jet of foam.

His first grip on the thing, he only got the handle, and so the blade swung back loose. But it was still enough to trace a line of red on the barber's cheek. Enough for the old guy to loosen his grip. Enough for Eddie to find a purchase, really get to work.

Using Jasha's keys, Sweeney locks the warehouse behind him. Turns to face a blinding Brooklyn morning. Nearly lunchtime. Cars idling by, and a distant hum from the BQE. Improbably, it's still just an average American day. Another in a near-infinite series.

Some consolation to think that his was almost certainly not the most evil act committed in the borough this morning. Indeed, according to a certain Old Testament, Hammurabi view of justice, what Sweeney did was downright righteous.

Ambling slow toward his rental car, he holds this fragile thought as long as he can, tends to it like a lit match in the wind. On the way, he lets Jasha's keys slip discretely into a storm grate.

He gets in his Honda, pulls away from the curb, studious with his blinker. Five blocks along, he wads up the cap and jacket and dumps them in a public trash bin. Two blocks after that, he finds another bin for the blood-spotted chamois cloth.

The smart money would tell him to get rid of his pistol, and as soon as possible. But not yet. Just…gimme a minute. He's shaky, and finds street parking on Verona beside Coffey Park. Lights a cigarette. Stares.

You're out there in the blue, Sweeney. A smile and a shoeshine.

Eddie was Breetvah? Fuuhhuck me running.

Is Breetvah?

Breetvah, who has kidnapped Aggie and Elizabeth. Couldn't be. Why would he?

If true, it changes things.

What reason would Jasha have to lie? No reason. Although and of course, people don't *need* a reason.

If true, it changes…everything. It also, yeah, makes a certain kind of venomous sense.

One of Eddie's own theories: Nobody knows nobody.

It's the kind of meaningless axiom we stumble across twenty times a day. Never rains but it pours, a bird in the hand, takes one to know one. But accept *this* little chestnut at face value—nobody knows *nobody*—it's enough to kill you slow, drown you in crushed ice, burn you from inside out.

Seven billion people in the world, and all of us preaching, kissing, fucking, juggling on stages and texting in cars, begging to be appreciated, praised. Alarums and excursions, flattery and insult, thieving and giving, fistfights and hugged reconciliation, and yet we're all still hidden from each other. A wife votes Democrat, never telling her Republican husband. A priest delivers the host with a tremble, but jerks off three hours later with jumper cables clipped to his nipples. The brutish football coach likes to slip, evenings, into his wife's panties, and a beloved cousin, your wingman, the confidante of your life, moonlights as a Russian psychopath.

Save it for later, Sweeney. It don't help you with Aggie.

Unless it does.

Among the various ambushes of the past forty-eight hours? Jasha's comment about Bytchkov lighting a candle for Sweeney's death day. August 12.

He's been inclined to resist the notion that his death was

unduly meaningful. Sure, there are a few out there to whom his existence meant something. His mother, sister, Eddie. But everybody else? Forget about it. What's that saying? The cemeteries are full of indispensable people.

Tina's phone sits face up on the seat beside him.

What the hell. They had a thing.

He hits the starts button. Gets her password screen. Punches it in…0812.

And sonofabitch, it works. Just like that, her phone's alive in his hand. A window into her life. Bank accounts, browsing history, Facebook. Just like that, he's got it all.

With the tip of one thick, ungainly finger, he touches an e-mail icon. Inflates a list of her most recent messages.

First three are from Gap, Pottery Barn, Macy's. Light blue, and unread.

Below them, a personal note. The text in gray, having been opened.

Adamo, Eddie
RE: Georgie
Yesterday, 11:32 PM

"Sorry about your brother. We'll take it out of Moretti's ass. Text me after you get the stones. E."

Eddie.
Cousin Eddie, who moonlights as Breetvah.
Breetvah, who has kidnapped Aggie.
That Eddie?
That Eddie.
Playing the same note (revenge as consolation) that

Sweeney had offered Tina in the hotel room. And even through his umbrage, his sense of betrayal, Sweeney enjoys this slight, serendipitous connection to his cousin. Great minds, and all that.

The initial spray of barber's blood ebbed fast: a shower to a leak to a dribble. The old man was astonished, then not. Acceptance faded to melancholy. His eyes fixed on the blade in Eddie's hand. The sight drew a smile. It's how he'd made his living, right? That razor? Which made his an ironical kind of death. He breathed one last, effortful word, the syllables bubbling up past his larynx: "Breet. Vah." Then stiffened. Died.

Eddie, on the other hand, was as alive as ever. Bloody as a newborn. He'd done it. Finally, thank you, Jesus. He'd made it. Entered the ranks of the truly badass. Murderers. *Big* time, man.

From this moment, he will trail behind him—in the manner of all murderers—an entire civilization of poorly paid detectives, tired forensic specialists, hack journalists, memento collectors, mourners, macabre mob aficionados, an invisible bleacher's-worth of…devotees? A good word. He'll take it. Hundreds of people, maybe thousands, who will find themselves in some ways *devoted* to this moment.

Assuming he could get away with it. So first thing? He walked to the door. Left some bloody sneaker prints but nothing to be done about that now. Remember it for next time. Shoe covers like nurses wear. He covered his fingers in his sleeve and twisted a deadbolt, locked himself in. Turned off the lights. A pool of blood around the barber went metallic in the dusk.

Next thing? Wash your hands, face. He pulled off his blood-stained hoodie. Found a garbage bag full of hair. Dropped the hoodie in, twisted the bag tight.

Final thing, misdirect. Give those legions of cops something to chew over. Some place to look other than the Italianos.

It needed a pen, or a pencil. A brush. A shaving brush. Write something. Something in Russian. What's he know from Russian?

Vodka, Stalin, Leningrad.

Breetvah.

He dabbed the brush into the pool of barber blood. Touched it to linoleum and made it halfway through the capital B before his ink ran out. Dabbed it down again. Got creative with the double Es.

It took him about ten minutes and most of the blood, but then…well *done*. Well done.

Then: What the fuck's it mean?

He found door keys in his barber's pocket. Dumped the brush in the bag with his hoodie. Unlocked the door, locked it again behind him. Head down. Play it casual. New York at dusk, nobody notices nobody.

His dark pants glittered under streetlights. Stay away from the subways.

A city full of the petty criminals, pickpockets and shoplifters, gangbangers playing it tough and tough guys falling flat. Bartenders aspiring to bodyguards and bodyguards playing sycophants until they can segue to extortionist. None of that's Eddie. Not anymore.

It was a long walk back Bay Ridge, and he was twenty blocks into it before he found the razor in his pocket.

Call it a souvenir.

Worst news in Marilyn's life, it's always come to her over the phone. Her experience, people pass along good news in person. They want to see your face. Bad news? It slips most easily through a phone line.

Her mother's first cancer report: "They say it's in both breasts, but you know, they're optimistic." And six months later? Her father, sobbing from Mayo in Minnesota. "She's gone." Ted's first phone call from the jail in Yonkers. "Yeah, hey, you're going to have to come up and bail me out." Then again, from the DA's office in Midtown. "They're saying Montana."

And now she sits in her prowler, staring out past a bug spattered windshield (grasshoppers caught under the wiper blades) toward a parking lot gone sepia in the heat. The road dust lies low in an inversion. Her cell phone cupped in both hands like a religious artifact. She's in the midst of a moment of vertigo, a disconnect so profound it nears nausea. Rachel Aniello in Montana. In a deputy's uniform. You never get used to it.

She has four messages, all from Ted. And all of increasing length, complexity, and apparent implausibility. From the first call-me-back to the last, which fills up the entire allotted three minutes of memory, and ends with the words, "which means, yeah, he's this goddamn psychopath or something, and must have a grudge against me long as your fucking arm to be doing what he's doing, and you know what really gets me, the thing I can't figure out, the thing the breaks my heart? Is that I...." Beeeeep.

Marilyn's prowler has become a trawler. She's lashed to the steering wheel in a storm, tossed through rolling troughs steep as canyons.

Sweeney in New York. That's the first thing. Her hunger not only for the background detritus of the city—the pneumatic wheeze of busses, distant Spanish; passing sirens (all of it hitting her ear the way drops of water find a cupped palm)—but for Sweeney's tone as well. That hint of Cosmo. This more than anything. A little of the old Brooklyn coming through, a little fuck you. Not just the accent (although that too), but the confidence. Even those words, "breaks my heart," were spoken with his old swagger, a self-depreciating I'm-just-fuckin-witch-ya kind of lilt.

That man, *that* man...

To her genuine astonishment, turns out she's missed him so goddamn much.

Counts Enemies, flipping through his CDs, says, "You got any hip hop?"

"What, I'm black, I got to be into rap?"

"Before I bust into a place—and granted, it's been a while—me, I like to get my bounce on. You know. NWA, Eazy-E. Older stuff. Get some *anger* running through. It helps."

"How about Curtis Mayfield?"

"Seriously?" He finds the CD. Tilts it up to the light for scratches. "Yeah, this'll work."

They sit listening to the bass line of "Pusherman." Counts Enemies nods. "Yeah, this'll work."

"Lot of people don't hear the sour under the sweet."

"So how we doing this?"

Merchant knows all the trailheads in Paradise Valley. Has his favorites, but he's hiked them all. His first year in Rockjaw, Jack Creek was his introduction. A quick drive from town, it picks up the dog walkers and geriatrics. Picnic tables and fire pits. But you get tired of dodging dog shit, so Merchant left this particular trail behind. He still remembers this cabin, though. Hard to forget it.

Couple hundred yards up from the gravel road to the trailhead, it stares down over the valley with unblinking windows, the leering teeth of a two-story porch, a patrician air of tolerance, silently suffering the parade of unwashed heathen treating themselves to a hike.

They're parked a quarter mile away. Counts Enemies says, "So if it's just the two of us, the only way we can do it where the hostages don't get killed, we set up a sniper post, wait until the guy shows himself. *Pop*. Done."

"There's a chance it might not be the right guy, yeah?"

"So we watch the house until we can verify the hostages."

"No time."

"Knock on the door. The guy answers, we shove a pistol in his ear."

"Might be more than one."

"So call the cops. Tell them you saw a guy dragging a woman in there against her will. Probable cause. Let the locals do the work."

They chew this over, staring at the house. They both come to the same conclusion at the same time. The only real option. Let the locals take over. Counts Enemies has his Glock, but drops it back into the canvas sack. Metal knocks against metal. "Ah well. That was going to be…"

"Yeah."

Merchant's cell phone rings. He checks out the number. "Speak of the devil."

"Who's that?"

"Marilyn Sweeney." Merchant shows him the number. "The locals."

Even the worst of us are restrained by circumstance, chained by cause and effect, shackled by rhyme and reason. But what if there is no rhyme, no reason? What if there is will but no conscience? Eddie Adamo at his worst? It needs a macabre highlight reel. Sportscenter meets the Oscar death montage

One o'clock in the morning, Eddie and Nose, having just locked up the tire shop, stand in the cold, adjusting to the city's near silence. The echoing growl of engines, distant laughter, garbage trucks. They could see their breaths. Nose shivered deeper into his coat, said, "D'you hear about that Russian guy? That barber?"

"What about him?"

Three days since Eddie's visit. After Eddie had given Nose his report ("Leave the guy alone a while, is my advice."), there'd been nothing. No obituary, no crime report. Nothing. Was it possible that the guy was so isolated, so alone, nobody even checked in on him? Solitary old fuck, deserved what he got.

"Somebody punched his ticket." Nose drew a finger across his neck. "I guess I weren't the only one he pissed off."

"Too bad."

"Gutted like a fucking pig. Plus, I heard they cut his balls off."

"Jesus." All this news to Eddie, of course, but he didn't miss the note of admiration in the Nose's voice.

Nose never smiled, but now the slabs of his cheeks twitched. He rubbed his hands together in a way that suggested pleasure. He was a minor leaguer who'd just been given inside dish about the Yanks. "Jesus is right. This world we live in, kid. I swear."

Twenty hours later, in a mist of rain, Eddie stood under an umbrella, staring up at the second story of a Russian restaurant. On the gray awning, in English and Cyrillic: "The Russo-America—Fine Cuisine." Women in black moved past the windows, faces hidden under veils of dark lace. Radishes in sour cream, crunching under white teeth. Chilled vodka sweating in shot glasses. The sound of an accordion, a muted trumpet blowing slow and sad. A *semi*-Orthodox wake.

As the rain drifted past, Eddie folded his umbrella, shook his last cigarette from a crumpled pack. Watched as the barber's capo, the pudgy commie with the cane, staggered out of the restaurant. Misread the three steps and lunged forward onto an absent fourth. Caught himself against the railing, hung there for a while. Straightened, touched his fedora. Looked around, pleased with the world. Wobbled down the sidewalk. Turned into an alley. Cue the sound of urine splattering against garbage cans.

Eddie with his razor, held low at his hip, stepped up behind. "Nice night."

The Russian started a little. Dick in hand, drew a wet zigzag on the wall. He saw white teeth in the gloom, and returned the grin. "Nice night, yes. Indeed." A cultured voice, measured. Careful with the sibilants in the way of a practiced drunk.

Later, Eddie rested the Russian's head (surprisingly heavy) wetly on a garbage can. Turned it toward the street, just so.

Tucked a note into the man's mouth. "Breetvah." Took a few steps back and bent to touch the man's wrist, his lapels. Found the gold watch and an envelope within the jacket, thick as a Louis L'amour novel. *Indeed.*

Eddie, given his nose for a buck, an oenophile of opportunism, started hanging out in Brighton Beach. All the good music was out of Seattle, the beefiest cabernets were bottled in Napa, and the smartest cons were being played by the Russians. A dog to vomit, for an aspiring wise guy, you go where the money is.

He found his bar on the boardwalk. Nice weather, they opened up the French doors to let a breeze through. Three, four times a week, Eddie picked up the N train to Coney Island, took a walk down the beach toward his Absolut on the rocks. Turns out, American Russians don't fancy Russian vodka. Something about leaving the homeland behind. Instead, they go for Absolut. The afternoon bartender had this little chip on her shoulder, and gave him his drink with her upper lip one twitch away from a sneer. Short little sexpot, with a cascade of black curly hair halfway to her ass. Sexy as hell. She kept some hand weights behind the bar, and worked on her guns when business was slow. Her name was Raisa, and in addition to Russian, she spoke Spanish like a Spaniard, English like a professor. But kept the TV tuned to insipid Mexican soaps operas.

Took some time, but Eddie finally found the spoon to crack her shell. She was waiting for him to buy her drinks. Shot after shot of vodka, and Eddie tipping big with each shot. They don't go for subtle, the Russians. After her shift was over, took their private party to a table by the jukebox. Drank, and developed a rapport. They only screwed the one time (two nights later, Eddie held her ankle up to his ear like it was a salute), but respected each other as fellow aspirants. They *wanted*.

Raisa came to know enough about Eddie—the tire shop, Nose, his cousin Cosmo—such that when Bytchkov and Jasha finally dropped in for a snort, she could give Eddie a meaningful tilt of her head. *That* guy.

Eddie went for a leak, came back to read his paper one stool down. Took his time with the business section, eavesdropping. Finally, through the guttural gargles, he heard his word: Breetvah. Heard it again, punctuated by an approving palm slap hard to the bar. Then again, as Bytchkov and Jasha touched their shot glasses, drank fast.

Eddie folded his paper. Said, "You know Breetvah?"

Bytchkov turned on his stool. "Excuse me, we are have our conversation. Not you."

"Me, I know Breetvah."

Bytchkov stared at the toes of Eddie's cheap sneakers and moved up, laying down judgment. Then dismissed him with a puff of air through hairy nostrils. "I do not think so."

Suave, nonchalant as hell, Eddie dropped a heavy gold watch on the bar. "We should talk, Mr. Bytchkov."

Eddie over the next six, seven years? His jawline goes loose and his shoulders go hard, and he coughs like a consumptive, squinting through the smoke. Working over his razor with the tired, jaded eyes of a sweatshop seamstress. His foreman and conductor, Grigory Bytchkov, pointing the way according to his own arcane agendas, his own opaque and particular reasons: This guy, that guy, him over there. And Breetvah, of course, blooms. A man over whom neither Bytchkov nor even Eddie Adamo feels like they have complete control.

Finally, here's Eddie in his early forties. A nice Sunday morning in Brooklyn. A doorbell, and Eddie comes to the door in a cardigan. Gray at his temples and a pair of reading glasses hooked to his shirt. Time beats us all in the end, even the arrogant, even the murderous. Which is perhaps a consoling thought for the rest of us.

Eddie had the Sunday crossword folded under one arm. "Donnie, great to see you. Thanks for the call. Marky, great tie. Come on in. Let me get you a cup of coffee."

Donnie Moretti, breathing hard after a brief walk from the curb, said, "Thanks, yeah. Coffee." Beside him, Marky Schena, in his suit and silk tie (a clothes horse in the tradition of Tony the Trigger) failed to return Eddie's smile.

Between the two men, a guy Eddie didn't recognize. Russian, from Eddie's quick glance. Confirmed by the accent. "Pleased to make your acquaintanceship." A dry handshake, spotless fingernails. A flinchy, pleading way of glancing at Moretti: Are we partners or am I a hostage or what?

Eddie called into the house. "Tina? Coffee?"

From the kitchen: "What, are your legs broken? Get it your own fuckin' self." She came to the door between rooms, wearing yoga pants and a sweatband. "Oh, hey. Donnie. Sorry about that. Yeah, I'll get you some coffee."

Settling into chairs, Eddie said, "Apologies for my wife. She don't got no manners."

Moretti made a sympathetic gesture. What're you gonna do.

Eddie poured cream, offered it around. Stirred a spoon into his coffee. Set it smoking on a napkin. "Gentleman?"

Moretti didn't drink coffee, which Eddie well knew. But it had been offered, and this was another man's house. He took a sip. Which told Eddie volumes about the errand. Moretti needed a favor. Big one. "Word has it, Eddie, you got an inside track to this guy, Breetvah."

"Who now?"

Moretti gave him a look. *Please*. "Word has it, this guy Breetvah, he's moved some stones. He's connected that way."

Eddie played it quiet-and-reflective.

"Me, I can go find a buyer for a couple rocks here and there. But we got a big order here. I need an introduction."

"How big's the order?"

Moretti tried on his version of a grin. A rictus of lips pulled back with fishhooks. "Show him there, Marky."

Marky produced a cheap black velvet bag from his jacket pocket. Worked at a knot and tipped the mouth toward the table. Spilled a few stones.

Eddie swallowed.

Marky rattled the rest of the bag for effect. Fed the spilled stones back into the mouth and made the bag disappear again.

The Russian had watched the bag the way a cat watches a can opener. Once the bag was out of sight, his eyes went back to Moretti.

Okay, so the Russian was here buying....what, exactly? Maybe influence. Moretti's connections. Him and de Blasio have had lunch. Leverage to fast track his American citizenship, a string of no-show management positions. But membership in this club would be contingent upon liquidation and laundry.

The machinery behind Eddie's eyes picked up speed. Turbines hummed, fans kicked in. You could almost smell the ozone-stink of burning wires, insulation. "I can make an introduction."

Moretti: "When?"

"Couple days? He ain't in New York, and he don't come into town that often."

"Couple days." Moretti frowned.

"Nothing I can do. Also, all due respect Donnie. He gets twitchy around his, you know, peers. The fewer people meet him, the better. He's going to want to see your buddy here, so they can speak Russian. See who they went to grade school with, or some fucking thing. And he'll tolerate Marky here, cause he knows you need to represent. But it might be better if you sit this one out."

Moretti studied Eddie. Came to a decision. Nodded once, quick.

And in that moment, Moretti lost his rocks but saved his life.

The old days, Moretti ran his business out the back of an Italian restaurant. Maybe he's still got it. Anyway, the kind of place that left a residue, a slime on the skin. Moretti's wall-eyed nephew behind the bar; osteoporotic aunt for a hostess; a nine-year-old nail biter for a busboy. The restaurant sat over a soundproofed basement where Donnie used to conduct his Q & As. On the occasion of Sweeney's one and only visit, an informant had sat chained from the ceiling, hanging like beef, unconscious, one eye out of its socket. Moretti passed Sweeney some homemade brass knucks. Folded them up in Sweeney's hand like a grandmother passing along nickels. "Feel like breaking some cheek bones?"

Sweeney finds Moretti now under the fluorescents of his own Bay Ridge Hardee's. From the street, he's hunched like a moist toadstool, food tray picked clean by fat, agile fingers. Nothing left but crumbs, a sprinkle of salt, a smear of ketchup.

Coming in the door, Jimmy Rugg stands up quick, blocking Sweeney's path. He's got this look.

Sweeney, "What?"

Jimmy Rugg pats him down, and he's not gentle with it. Hands hard against Sweeney's ribs, inside his legs. He steps back. Tilts his head. "We've just buhheen sitting here, me and Lucho, thinking about that trick you pulled."

"Which trick now?"

"That one where you made everybody think you were dead."

"Ah."

"Lucho had to point it out, what kind of cold, *cold* blooded shit that is, man." Rugg is angry enough, maybe he's on the edge of tears. "Took me a while, but that shit? That's juhhust unforgiveable. It just is."

Sweeney spread his hands. How do you respond to unforgiveable?

"And that thing you said about grabbing lunch?" Rugg broke his gaze. "That's a dick thing to say, man. You just needed to know that. You ever need backup, don't look my way. That's all." He jerked his head back at Moretti. "Donnie? We're over here you need us."

Unstable now, wobbly, Sweeney pushes past Rugg to approach Moretti. Supplicant before the Pope.

Moretti was never a looker, but this light's doing nothing for him. Complexion like sandpaper coated in Elmer's glue, cellulite in the jowels, bags under his eyes. A cheap chrome cane against the wall and, with one leg stretched out long, fabric hiked up to show a shin swollen under orthotic hose. Sweeney feels a twinge of sympathy. But then, no. Careful with that shit, Sweeney. There's no advantage to sympathy. Wave it away like it's a bee.

"Them guys there," Moretti says, "they're some kind of pissed at you. You know that?"

"I got that feeling, yeah."

"Jimmy Rugg, sweetest man on the face of the earth. You know what kind of asshole it takes to get Jimmy Rugg pissed at him?"

A rhetorical question.

"Me, I got no problem with what you done. I'm a, what's that word, that word you and Eddie was always throwing around. Sounded like pig, only had an R in it."

"Pragmatist."

"Yeah, that's me. I'm a pragmatist. Do whatever you got to do to get the job done. You didn't do nothing against me and mine, so far as I'm concerned we're all in good shape here."

Nothing Sweeney hadn't expected. "Reason I'm back in New York, Mr. Moretti, I got me a problem. I hear you got one, too. So I'm wondering if you'll let me help you with yours. And I'm hoping maybe you can help with mine. Maybe we can *quid pro quo* us some solutions."

Moretti stares at him with cloudy eyes, dead as a snake shedding its skin. "Do fucking tell."

Marilyn is fond of Cal Merchant, but cautiously so. There's something, something...He makes her feel a bit of a fraud, honestly. She sees measured respect but never anxiety. The sheriff's outfit, the pistol, the badge: you get used to a certain deference. But Merchant's default attitude is bemusement. Here's Sweeney's ex, playing cop. To her credit, she realizes that she wouldn't be so sensitive if there weren't some truth to it.

Coming up to him, she pulls off her vest, unripping Velcro. She pinches up her sweaty blouse, airing out the sweat under her arms. "Hot day."

A ring of ponderosa pine saplings were planted when the asphalt driveway was laid down. Merchant stands among them, inconspicuous, watching the bizarre of flashing red and blue lights. A parking lot of sheriff's deputies, staties, an ambulance. Slow news day in Rockjaw. "They're saying it might get up to a hundred."

"Where's your friend? The guy with the braids?"

"Hitchhiked back into town. Said something about Greyhound."

"You got his information? We might need to get in touch."

"Yeah, I wouldn't do that."

"Might need to."

"Don't." His face pleasant but his tone cold.

"Last time I checked, Cal, I wasn't working for you."

"Big day for Park County law enforcement, yeah?" He might be giving her the temperature again.

She rolls with it, for now. "You heard about the floaters? You ain't kidding."

EMTs emerge from the basement's sliding glass doors, aluminum gurney between them. On the gurney, Aggie's unconscious, face hidden by an oxygen mask. Forearm pierced by a saline drip.

"She was in there alone? Her daughter wasn't with her."

"We found ropes around two poles. But yeah, just Aggie." She considers for a moment, weighing her words. "And a warm cup of coffee in the kitchen."

"Okay."

"So he saw us coming. Slipped out the back. Little Dry Creek trailhead's just over the hill thataway, maybe he kept a car parked."

"Ted's cousin."

"He told you that?"

"He gave me the name. Cousin wasn't too hard from there."

"You're good at that, I guess."

"What I do."

Reluctantly, resisting the urge to push back, fighting her own umbrage over Merchant's missing Indian, she says, "Thank you for helping him."

Merchant reaches over to knead her shoulder a bit. "You're welcome. I'm always here for you and your man."

"Well, he's not...I'm not..."

"No?" Merchant, pleasant. "Whatever you say." He touches a forefinger to an imaginary cowboy hat. "Ma'am. I got some things to do. Left a pot on the stove. But you call me when you track down this piece of shit. I want to be there."

It all comes down to cell phones.

Here's how quickly life changes. You're standing on a highway berm, listening as a Harley chugs and burps toward you, sound waves compressed into a rising scale. Then the bike flips by, and the waves elongate, descend and disappear. That's life before cell phones, life after. Miracles.

No snake without its garden, though; with the miracle comes the digital presumptive guilt called homeland security. Life is reduced to a string of zeroes and ones, and everything about us (Netflix, Amazon, Gmail) available to the suspicious with the click of a mouse. On his bad days, Sweeney considers himself less citizen than subject.

He drives around Grand Army Plaza a couple full orbits, trying to choose between Prospect Park and the Botanical Gardens. Figures the park's likely crowded with the last of the lunchtime joggers, decides on a sliver of green space beside the Gardens, a bench looking down on the Eastern Parkway. Right where the cars start to speed up, released from the roundabout. Used to be a favorite place with his sister's kids. Good set of swingsets.

He settles in and spreads out a little. Breathes.

He's been putting it together from Eddie's perspective; Maybe he's got it close to figured out.

So Eddie steals the stones from Moretti. But the only way he can get away with it, given Moretti's personality, is if

Eddie's already dead. Otherwise, it's Jabba the hut and Han Solo. Eddie's getting hunted down, put in carbonite, displayed behind the throne. Or, very least, dumped in the Hudson.

Okay, so Eddie's dead. But if he's dead, how do you go about moving the rocks? All his old contacts will be kaput. It's a dilemma.

But maybe one solved by his old partner, the Laurel to his Hardy, good old Cosmo.

Who's apparently got this whole other life now. In Montana.

So how do we deal with that?

And this is where Sweeney's logic breaks down. He doesn't see it, can't understand. If Eddie was in a jam, why not just *ask* for help? Why all the bullshit? Photos in envelopes and Tina's elaborate lies. It don't make no kind of sense.

Sitting on the bench, holding Tina's cell phone, Sweeney feels like when him and Marilyn were first dating. That nervousness. But now, what's he got to be nervous about? It's just Eddie.

Only of course it's not. He's truly got no idea who this guy is.

Fuck it.

He lights up Tina's cell, punches in her code. Dials Eddie's number.

A distant bring, bring, bring. A click, background noise, then that familiar, familiar voice: "Tina? Where the *fuck* you been?"

~

He knows that voice. *Knows* it. The smooth buildup with a bullying catch at the end. "What's up, cousin?"

Eddie, walking fast and breathing hard. Background static of wind and branches slapping. "Cosmo?" It takes him a few breaths, but he eventually manages the warmest kind of chuckle. "Shit man, how are you?"

"Pretty good, pretty good. How about you?"

"Not bad at all. So."

"So."

A chuckle. "So how'd you figure it out?"

"Tina's phone."

"*Her* phone?"

"Password's the day I died."

"Treacherous bitch." He says it pleasantly enough.

"Aggie okay? Elizabeth?"

"Your girls. Yeah, they're in one piece." A long pause while he walks. "Speaking of treacherous bitches, though."

Sweeney has…Jesus, Sweeney has questions. He's got questions the way you got forks and knives in a kitchen drawer. Stacked, compartmentalized. Best to go at it obliquely. Opt for light banter. "What I want to know, Eddie, when'd you learn Photoshop like that? That picture with your throat cut? Brilliant."

"Photoshop my ass, that shit was *real*. Took me and Tina something like two hours with her mascara pencil. Three bottles of ketchup."

"Well, good job. Well done."

"Got the idea from my cousin. This guy, we used to be tight. Die for each other kind of tight. Until the day he skipped town. Made everybody think he died. Can you believe that? Nice funeral, though."

"Yeah, I was there."

"No shit?"

"Gray limousine out front."

"I *remember* that. I do. That was you, huh?"

Something in Eddie's tone—wistful surprise at a shared memory—makes Sweeney recall Jimmy Rugg. Which in turn forces him to linger, once again, on his guilt, or the absence of it. His principal consolation has been the image of himself as hero. He's been sacrificing. For his family, for those Russian kids. And sure, that's not wrong, but maybe it's not entirely right, either.

Sweeney's next thought? Who is it that put him in that position in the first place? Who introduced him to Bytchkov? Who wanted to kill innocent kids? For that matter, who is it that stole the station wagon?

Eddie: "Hey Cosmo. One thing I been wondering about? You still got my rocks?"

"Yeah, I got em."

"You feel like walking them over to midtown? Zakayev can move those stones for you slick as snot off a doorknob. Guy's got cash, and this whole team of cutters in Tel Aviv."

"What's in it for me?"

Eddie has anticipated the question. "Now that we're back on a first name basis and all, I'll go in for half. Right down the middle. That's the kind of forgiving kind of guy I am."

"Aggie slipped away, huh?"

Three thousand miles east, Sweeney hears a Montana car door slam. The background noise diminishes. Eddie jingles keys, and the engine starts. "Maybe. But me and Elizabeth—what is her name, by the way? Bess or Betsy or Elizabeth or what?—me and her, we're still tight. Figured I'd better, you know, diversify my investment, find her a storage shed somewhere. Good thinking right about now, yeah?"

"Jesus, Eddie. What *happened* to you, man?"

"No, no. Don't lay this shit on *me*. I been betrayed at every turn. Do *not* lay this shit on me."

"Yeah, we'll talk betrayals."

"You planning on being a *good guy*, Cosmo? A *nice* guy? Move those rocks for me?"

"I'm coming back to Montana, Eddie. First flight I can catch. Best I can do, Eddie, very best, tomorrow night I put the rocks in your hand. You can go move the rocks yourself. Start from scratch. What do you say?"

The sound of the car engine rises and falls. Tires crunch through gravel, transition to asphalt. "What's your cut?"

"Ten percent. Pain and suffering surcharge."

Finally: "I'm good with that."

~

Tina's call comes just as Sweeney's stepping onto the curb at Laguardia. He waffles for a second, then decides, screw it. Take the call, Sweeney. Get this over with. "Hey."

"Jesus, Cosmo. Finally. *Fin*ally. So, you meet with your fence?"

"Nah, see, here's the thing. I'm flying back to Montana."

"Wait a minute, now just. Huh...? "

"Heading home." He hands the driver a pair of folded bills. "Keep the change."

"You still got them, though? The diamonds?"

"What diamonds?"

Sweeney holds the phone away from his ear, anticipating the screech. *Motherfucker sonofabitch bastard cocksucker. Whatdoyoumeanwhatdiamonds?*

"Those diamonds that weren't ever yours to begin with?

Dug up by a ten-year-old in Siberia or some place? Those diamonds?"

"*My* diamonds. *Mine.*"

"Gone like they never were. Phhsst. Think about it like that. It'll help. Go home, is my advice. Repair that back door. Start over. *Earn* some money. Maybe get a master's degree."

"Oh fuck you, you sacrimonious piece of shit. Fuck you…"

She starts to cry.

He waits.

Waits for his own sympathy, for the hard bolus of callused distance to open up into tenderness. The puddle of saltwater he's recently reacquired for a heart, maybe it'll shiver slightly. "Sanctimonious, you mean to say."

"What?"

"You said sacrimonious. You meant sanctimonious. Or maybe acrimonious."

"Cosmo…" She cries harder.

"Call Eddie. He'll explain it better than I can."

"Eddie…?"

Gently, he presses fingertip to screen, ending the call.

The first trash can he sees, he lets her phone slip from his fingers, tumble down between coffee cups and damp newspapers.

Sweeney glances away, looks up at the terminal signs. Hangs a left toward security.

~

When were him and Eddie closest? If this is the nadir of their partnership, what was the apogee? Jet Blue to Minneapolis, he settles on the time they stole that taxi.

A cold night in February, thick heavy flakes falling, they

had an Armenian attorney trussed in the trunk. They rode around in Brooklyn and Queens hitting ATMs with the Armenian's cards. Finally, they'd driven out to Long Island to lean the lawyer up against a boardwalk rail.

Eddie had photos from the guy's wallet. "Nice family."

Shivering, still cramped into a hunch, the Armenian sobbed. "Please…"

"Yeah, we got a nice family, too. And you messed with ours. Happens again? You miss another payment? Your kids are taking their own little joy ride in the trunk. But they'll be riding around with pieces of you for company. Ears, nose, balls. Capisce?"

That wasn't the good memory.

No. The drive back to Brooklyn, that was the memory. Snow falling slow in the headlights and the dawn light gradually pulling a gray curtain over the BQE. So quiet, so peaceful. They might have been in a balloon floating over this sewer of a city, bouncing on a cushion of privilege. They had earlier split the cash into halves, and Sweeney still remembers the weight of that folded paper in his shirt pocket, the sense of accomplishment it brought, the calm arrogance of their entitlement.

"There are days," Eddie finally said, "when I regret not going to college. But today, Cosmo, today is not one of those days."

~

One o'clock in the morning, Sweeney catches the Spur ten minutes from closing. His favorite bartender in the entire world, Rosalee, is eating a spinach salad at the end of the bar. Her husband drinks a beer beside her, shelling peanuts. Both heads tilted up toward the TV. On the tube, late night noir: rain and umbrellas, tears and a tragic sax. The sound of a car crash, breaking glass, a scream.

Rosalee used to teach Home-Ec at the high school, but gave it up when it became clear that drawing draft beers and rolling out Bud Lite kegs paid better. She's the mother half these drunks keep forgetting to call on mother's day. They tip her out of gratitude and guilt. She brings in bran muffins, cookies. In the winter, knits caps for the regulars. The smallest gesture of goodwill tilts these sots over into sobs. Her husband, Ray, is a retired switchman. A beard the color of a red fox dusted with snow, and a SnapOn cap to cover his baldness. Nice enough guy until you see him next to his wife and realize, by the juxtaposition, what a grumpy prick he is.

Ray nods now, says Sweeney's name; goes back to the TV.

But Rosalee is up quick. "Teddy!" Hugs him like he's her brother stumbling in from a blizzard. "Scotch?"

"Double."

"That kind of night, huh?" She gives her sympathy. The best bartenders don't have to fake it.

"You got no idea."

Against the back wall, rotating around the nearest of the two pool tables, Sweeney's cousin Eddie chalks a cue.

Sweeney's first view of his cousin in ten years, but he willfully makes it a glimpse, an incidental catch while he passes over the larger landscape. He studies Rosalee instead, pouring his drink. The gurgle of booze through the pour spout, then another. She tilts the bottle upright, and down again. A triple, at least. A veritable schooner of Scotch. Sweet*heart*.

Handing it to him, she says, "Any of it true, what that guy's saying?" She tilts her head toward Eddie.

"What's he been saying?"

"Weird even saying it out loud. But. How you used to be in the mob? or something. How your name's not really Ted Sweeney. Silly, right?" She waits for his reassurance.

It's a moment like trying to start your car on a cold day. The few seconds of uncertainty as the engine stutters and stumbles, works to find a rhythm. That moment when it could go either way. He swallows a good third of his Scotch, says, "True, yeah."

"Dude," she says, and though she's pushing sixty, the word comes readily to her lips, "that is bad *ass*. Ray and me were talking, we can't believe how you've been holding out on us."

"Holding out?"

"I mean, stories, right? The stories you could tell."

"Well."

"This one's on the house." She raps the bar with her knuckles. "Next one, though, you spill some dish. New York gangster kind of dish. Promise?"

He makes the promise, and takes up his drink. Raises it to her. "Thanks for this." He puts a little extra on the first word, trying to freight it up with meaning.

Floats back toward the pool table on a cloud of surreal. Could it be that simple?

Eddie has dropped the five ball and is eyeing the six, scowling. Chalks his cue again, perhaps out of nervousness (though he hides it well), and blows on the tip. "You're looking good, Cosmo. Fit."

~

Eddie Adamo, cousin to Cosimo Aniello, wears a white dress shirt and faded black jeans, a wide leather belt and cheap sneakers. In most of Montana, his dress choices would read as New York hip. Fresh from New York, Sweeney sees panic and improv. Maybe the shirt was starched when Eddie put it on, but that was yesterday. He could use a shave. But these are cosmetic flaws on what is still an essential air of cockiness. His Eddieness. The extravagant self-possession that draws you into his orbit, that forces you to pander to him, perform for his opinion.

Eddie offers his hand. And *here's* a tense moment, each of them considering the gesture. The implications should Sweeney accept, the repercussions should he refuse.

Finally—it's his *cousin*, man—Sweeney steps toward the outstretched hand. He lets instinct and muscle memory make his decision. The two men grip hands hard enough to grind bones, then...

Then they're hugging. It happens of its own accord. Eddie pounding Sweeney on the back, Sweeney clutching Eddie tight, saying, "You bastard, you bastard."

Eddie coming back: "Cosmo, man. *Cosmo.*"

They break apart, and Eddie takes Sweeney by the shoulders. "You know what you did to me? Dying like you did? You got any idea?" He slaps Sweeney lightly on the cheek. "Huh? Cosmo?" Then again, harder. And once more, harder still.

Sweeney stands there, taking it.

"You got no idea. *No* idea."

Sure, they used to be tight. Tighter, maybe, even than Sweeney had thought. He's touched.

But no, Sweeney's misreading it. "Me and Bytchkov were this close, *this* close, to having our own thing. Italians and Russians? We were making history, man. Till you fucked it all up."

"Just trying to do the right thing."

Eddie bares his teeth. For a moment, he's speechless. What the hell just came out of Cosmo's mouth? He visibly inhales. Lets it out slow. Says, "You still shoot pool?"

"Of course."

"Rack em. I'll break."

"Eight ball?"

"Why not."

Eddie's got five bucks worth of quarters on the rail. Sweeney drops in a dollar's worth. Fills the rack.

"I love this game. Love it." Eddie breaks hard. "Lot of guys, they only shoot for money. But me, I'll shoot anytime, anywhere. The *game*. Know what I'm saying?"

"I think so, yeah."

Eddie has improved his stick in ten years, but so has Sweeney. Eddie drops three balls on the break, then runs the stripes down to the eight ball. Sweeney takes over, empties the table. Pops the eight in the side from three inches away. The good players make it look easy.

"Nice."

"Rack 'em."

Eddie deposits his quarters then bends over the table, placing balls into the rack. "So. My rocks?"

Sweeney digs into his pocket. Sets a Ziploc bag on the rail.

Eddie lets it sit there. "Second half when that girl's safe?"

"Minus ten percent."

"Trunk of my car. Black Mazda on the corner of Callender and Second. Keys on the left front tire. Mind if I break again?"

"Help yourself." Sweeney has his cell phone. He speed dials a number. "Yeah, hey. It's me." He passes along Eddie's directions. Then: "Look in the trunk."

Eddie chalks his cue. Breaks hard. The one and three drop. "Not about money, not about getting laid, living an extra year or two, gluten free diets, some such shit. I mean, our lives are gone like *that*." He snaps his fingers. "The game. And if not that, then what?"

"Eddie and his theories."

Eddie considers an angle on the four ball. "I want you to go back to New York with me."

"Yeah, right."

"I'm serious."

"You're dead. Me too, for that matter."

"That's what's so perfect, right? Me and you, the ghosts in the machine."

"I don't get it."

"Breetvah, *he's* alive, though. And now that we got some scratch, we can set up our own little army. Eddie and cousin Cosmo, kicking ass again." A pause, then: "Not like you got anything left for you here."

Sweeney has an epiphany like an overinflated balloon popping in his face. "So that's why all the envelopes, why all this…" He makes complicated, mixing-bowl gestures with both hands. "You been trying to burn my bridges."

Eddie touches fingertip to nose. "But I mean, hey, turns out, I did you a favor."

"I don't know what…"

"That girlfriend of yours, man."

"Aggie's all right."

"You want to know how I found you? She ratted you out, man. Called the *New York Times* to sell a story. Guy she talked to, the reporter, nice guy, he owes me a favor, he passes her name along. I call her up, offer her fifty grand for your address. And she *gives* it to me, Cosmo. Has no idea who I am, what I might do. You ever want to know what your life's worth? That's it. Fifty grand. What kind of woman pulls that shit?"

"She's had a hard time."

"Fuck, man. Who hasn't? That's no excuse." Flustered, Eddie scratches. "Shit."

Sweeney's phone buzzes. He glances at a text. "Elizabeth's good."

"Right. So. Second half?"

"They'll be bringing it."

"They?"

~

As choreographed by karma, the front door opens on the beat. A whiff of cold night air, a wedge of streetlight, and Marilyn. Out of uniform in Wranglers and a Carhartt sweatshirt, she glances at Eddie and Sweeney, turns to the bartender. "Hey Rose. Mind if I ask a favor?" She bends close to the bartender. Slips her a folded bill.

Rose, half offended: "You just need to ask, sweetie." But takes the bill. They always take the bill.

Eddie watches as Rosalee and her husband step out of the bar, leaving him alone with Sweeney and Marilyn. His eyes ping pong between them. Going for insouciant, he steps around the table, picks up the bag full of stones. He gets the sense, this ain't entirely his game anymore.

And yeah, no kidding. Behind Marilyn, the door opens again. Lukey Ray. And behind him, Mike Patriso.

Eddie says, under his breath, "Fuck!" And spins toward

the back door.

But more bad news, that door is opening as well. Sweeney's buddy comes, that black guy Cal Merchant, followed by Jake Leon and, behind him...who's the kid? Maybe a Moretti. There's that same unfortunate recession of a chin, overshadowed by the eaves of a thick, Tom Selleck mustache.

Eddie makes a motion, reaching behind him toward his belt, toward the inside of his back.

The good news about those hide-a-holsters? They're hidden. Bad news, they're awkward. The furthest thing from a fast draw.

Merchant sees Eddie going for a gun and rushes forward three or four paces, wraps his arms around Eddie in a bear hug, trapping Eddie's arms next to his body. The momentum carries them both against the cue rack. Sticks tumble and bounce, rattling to the floor.

Eddie stands quiet, head low. Merchant inches his arms down until he can grab Eddie's piece. Eddie says, "Love you too, brother."

"Cracker." Merchant comes out with a snubnosed .38.

Eddie looks past Merchant. "Cosmo. What'd you do to me, man?"

Marilyn slips in under Sweeney's arm. "You're looking good, Eddie. Fit."

"I just said the same thing about Cosmo."

The out-of-towners all have pistols, and they're all pointed his way. Four barrels, and Marilyn hasn't even produced hers yet. Eddie raises his arms without being asked, touches the back of his neck.

Lukey Ray steps forward with cuffs.

"Hey Lukey."

"Eddie. You got the stones?"

"Hip pocket. No, the other one."

Lukey passes the Ziploc to the kid with the mustache, pulls Eddie's arms behind him. "Let me know if these are too tight."

Eddie says to Sweeney, "Moretti giving you better than ten percent?"

"I'm not getting a dime."

"The fuck, then, Cosmo." Eddie, genuinely flabbergasted.

"Other things are on the table."

"Hope it's worth it, whatever."

Sweeney takes a breath. Starts forming the first syllable of his justification. It's important that he gets this right. He wants it to start with not-my-fault, ramble around to making-the-best-of-a-bad situation, then add something about responding in kind. It's important to him that Eddie should see his side. But Sweeney's only just opened his mouth when the Moretti kid blindsides Eddie with a hard right. Jumping up slightly to put his weight behind it.

Eddie, hands behind him, has no room to maneuver, to defend himself. The punch opens up his eye to the bone and sprays thick drops of blood across the green velvet of the pool table. He drops like he's been shot.

Sweeney flinches hard on Eddie's behalf. Has to fight every urge, every ingrained twitch and jerk, not to jump to his cousin's defense.

The kid grins wide, makes a pained motion with his hand, like flicking off water. "Wow!" *Heavy* accent. "That is a good clock."

Cocky little shit. Sweeney, on the balls of his feet, clenches his fists. Okay, okay, settle back. Easy now. Swallow.

His reaction gives him some glimpse into the upcoming legion of sleepless nights marching his way. Fuhhuck.

Sweeney? Can't win for losing, man.

Marilyn, who knows him better than anyone—after all these years, why deny it—tightens her fist on his back, fingers clenching at the fabric of his shirt.

Eddie pulls himself to his feet, straightens, but with limited success. His eyes focusing some other kind horizon, one knee not locking too well. "Cosmo..."

Sweeney says, "Yeah, Eddie. Me too."

~

Eight o'clock in the morning, Sweeney sits splayed on his couch, fallen in the posture of a man punched in the nose. Every stool in the world's been slipped treacherously out from under him. Staring for hours at this empty, *empty* goddamn life, Zeke asleep beside him. The dog blowing at his cheeks, paws twitching. Chasing rabbits. Envy the creature his obliviousness.

Through the window, past the grime on the glass and the blur of his own sleeplessness, he watches as Marilyn's cruiser eases up next to his truck. A car door slams. Ten seconds later, her knuckles are dancing a cheerful shave-and-a-haircut rap on his back door. "You awake yet?"

He swallows. Tries to call out her name but manages only a croak.

She's not bashful about unlatching his bungee cord, though, letting herself in.

Six hours now it's been. Six hours' worth of maudlin memories, scrolling newsreels of disappointment and self-flagellation. He'd like to cry. A good sob might be healthy right about now. Balance out the humors. But no. He's got a problem with tears. Like nausea, he resists it. The mechanism is missing, or rusty from disuse.

Certainly, he can't cry in front of a woman. Even (or especially) this one.

"Jesus, Ted." Marilyn stands in the doorway, taking stock. A bottle of Johnnie Walker Red, closer to empty than full; a shoebox full of snapshots, photos scattered like chips from a burst bag; the polished bone-handle of his old .357 half-hidden under the sofa.

She hunkers down low, lifts away the Scotch glass. Takes the hand, skin chilled by the drink, and pulls him to his feet.

"Marilyn." He resists.

"None of that." She leads him toward his bathroom.

"Marilyn…" His mouth works around the next words: I killed Eddie.

"He had it coming." She starts water in the tub. Then, in the gathering steam, undresses him. Pulls his arms through their sleeves, unbuttons his pants, slips them down his narrow hips.

He stands naked before her. Her gestures oddly sexless, those of a sister rather than a lover. She's tending to him, taking care of him.

He had it coming. Four words, five syllables. As absolutions go, of course, they leave something to be desired. But he'll take them.

He slips into the bath with an animal's dumb sense of release. A few minutes later, he's dimly aware of the sounds of Marilyn tidying up. The rattle of glasses, the running of water. A pan clanging.

The bath comes close to sobering him up. He can, at least, manage a shave. Stare at himself in the mirror. He swings the hinged wings forward to create an infinite series of Ted Sweeneys. Through the steam, he considers the lopsided inconsistencies. Left profile, right profile. His boxer's nose. Getting old, Sweeney. Which is more than you can say now about Eddie.

Sweeney closes the paired mirrors, pulls himself together again.

In the days to come, he will be carried along in the gradual recoupling of his life, the hemispheres brought together in a bloodless but painful series of affirmations and denials, handshakes on the street, a few firm rebuffs from the churchgoing crowd. A front page story will give a modest condemnation of his criminal past counterbalanced by a flattering take on his community work. The soup kitchen, the library. Things will change for him, of course, but only time will tell how profoundly. The jury is out.

Tomorrow he'll pay a visit to Aggie in the hospital, find Elizabeth dozing beside the bed. Elizabeth, who will come into his arms with the innocent eagerness of a twelve-year-old. "Teddy..." Hugging him at the neck, pulling him down toward her, toward her tears. "He's gone? Marilyn told me he's gone. He's really gone?"

Aggie will refuse to meet his eyes. The hottest accelerant for outrage? Guilt, of course. Aggie with her hand pierced by an IV drip, her wrists bruised by Eddie's zipcuffs, squares of white tape over the cuts above her eyes. "Get out of my sight."

He used to believe that the friendship of men is built on an armature of respect hidden under a veneer of disdain. But if there's anything to be learned here, perhaps it has something to do with the inevitability of betrayal. The biological mechanism of it. Back when the species was new, right after our first handshake, the first vow, there was that first broken promise. You'd have to say that the friendship of men, then—while including respect and disdain, sure—is all balanced finally on a circus ball of forgiveness.

Sweeney's got to work on that.

Grigory Bytchkov's a well-liked man. Cheerful. Which people appreciate, corrections officers and inmates alike. The most genial turd in this particular bowl. Sing Sing, A-Block, M-Gallery. A cavernous, echoing space of angst and anger, petty revenge and tiny scandal, all of it pinched up into a stone-walled mason jar and shaken hard.

Coming out of the tunnel entrance, dig the four stories of cells looming overhead. Stare up too long, they want to avalanche down. Take a half step back. To the right and left, the block disappears into hazy distance. Six hundred and eighty men housed here. Six *hundred*. And eighty. Murderers, rapists, pedophiles. Each floor is sectioned into galleries, and at least four times a day (three meals, plus rec time) these men are herded back to their cells. Gray bars grind close.

And these cells, man. Seven feet long, a toilet, a sink, a cot. Maybe a clothesline for laundry, wet t-shirts, extra pair of pants. Run your fingers up the wall, count the cracks. Do the math until your bid is up. Number your grievances. Ten locked metal doors between them and us.

Out in the hall, the corrections officers in their grey uniforms rotate through, clipboards held up like breastplates. Head count four times a day. Slow as third graders most of these guys, moving their lips as they count. Batons clipped to their belts. Notepads in shirt pockets. After the first few minutes of a shift, you fail to notice the odor of bodies, the testosterone stink in the air. If you're a corrections officer, you're too busy fretting the clerical details to consider, yet again, whether this is maybe the best possible way you could be earning a living. Ball breakers up the ladder, murderers down.

If you're an inmate, and after you get used to it, life could be worse. Nights are noisy but the food is free. And if you understand the most efficient oil for these sadistic gears, you can pass your time reasonably well. Bytchkov eats with the whites (as he must) but makes it a point to sit closest to the blacks. He doesn't smoke, but gets cartons of Newports from his wife, passes the decks out as favors. He's well liked and mildly feared.

Like everyone else in Sing Sing's max wings, after breakfast, lunch, dinner, he's reluctant to step back into his cell. Give me an extra five minutes, CO. Another two minutes. Sixty, seventy men milling around, knotting together to slap hands, exchange god knows what sort of contraband. Cigarettes and dope, mostly. It's chaos and confusion. A college dorm room meets a street riot.

This particular day, after lunch, there are two COs on the gallery. Half a dozen guys under keeplock, but the rest out in the corridor. "Back in the cells, back in the cells, back in the cells." A CO walks along, dragging baton against bars. Turns on his heel at the far end, starts making his way back. "Step it up, hurry it along. I ain't asking twice." His voice dull with routine.

Behind him, at a moment when his body blocks the vision of the second CO, a handful of prisoners tightens together into a knot. There's a guttural scream, a shout, a babble. And the men flare again, flushing like birds.

To reveal Bytchkov flat on cement, one hand held to his neck, mouth working. Under his hand, the stub of a plastic toothbrush. One end of it melted and sharpened to a point, hard enough to scratch cement. A skewer that's violated Bytchkov's carotid artery as readily as room-temperature butter.

The first initial spray of blood hit a dozen different men. No telling who might have been responsible, who might have first held Bytchkov's head, his arms, who might have worked the shank. And by the time the two COs reach his side, Bytchkov's well past being able to point a finger.

Shame. Nice guy.

Thirteen hours later, one o'clock in the morning, the night shift CO pauses three times in front of three different cells, passing along three packs of smokes, slipping them through the bars. Under the cellophane, dime bags of high-octane coke and folded, twenty dollar bills. Her whisper, three times in a row: "Moretti says thanks."

Walking to his truck in the parking lot of the Rockjaw hospital, just after visiting Aggie, Sweeney's phone rings. He glances down. A 212 number. New York. Maybe it's Tina, maybe his sister, maybe even *The New York Times*. The last isn't inconceivable. He's got a pretty good story to tell.

The number, and the number of names that could be associated with it, reminds him unpleasantly of the duties that his resurrection will now insist he perform. He'll have to get hold of his sister, for instance. And sooner rather than later. Perhaps tonight, perhaps tomorrow. After the initial shock, she'll have to be kind to him, won't she? She'll have to allow him back into her life, yes? He's uncertain. Not sure he'd do the same, if he were in her shoes.

Normally he'd ignore the call, check his voice mail a few minutes later; but he's inclined now to get this over with. To start as soon as possible swiping an eraser at the ghostly marks of his various misjudgments. "Yeah, hello, this is Sweeney."

The voice, grumbling and phlegmatic, knocks all his other concerns off the table. "That what you're calling yourself these days?" Donnie Moretti says. "I was wondering about that."

"Donnie, what can I do for you?"

"No chit chat, huh, Cosmo? No how-you-doing, nice-day, sun-shining-where-you-are?"

"What can I do for you."

"You can tell me where my fucking goods are, for one

thing. Yeah, you can do that for me."

Sweeney feels a cold stone slip down into the quiet pool of his stomach. "You don't have that bag? I gave it to that Italian kid, your nephew or whatever."

"Yeah, well he ain't picking up his phone. Neither is Lukey, neither is Mike, none of those fucking guys. Nobody's picking up their phone. Only person in Montana with his phone on is you."

"I gave them the rocks, Donnie. Swear to god."

"Don't say rocks." This is Moretti, cautious of their cell phones. "But yeah, I know that much. They called me this morning. Three thirty, woke me up. Which is fine, that's what I told em to do. Said they got em, and they got that worthless sack of shit cousin of yours cuffed in the backseat. They're finding a dirt road somewhere, taking him up into those mountains"

"I don't need to hear about any of that."

"…and that's the last I heard. So I'm sitting here thinking maybe all you guys got together on a double cross. Like you're all one big happy family on the way to Mexico and here's Donnie Moretti back in Brooklyn, holding his dick."

"You got to ask yourself, why would I bring this deal to you then turn around and cross you?"

"You got any better ideas?"

"…Uh. Fuck."

"What."

Sweeney stares past the top of the hospital toward the Absarokas. The closest peaks. "They cuffed him in the back seat."

"What I said."

"Eddie keeps a handcuff key in his back pocket. Used to, anyway."

Moretti makes a noise like he just swallowed a fly.

"I'll look around, Donnie, see what I come up with. But maybe those boys of yours aren't doing too good."

"You didn't think to mention that little fact earlier? The handcuff key?"

"I gave you Eddie, I gave you the stones. Don't blame me if those fucksticks you hired couldn't keep hold of him."

"Fucksticks."

A delicate matter with Moretti. Balancing your legitimate outrage against Moretti's capacity for insult. "No disrespect, Donnie."

Moretti sighs heavily. "I know, I know, Christ. Cosmo. What the fuck."

"I'll keep an eye out. Who knows, maybe they got stuck in the woods out of cell phone range. Maybe they're hiking home. Even now, right?"

"Maybe, maybe."

"I'll call you, I hear anything."

After hanging up, Sweeney lets Zeke out of his truck to take a leak. He sits up on his tailgate, considering the mountains. Eddie on the loose. He takes his own internal temperature, finds two distinct reactions. The first? Good for you, man. I got *that* off my conscience Call this one relief. The second? Eddie out there, with a fresh and vivid hatred for all things Sweeney. What comes next? Dread.

For now, though, and oddly enough, relief wins out. "Let's go Zeke."

~

For Sweeney's money, nothing beats September. The hot, airless days of August sweeten and swell, the cottonwoods do their thing with the yellow; the velvet comes off the antlers and the brown trout start sweeping up redds. Tourists are a distant theory and the air is crisp enough to suggest a chill even while it's warm enough for shirtsleeves.

He's in a good mood as he unlocks Marilyn's door, pushes forward with his laundry basket. Humming an old Stones tune. Breaking out into occasional lyrics. "But if you try sometimes, you just might find…"

Zeke explores the kitchen, makes friendly with the shih-tzu, nose to ass. Gives the cat a wide berth. Settles in on a now-familiar corner of the couch.

In the cramped laundry room, Sweeney empties out a month's worth of old shirts and jeans. Pours in the Tide. And while the machine chugs, he comes back out to sit beside Zeke, comfortable with the remote and one of Marilyn's beers. Turns on *Days of our Lives*. "What do you think there, Zeke? Are Jennifer and Jake getting back together, or what?"

He's developed a fondness for these sappy serials. They do seem like the essential gist of some damn thing. Happiness always *juuust* out of reach. Ain't that the way it is? The good life evades us all. Even now, and now, and now. We ripe and ripe, then we rot and rot, and then…

"Big day, Zeke." One month after Moretti's phone call. Thirty days since Eddie disappeared. Since they found the abandoned Taurus up Jack Creek; only a few hundred yards, in fact, from the house Eddie had used to hold Aggie and Elizabeth. The Taurus with all four doors open and the headlights going dim. Lukey, cold behind the wheel with his throat cut ear to ear and his shoulder holster empty. Mike Patriso half out of the shotgun side front seat, a single hole neat in his left temple, messy on his right. It doesn't take a genius to read the forensic narrative. Jake Leon, in the backseat and still in his seatbelt, three holes in his ribs, each one popped close enough to leave powder burns. And the Italian kid, Domenico, twenty yards away in the trees, stretched out on the wooden bench of a picnic table, a single hole in his gut. Breathing, but only just. The only mystery, why Eddie would leave the kid alive. Maybe a message to Moretti. If so, it's illegible.

Domenico was discharged from the Billings Clinic last week, minus a spleen and a couple feet of small intestine, and owing six liters of blood to the good people of Montana. He boarded the plane back to Brooklyn using a walker.

Eddie? Eddie's on the run and the most wanted list. Which is, yeah, odd. Pulling up the FBI web page, that's cousin Eddie, man. Big time. *Biiig* time.

For now, Sweeney's not too worried about it. With the diamonds in hand, Eddie's got the means to do some damage, and certainly the incentive, but you got to think he's too busy keeping his head low to worry about revenge. For now. And for now's good enough for Sweeney.

Now it's thirty days later, and Sweeney's been promising himself, you make it thirty days, if Eddie doesn't turn up, if Moretti doesn't come at you, you can give yourself this moment.

He stretches out his legs to reach into the pocket of his jeans. Finds Aggie's old ring box, the crushed velvet from the jewelry store. He cracks it open and tilts it out over his open palm. Catches a loose stone. *The* stone. Tina's sample.

Hefting it in his palm, it feels heavier even than he remembered. He pinches it up between thumb and forefinger, holds it close to one eye. Tilts it to the light, squinting through the sparkle, the opaque gray.

And damn. If he makes an effort, he can see shapes in the heart of the stone. Tiny occlusions. Julietta had mentioned them. Past the oblique, prismatic glitter, under the compressed layerings of carbon, he can just make out two slivers of geometry. A horizontal bar that looks, without much imagination, like the roofline of a cabin. And beside it? An incomplete triangle that might be the crest of a pine tree. Put them together, they resemble a certain amount of hope, maybe a slight measure of melancholy.

Put them together, they look like a life.